Unmoored

Wrecked

Ellie Pond

Illustrated cover design by SJ Fowler

Object cover design by Melissa Doughty - Mel D. Designs

Copy Editing: The Word Faery

Proofreading by Lori Diederich

Chapter 1

Lost at Sea

Haley

I'm gasping. Never a good thing when you're trying to swim. The darn life vest is strangling me, and it's impossible to dive underwater. But I'm doing my best. If I take it off, Zane will explode, and it's best we all keep ourselves focused, searching. Not that I know what I'm looking for, not really. But if I've learned anything over the last few months, it's to expect the unexpected. Sam turned up. He's alive. Just because the Rock Candy's gone doesn't mean that Calvin and Easton are dead. They might have gotten it running and are heading around the other side of the island to pick us up.

Why wouldn't they go the other way toward us? There could be a reason, a really smart reason, that only someone like Calvin would know.

I've never been an overly naïve-positive person. I wanted my mother to get better when she was sick. But the odds weren't in her favor. And I knew that she might not make it. I was expecting it when she told me the doctors said she didn't have much more time.

There's no way they got the ship running. It was still months away from being done. That's what Calvin and Sam both said. And done, by any standard, wasn't taking it for a joyride around the other side of the island.

Reality sinks in—the pirates we've heard on the VHF radio are most likely responsible for the yacht being gone.

The guys have to be okay. They have to be.

The water is siltier than normal. But that's not surprising; there's nothing for it to flow against. They must have had to really tug the Rock Candy out of its home in the reef. Still, little fish dart through my legs, swimming away from me as fast as they can; they're as confused as I am. How could the yacht be gone?

"Haley!" Sam calls from not far away. His head bounces above the waves.

"I'm here." I put my hand in the air and wave it. "I'm here."

"See anything?" He takes powerful strokes over to me.

"Nothing."

Zane joins us.

"We should go back. Let Dante know. We'll need to make the camp beach look as empty as possible." Sam reaches his hand out to me.

We head back to the beach where the guys have tied up the raft. I drag myself out of the water onto the thin strip of sand near the bluff. The swim has left me exhausted. But then it's more than the swim making my lungs burn. Anytime I think of Calvin or Easton, I seize up.

"Did you go to the cave?" I ask Sam.

"No, but I think we should take the tender closer. I want to see if the WaveRunner is there."

Zane's already got one of the ropes untied. Getting the rubber bottom of the tender secure next to the bluff was hard. I'm hoping that we can make it out of the opening the Rock Candy was sitting in.

"Here, Little Bird, take this rope, and I'll get the other one."

Sam has the outboard motor tilted up. "I'll give you a push and swim out when you get past the reef."

"No, you get in. I'll push," I say.

Sam flicks his head to me. "Zane can do it."

I'm chewing on the side of my mouth. Sam didn't see how Zane has become a better swimmer over the last few months, but I'm still a better swimmer. "Okay. Be careful."

"Always, Little Bird." He tosses the second rope in and gives a good push, letting us drift through the channel. It gives us enough depth for Sam to drop the outboard motor. There wouldn't be enough room for Zane to jump into the tender here. He'll have to swim out to us. My eyes sting, and I'm barely holding it together, watching Zane get smaller as we zig through the reef.

Sam turns the boat into the waves, holding us in place, waiting for Zane. I can't take my eyes off him. He's wearing a life vest. I watch, swimming every stroke with him until he's at the edge of the tender.

"Give me your hand," I say.

Zane gives one hand to me and grabs the side rope of the tender, flipping himself in. "I'm good." He says to Sam, "Let's check the cave. We won't be able to get in it with the tender, but we should be able to see if the WaveRunner is there."

I hold my breath until we can peek into the dark opening. "I don't see anything."

Zane moves to the side. "I don't either. I'm going to——"

I jump off the side of the tender before Zane can do it. Both Zane and Sam are yelling at me. I stop for a second and wave back at them. "I'm good, I'm good. I'll be right back."

A wave crashes over my head, and I suck in a mouthful of water. I've always preferred swimming underwater, but that's impossible with a life vest on. I sputter out the seawater and swim freestyle to the cave.

In my head, I was a good swimmer. But that was before I saw how effortless Easton made it look. I'm sure I'm splashing more than a toddler in a kiddie pool as I grasp for the water with my hands. It's moving me forward, though. So that's something. But darn if this damn cave isn't a lot farther away than I ever thought it was.

It's only the second time I've been in it. The tide wasn't as high as it is now. Entering the cave, the water temperature drops. There's something more terrifying to me about swimming in water where you can't see the bottom of the seabed too. Dappled sunlight bounces on the waves as they crash against the walls.

I had heard Zane talking about sinking a carabiner into the wall to secure the WaveRunner. The WaveRunner is gone. But on the wall, hanging from the carabiner, is one life jacket. One? I make my way onto the rock shelf and reach up. The jacket is tied with three different types of knots. I'm not sure what they're called. This is one of the thousand times that I wished I knew more about the exterior of the yacht than how to set a table. But still, it feels like a message.

I unhook it and take the vest, then take a look around underwater. There's something dark and large down there. A box? I'm fighting not one but two life vests to see what it is. But I lose and they burst me up to the surface. I gulp air and head back down. I can only pull myself a few feet. The box is large and dark and covered with seaweed. Whatever it is has been down there a long time. And it can stay there for a while longer.

I bounce to the surface. I can't do that again. It's taking too much out of me. It also has nothing to do with Calvin or Easton or the Rock Candy.

I head back to the tender. Each stroke on the way back is like fire shooting through my shoulder blades. By the time I reach the tender, there's no hope for me to be as graceful as Zane was getting in. I hold my hands up like an overtired child, and Zane and Sam pull me into the boat. Once I settle on the bench, they're scowling at me. Zane has his arms crossed over his chest. Sam has one hand on the tiller, and his lips are in full pout. He has no idea how handsome he is when he's mad.

"I could have—"

I cut Zane off. "I know, but I can swim too. I found this." I hold the life vest up. "It was tied to where the Wave-Runner was."

"Easton—he never takes the life vest with him."

"The WaveRunner wasn't there, but there's three fancy knots in the vest, ones that I don't think Easton would have known."

"Could be they left it for us as a clue. Letting us know they have the WaveRunner." Sam maneuvers us away from the cave.

I wring out my hair and use my T-shirt to dry my face. I'm holding the spare lifejacket on my lap like it's a teddy bear. My stomach clenches. "I like the idea. But if they have the WaveRunner, why didn't we see them on our way here?"

"They wouldn't want the pirates to follow them back to camp," Zane says.

"All right. Well, let's go get them."

"No, Little Bird. I think what Sam said before is the best. We need to get back to camp and make the beach look as empty as possible."

"But what if they're hurt?" I'm shaking, even though I'll be dry in a few minutes from the beating sun. "We have to go after them."

"No, we have to get you back to camp. Then Sam and I can come back out."

"That's a waste of fuel and time, and we only have so much fuel. We should go now." I point to the beach around the bluff where Zane found the eggs. Chicken Beach.

"Is the gun still at camp?" Sam asks Zane.

I clutch the spare vest in my lap tighter. "There's a gun back at camp?"

"Yes."

"And why didn't you tell . . ." Now isn't the time to be mad at them for being overprotective assholes. I've known for a while that they were trying to keep me off the boat and back at camp, and I suppose it makes sense now. There are a lot of fates that I never wanted to befall me, and I can't be mad at them for not wanting me to be captured by pirates either. But then, I didn't want any of us to be captured by pirates. "Fine, let's go and get this gun and go and find Calvin and Easton."

They both stare at me like I've asked them to watch *Poltergeist* in a haunted house on Halloween.

Chapter 2

Salvage

Dante

Penny takes off running for the beach, her tail wagging, barking her happy bark.

"Where are you going? Get back here!" I yank the pot off the potbelly stove and chase after her. Getting to the beach, zigging and zagging through the brush, takes me longer now. She's darted down the old path.

When I catch up to her, she's barking at the waves. "Have you got dementia, old girl? They won't be back for a —" The tender appears on the horizon. It's too far away for me to pick out who's in it other than Haley. Her hair keeps getting blonder the longer we're here, and it's waving in front of her face. Another second and I realize it's Sam and Zane too. This can't be good.

I wade out, ready to take the rope from Zane. Their faces range from stoic to devastated. I have to really focus on holding Haley's eyes. This is bad. Really bad. I look away to haul on the rope. I get ready to loop it around the big rock, figuring we're going to need it to go back out soon.

"Don't tie it off. We need to haul it up. Hide it even better than normal," Sam says.

"Okay, you going to tell me what the hell is going on?" I'm holding tension, anchoring the tender as best as I can against the waves while Zane helps Haley out. She's loaded up with the backpacks they took for the day. All the supplies are dry, but the three of them are not. "Did you flip out of the tender?"

Haley shakes her head, her hands over her mouth. "Rock Candy is gone. The only thing we found were cut ropes and a life jacket in the cave. WaveRunner's gone too."

"Fuck." My stomach tightens. "Pirates?" I don't know why I'm asking because of course it was fucking pirates. Calvin and Easton didn't just take the rotting hull for a joyride. Damn them.

We all knew the beach was a safer place. And yet Calvin had to work all night.

"Let's get the beach clear and then fill Dante in with the rest we know." Sam's already working on the outboard motor.

Zane comes shoulder to shoulder with me, his arms full of the bags. "I'll help you with that in a second." He places the bags above the tide line. "Little Bird, why don't you take Penny back to camp? We'll be up as soon as we can."

"Zane, I can help." Haley picks up all the bags Zane dropped. "I'll be back for a second load." Her shoulders are slumped, and her eyes are red. But she's not crying. Not yet.

"Thank you, Haley."

"Come on, Penny."

I ache to go after Haley and pull her into my arms. She's tough, too tough for her own good. I should know. I've pushed my own emotions aside during too many tragedies, but it's different when you watch someone else do it.

After she disappears into the undergrowth on the way to camp, Zane turns to me as we guide the tender in. He shakes his head no. Like that's enough of a fucking explanation.

I grunt. I grunt in a very Calvin way. "There's no fucking way the two of them are dead. They would have figured a way out."

Sam, being Sam, has the outboard motor all by himself as he sinks into the sand with each step. "It's possible. But not probable."

"What the fuck, Sam?" I've got the side rope of the tender, and Zane's got the other half. It takes us a minute to catch up to him. When we've got the tender positioned to get ready to cover with brush, I tap Sam's shoulder. "I said what the fuck. Do you have any evidence that the Viking and Swimmer Boy are dead?"

"No," he says.

"Well then, that's what we're going to go with. If we act like they're dead, it will crush her. So they're not dead."

"What are you, the bloody King of England?" Zane tosses another brown palm frond on the tender.

"No, but I'll protect Haley's heart like I'm an emperor. So don't push me."

"She's an adult. Treating her like a child isn't going to help anything," Sam says, his hands on his hips. "We need to pull up the fish weir."

"Fuck we do." Has he gone completely mad?

"We can't let them see where we are," Zane says. He's on the side of the captain, of course. He's still got some hero worship going on.

"It's sticks in the beach. Come on, man. If the pirates have any sense about them, they're not going to believe that boat got here by itself." I'm not letting them touch the damn thing. We've finally got it perfected so it doesn't capture too much.

"We're going to have to move it eventually anyway, Dante." Zane's looking over at me with his big brown eyes.

"Stop. Just stop." I grab both Sam and Zane by their wrists. Sam's eyes flick to where I'm touching him, and I let go. "Fine, just come down here with me." I march to the beach and turn back to face the jungle. "We've done too much damage. Pulling up the fish weir isn't going to make this place look wild and untamed. Look." The two of them look up at me. The area along the jungle's edge is trampled. It's going to take years for it to appear the way it did before we came here. The dead fronds on top of the tender look like a pile of dead fronds covering something. There's nothing natural about it. "Sure, if someone just glances over, maybe they wouldn't notice anything, but if they have half a brain cell, they'll figure it out. Pulling up the fish weir—how we get most of our food—means we've got half a brain cell."

Sam shook his head. "Damn. Can't you just follow orders?"

"Not when they're fucking stupid." I turn to Zane, who is looking at where the jungle hits the beach.

"He's right, Captain. There's no amount of smoothing down the sand that's going to make someone think there isn't a herd of zebras living in the jungle." Only he said it the fucked up British way.

Sam blows out his breath and shakes his head. "Fine. We'll need to prepare in other ways, then."

"That's a jolly good idea."

I have to bite my tongue not to say, *"Why don't you just suck his cock then, too?"* Instead, I just nod and head into the jungle. I'm not sure what I expect Sassy to be doing when I get to camp, but brushing Penny isn't it.

The dog hates being brushed, but she's looking up at Haley like she knows she's in pain.

"Hey, Sassy." I loop my arm around her waist, and she glances up at me. Her eyes are more than red now. There are tears on the edges of her lashes. "Tell me everything." I'm pretty sure that I know everything, but I know her telling me will help her work through it.

"It was just gone."

Zane and Sam are behind us now. The way Sam has his shoulders arched, he wants to say something. I put my hand up to keep him from cutting her off. If need be, I'll go Viking on him. But he's smart enough to stop.

"We swam around, looking for anything that might tell us . . . well, anything. But we didn't see anything. Then I swam to the cave. Where I found the extra life vest. But no WaveRunner."

"Oh, right. Little Bird, you were going to show me what type of knots the vest was tied up with."

"Yes, I'm not great at knots. But I can try." Sassy grabs a piece of rope from the edge of the basket next to the ladder. "This should work." She tries for a few minutes. "Or not. I don't know my knots. This is so frustrating." She pulls on both ends of the strand, pulling it into a perfect square knot. "Wait, this is one of them. The third one. There's no way I'll be able to remember the others."

"Here, Sassy, why don't they make knots and you tell us if they look like the right ones?"

"Sure, that would be good." She hands me the rope. Sam and Zane find other strands.

I make a bowline. The hardest part is keeping Pepper from eating the ends as I wind it around. "How about this one?"

"No, I don't think so," Sassy says.

"How about this one?" Sam hands her one. His hand rests on her knee. She rubs her fingers over his.

"Maybe that might be the last one. It was a little more complex to take off."

"This is a sheet bend."

"This is good, Little Bird. There's no way Calvin put the WaveRider away at night. Not when Easton was there. And there's no way that Easton could know a sheet bend knot. Which means Calvin was in the cave after the pirates took the yacht."

Fuck me. I don't want to bring it up, but Sam's right, we shouldn't treat Haley like a child. "Easton did grow up on the water in Maine, and then they did have a small motor boat off the dock in Miami." And the second the words come out of my mouth, I want to pull them back in. Her shoulders slump. "Let's figure out the last knot."

My fingers are cramping when I give her a fourth knot. Sam and Zane are trying all kinds of knots as well. And we're all getting, "No, that's not it."

Finally, Sam hands her a knot that I've never seen.

"That's it!" Haley stands up, and Pepper dashes under the kitchen counter.

"That's a Zeppelin Bend. No way in the world Easton would know it," Sam says.

"Agreed." Zane tosses his rope into the basket and heads up the ladder to the sleeping platform.

"This is fantastic!" Haley's blue eyes light up. "We should go looking for them, like now. What if they're hurt?"

Sam flicks his eyes at me. Fucking coward. "I know you want to charge off, Sassy, but we need to be smart. They didn't come back here with the WaveRunner, which means either the pirates are after them or they think that the pirates might come after them." I put my hand on her knee. "Either way, we need a plan."

"We know this island better than the pirates. We can move around faster than they can," Zane says. He has the gun box under his arm as he comes down the ladder.

"We think we know this island better than them. But there were paths here when we got here. At first, we thought they were boar and goat paths, but we've only seen two boars. The paths could have been made by people." Haley's playing with a rope.

Zane nods. "Maybe, Little Bird. But I trust Calvin's tracking abilities. He said there hadn't been anyone on the island, not for a long time. Whoever wrecked the derelict might have started the paths, and the boars kept them up."

"The fact is that we know this side of the island really well, Sassy. And we need to set things up to our advantage." I lean over, tuck a loose tendril behind her ear, and kiss her cheek.

"Getting all of us captured won't help anyone." Sam kisses her other cheek.

"We get things ready here, and then we go looking for them." Zane places the gun box on the kitchen block counter.

I nod. But I can't think of a worse idea than us going looking for an Olympic swimmer and a Viking mountain man. Swimming back to port might be a worse idea, but just barely. I smile at Sassy. "Come on. Let's see what Ewok tricks Zane wants us to build."

Her forehead furrows.

Zane laughs. "We still have a saw and an axe, and I'm feeling a little crafty. I always love the one where the two logs swung together and crushed the storm troopers. Oh, Little Bird, tell me you've seen Return of the Jedi?"

She shakes her head. "Well, as soon as I'm done with Marvel, I will have to move over to Star Wars."

"First, we have some work to do," Sam says.

Chapter 3

Backward Thrusters

Calvin

I strip off the vest and grab the rope from the wall.

Easton glares at me in the dim light. The light from the pirates' boat reflects over the water to the entrance of the cave. I can't really see the glare, but his body language sitting on the WaveRunner is screaming it. I'm holding the line to the ring on the wall. If they come this way, we can either try to get around them or dive.

"What in the hell are you doing? Put the vest back on. I don't want to pull you out of the water," Easton whispers, which is ridiculous because there's no way anyone could hear us over the roar of the pirates' clunky engine. The damn thing is spitting and moaning. It's a hunk of junk. But it's big enough that they could pull the Rock Candy from the reef. And tow it. Maybe. They might burn out their own engine too. But then, they've got working radios and people on the other end of those radios.

"If they start shooting at us, I want to be able to dive underwater."

"Right. Well, give it here. I'll tie it to the WaveRunner."

"You want to tie the reflective surface to the black WaveRunner that hopefully will get us out of here without being seen?"

"Fuck, leave it."

"I was planning on it."

"What are you doing?"

"I'm tying it up."

"You think you're overdoing it a little?"

"You're the one who normally takes the WaveRunner back and forth?"

"Yeah. Me swimmer, you engine guy."

"Fuckhead." I'm not going to let the pirates take him, but every time I think he might not be an ass . . . "What's going to happen tomorrow? When the tender comes back? The boat is gone. They'll come in here and see the vest. Which they all know you never grab. So they'll assume the pirates found the WaveRunner. But if I tie the vest up with knots that there's no way you know, then they'll get the message we were both in the cave and on the WaveRunner."

"You are scary fucking smart. But you think they're going to understand it?"

"Zane." I incline my head in the dark at him.

"Fine."

Of course it is. There's a lot of swearing and shouting out on the yacht. No doubt they've found the bar. I'm hoping they get out of here with the yacht before the morning light hits. The last thing I want is for them to find us in a cave. An hour ticks by and then another hour. Easton jumps off the WaveRunner to stretch his legs while I sit on it, ready to go. I'm more than thankful to Zane for keeping both the tender and the WaveRunner gassed up.

And I suppose even happy that he dropped the damn thing over the side of the yacht. It's been really useful for the time we've had it. I still don't understand what the hell Zane was talking about when he said, *"I did the math."* The yacht could have ended up with a giant hole in the middle of the port side. But then, what the hell would it matter? It would just be less for the damn pirates.

There's a loud chunking and more shouting. "Fuck" in a thick accent that echoes off the side of the boat. And I'm wondering if we need to duck under the water, but then the engines of the pirate ship groan. Their thrusters are going full force. And the light changes. Bouncing off the night waves. We can't see the ship, either.

I look over at Easton. He's gone silent. We're both holding our breath, feeling the vibrations of the Rock Candy squeaking out of her hold in the reef. It's like a scratch of fingernails clawing at my skin. The excitement of finding the components. I fucking installed them. With the right tools, they're going to have the yacht up and running with not that much effort.

Lights flicker near the opening of the cave, but not close enough to give us away. Still, I'm clenching my sides, ready to ease into the water if I need to. But then the light's gone. The chugging of the pirate ship's misaligned motor isn't nearly as loud as it was ten minutes ago.

I'm next to the WaveRunner, but not on it. I crouch on one leg. There's no way they could hear us, but I'm still not going to yell. "I think they're gone, but we need to wait."

"Agreed. I'll swim out and see what's going on."

"No, there's no need for that. We wait. And when we get out, we go away from camp."

"Away?"

"Yes. If they see us, we don't want to lead them right back to the others, to Haley."

Easton nods. And that fucker, even in the dark I can pick out the glint in his eye that says, *I'm going to go do exactly what I want*. He can't listen to anyone.

He slinks over the side of the WaveRunner and into the water. "Part of the way," he says before slipping under the water.

I can't see him. It's too dark. I stare directly at the mouth of the cave where the moonlight and possibly the residue of the pirate's lights shine on the water. There's nothing, until I see his dark blond hair on the surface near the wall. He's treading water so that only the top of his head and eyes are above water like a wayward crocodile. I want to push him the rest of the way under. The fact that he can't ever listen to me at all is beyond frustrating.

After a few minutes, I lose him in the waves. And I'm starting to know what my mother felt like when my brother and I played dead man at the bottom of the farm pond. My eyes dart around the top of the water, waiting for any sort of movement, so I don't notice it when he pops up right next to me until he touches my shoulder.

"Fuck, I thought you drowned."

"Stop it with the wishful thinking, Green. I can hold my breath a long time. It's useful for lots of things."

Honestly, it's more frustrating that I don't want to hurt him anymore. "What did you see?"

"They've got her towed beyond the breakers, but they're not moving away. How long do we have in the cave before high tide fills it?"

"An hour. We'll be pruned, but we should be fine." Easton hops onto the water-covered ledge and I take a turn sitting on the WaveRunner. The most important thing is for the damn scavengers to have the boat hauled far enough away they can't see us. Far enough that when our crew comes back in the morning, they're not spotted by the damn pirates.

Easton eases back into the water and swims to the end of the cave. The thing with high tide is that there's room for the WaveRunner in the cave, but not someone on top of it. We'll have to tow it out of the cave and hop on. We're not far from that point now.

Easton swims back and his head pops up, but I'm expecting it this time. "I can't see anything out there now. We can take the chance and make our way out of here."

I tap the handlebars. "I don't want to have to pull this damn thing out."

"I don't either." Easton climbs onto the back of it.

There's no way to start the WaveRunner quietly. It's just not possible. I turn over the motor and ease us into the mouth of the cave. Easton's right; I don't see them right outside of the breakers, but that doesn't mean much.

He leans up and shouts into my ear over the waves and motor. "Can you stay close to the shore and then we can zip down to camp?"

"No," I toss over my shoulder.

"What do you mean, no?"

We've already been over this, so there's no reason to go into it again. I'm not leading the pirates back to camp. We left one of the two good pairs of binoculars on the back deck. Not the ones with night vision, but it's still dusk. They can see us if they want to. "No."

"Fucking Green," he hisses.

But that's how I feel about him now too. So yeah. If I'd listened to him, we would have been on the top of the boat when the pirates came barreling in, not tucked away in the secret connector between the crew area and the toy hauler room. We wouldn't have been able to sink quietly into the water and swim for the cave. We'd have been taken or shot. So no, I'm not explaining myself to him again. If I see so much as a pinprick of light on the horizon, I'm taking us away from camp.

We bounce on the waves, the kind of blows that have guests flying off when they're not holding on tightly enough. But I'm gripping the saddle tightly with my thighs. And there on the horizon . . . It's not a pinprick. It's two large dots. The pirate ship pulling the Rock Candy. They're close enough that I can make out the swoosh of the wave on the Rock Candy logo.

"Keep your head down." I turn hard toward Chicken Beach. There's no point in going back to the cave. We wouldn't be able to get the WaveRunner all the way in, not without it taking our heads off. There's a large section of bluff over here, just like on the way back to camp. We're exposed, no matter which way we go. There's nothing I can do about it. It's a quarter mile of rock on one side and the ocean on the other.

But the good news is the pirate ship is sailing directly away from the island. It's mostly the Rock Candy's aft that's visible. And there's really no reason for any of them to be hanging out there. Even though they haven't closed the toy hauler up.

"You drive this thing. I'll watch them," Easton shouts against the wind and the waves. I take one last glance. He's right. With the right course, I might keep them from seeing us.

We're about thirty feet from clearing the bluff when Easton stiffens behind me.

"What?" I glance back at him.

"Just go and keep your head fucking down. Go. Go! Go!"

I do that and hunch over the steering bars. Easton leans into me, flattening himself. There's no need to ask what he saw. I'm sure it involves a trigger. But leaning like we are gives a better edge against the wind shear, and I might be imagining it, but it feels as if we thrust forward.

I push on the throttle even more, and we clear the bluff. The beach here on this side is curved from the current coming off the bluff. If we stay in the water longer, shooting over the widest part of the beach, the run to the jungle will be significantly shorter. And that's what I aim for.

Rockwell is mercifully quiet, pressing into me. With the breaker waves and the increased speed, we're jumping all around, hitting the wells of the waves fucking hard. But I'm able to take us right up onto the beach.

I let the WaveRunner hit the shore and skid up the sand that the tidal action has pressed and condensed. I don't have to tell Rockwell to jump or run. I turn the machine off at the same time I'm rolling off it. I stumble for a few steps before I get my footing. I'm thundering for the jungle when I hear the shot.

Chapter 4

Cannon

Easton

Fucking hell. I'm right beside Green when the shot rips through my arm. I half step and stagger.

Calvin reaches for me and pulls me along. I shake off his grip.

"I'm good. Go, go." Reflex has my good hand holding the wet bloody mess of a bicep.

Another shot, and then another two rounds fire at our feet. The bullets shoot sand up into the air. A few more steps and we're above the tide line. The sand is loose, and each step is a slog.

"Keep your head down. We're almost to the tree line."

I'm pushing my legs, willing them to move. My primitive brain has taken over. I'm going. Left, right, left. More bullets spray across the sand and dry seaweed behind us.

"Fuck."

I glance at Green. Bile rises up my throat.

"Keep going."

I'm pulling through the underbrush, dry fronds

scratching and tearing at my skin as I dive in. Next to me, Calvin's breaking his own path. The shooting on the beach stops. Or it's hidden by the sound of the waves and the thudding of my heart in my ears.

There's two large trees. Not as big as our map tree, but big. I round one and wait for Green. He leans against it, looking down at his foot.

"Did you get hit?" I ask.

"Just a nick on the side of my heel. I've got scratches from the undergrowth that are worse. Your arm?"

"I'll look at it later. You ready? I'll let you take the lead." I haven't been over here. Not that Calvin has been here much either. Zane and Dante did most of the exploring. But Green's at least been on this side of the island, when he found the pomelos.

"There's a stream up ahead. We can follow it back to the mountain and head up it and get a view of this side. Maybe." There's a bluff in the way. It's the reason we didn't see the Rock Candy until we went into the cave. "They're not going to come onto the beach. If they've got momentum with the Rock Candy attached to their boat with the shitty engines, they're not going to stop. Not if they're smart."

The Rock Candy's a lot bigger than their boat. It could easily jackknife and bash into the side of their ship if they stop. Them launching a tender or a rowboat would be a mistake. But that doesn't mean they won't do it. I want out of here and as fast as we can get.

He nods at me, and I'm after him. The jungle smacks us around. Branches scrape and claw at our sides. I'm protecting my right arm by using my left one to cut through the brush like a sideways offensive lineman. And fuck me, I'm just trusting that Green is using that internal hunting and tracking compass he's got implanted in his brain. Because I've got no damn idea where we are.

On reflex, my left hand comes off my right bicep to catch a branch about to smack me in the face, and I grunt from the pain of releasing the hole in my arm.

Green glares over his shoulder. "You good? There should be somewhere to stop up ahead."

"I'm good." I squeeze my bicep, sealing the wound.

"Then shut up and stop squealing and stop stepping on every noisy branch."

I clamp down because now's not the time to lecture the Viking on his lack of empathy. But I do start watching where his feet are stepping and try to place my feet in the same places. There's the smallest possibility he might be right. We're moving a lot more quietly now. But his definition of close and mine are totally different.

My hand's clamped over the hole in my arm. I'm looking out for things I might use to help stop the bleeding. We've got nothing. I'm not even wearing a shirt to take off and make a tourniquet or sling. Green's wearing swim shorts. I'm wearing cargo shorts. Shorts I almost ditched back in the cave. I'm really thankful that I didn't. Then again, the thought of running through the jungle with my junk swinging around so I can use my shorts to stop the bleeding doesn't bring me any joy.

I have to catch another branch, and this time I manage to grit my teeth and duck out of the way of it. When we break through the scrub brush onto what could almost be considered a path, I slow.

"You need a break?"

"Did you ever consider becoming a runner?" I ask.

"I played ball."

"Right. Yeah, I need a minute."

Green glances at my arm. He yanks down his pants. From the pocket, he takes his ever-present pocketknife. He slices around the edge of both legs, taking them off. "Let me see." I don't wince when I remove my hand. He also doesn't react to my torn flesh. "Through and through. That's good."

I nod because he's right. It's better than if I had to go digging in my arm for a bullet.

He folds one of the legs of his shorts up and cuts it in two. "Hold this one on the front." He places it on the front side of my arm and another on the back, then he wraps the remaining one around my arm, securing the two squares of cloth in place tightly. The pressure brings a welcome new dimension to the pain.

He yanks his pants back on. The pocket now hangs lower than the legs of the shorts. They're more a tool belt for his knife. "You ready? I can hear the stream up ahead."

I close my eyes and block out the other noises, and only then can I faintly make it out. I'm a few steps behind him again. With the adrenaline vanishing from my blood, the throbbing in my arm increases. I'm dragging. No way I'm going to let Green know it. The competitor in me won't let that happen. Each step hurts more than the last one, but knowing the pirates could be on our trail makes it a lot easier to fight the pain. The jungle changes, opens somewhat, and damn if Green wasn't right. A stream appears on our left. It's running faster than the one near camp.

"The mountain comes down a lot steeper on this side," Calvin answers my unasked question. He bounds through the waist-deep ferns, avoiding them like he's skiing through a slalom course. "Try to keep from leaving a blood trail."

"I'll try to stop bleeding."

"Stop touching the plants," he barks.

I pull my arm close into my stomach. This is like the worst game of the ground is lava I ever played with Emily.

It's another half mile before Green stops again. It's hard to see anything, but the mountain has to appear soon. There are more rocks under our feet and less dirt, and the canopy is opening up.

Green stops at the edge of the stream. He focuses ahead and then back at the water. "You up for a swim? If they are following us, we can stop the trail."

"I'm always up for a swim. Even with one arm." I try not to think about what I'm saying. Fuck. I left my professional swimming days behind me before I even stepped on board the yacht. But a little part of me always thought that maybe I might change my mind. It's not realistic. I wasn't keeping up with the young kids, even when I trained every day. But having a hunk shot out of my dominant arm? There's not even a small chance of "maybe" left.

Green eases into the water. "There's a good step in over here." He turns and watches me as I jump in. My legs are fine. I don't need to worry about them.

Every scratch on my body lights up when water hits them. It's waist-deep in the middle and crystal clear, matching the other side of the mountain. It's cooler, though. Or that could be me, the hormones racing out of my body.

The cold water shocks my system. It's remarkable, the difference between the two sides of the mountain. Every scratch, every nick, is on fire. I duck my head underwater, holding my arm above my head, trying to keep it dry. I shake my head like a dog when I come out of the water, droplets rolling down my face. I run my fingers through my hair, slicking it back. Green's already thirty feet ahead of me. I have to double-step to catch up to him.

I glance back over my shoulder. What did I expect? To

see a troop of rebels chasing after us? But there's nothing, not even a bird.

The stream is deeper on this side. In places, it goes all the way up to my chest. But it's certainly easier to navigate than fighting our way through the undergrowth of the jungle or the ferns.

With a little effort, I catch up to Green. There are deep scratches all over his back, and his shoulders as well. We tread through the water, moving as silently as possible. Occasionally, one of us will touch a rock and it splashes. My heart thuds. I turn back to see if anyone has heard it behind us, though we're still in the clear.

The stream gets steeper as we get closer to the mountain, but on this side, there's no waterfall. The water slowly cascades down the mountain from side to side, sliding into a small pool with less dramatic effect than on our side of the island.

Green turns back and looks at me. "You ready to climb?" I look up at the mountain. "It's a lot worse than it looks," he says.

"I don't know about that because it looks damn bad. It's not quite a sheer bluff, but it's the closest it can come to being one. Not sure how I can do it with one arm." Rock climbing has never been my forte. Sure, I've done it over the years. It's good training. I'm not afraid of heights. At least, I tell myself I'm not. I'm afraid of falling.

"You can do it," Green says with authority.

"Sure, I can. Let's go." We leave the stream on the opposite side from where we entered. There are fewer ferns here and a hell of a lot more sharp rocks.

Green takes the lead. We're still well under the canopy, and I'm just hoping that when we get above it, we're not sitting ducks, beacons of light shining on the mountainside, attracting the pirates to our location.

We head up. The climb isn't too bad to begin with, and I try to remind myself to not use my right arm. But it's damn hard. We get a quarter of the way up. The slope is a slow grade to begin with, but when Green pauses on a ledge and I get a good look at what's to come, I realize no fucking way are we a quarter of the way up. We're not even an eighth. Quantifying it is just damn stupid at this point.

"You okay to keep going?" Green asks.

"What choice do we have?" I reply.

"Go back down? Make camp? Give it a day or two. Hope that they leave and haven't taken the WaveRunner or shot it full of holes and we can get back to camp that way."

"Is this how you came when you got the pomelos?" I ask.

"Not exactly here—a little bit farther down the mountain. But there's a field of thorn thickets that lasts for acres. When I came down from the pomelos, I came back this way —that's why I never got as far. We're not exactly dressed for a thicket of thorns."

"We are not," I reply.

Chapter 5

Casting Off

Haley

I've got two water bottles and a bunch of jerky in my backpack, plus the first aid kit, a knife, and some spare clothes for Calvin and Easton. I'm standing in the middle of camp, my eyes clenched. What else could we need?

No one else is anxious to go. Dante's collecting all the extra stakes Calvin made from the fish weir. Sam's on top of the lookout stand. And I'm not sure where Zane has got to.

It's just Penny and me waiting to go. "We need to get moving. They're wrong about this," I say to her.

Penny cocks her head at me and lies at my feet, her head resting on her paws. If ever there was a "yup" from a dog, it's now.

I clear my throat. "Hey," I say. There's no response. The three of them had been whirling around the camp like moths while I collected the supplies, and now there's no one. "Hello?"

Where have they gone? I know Sam can't hear me up

on the platform over the wind, jungle noises, and the ocean's roar. But I yell, "I'm going. Anyone who wants to go with me can. Or not. But I'm going."

I haven't lost my common sense. I won't go alone. But it's something my mom did when I was just old enough to stay in the house by myself. I'd tell her I didn't want to go to the store. She'd wander around finding her car keys, her cloth bags. She was one of the first to bring her own bags to the store. It sent me into a spiral of embarrassment—her neatly folded canvas bags with pictures of a cartoon earth with big burly arms giving a thumbs up.

I still have those bags—well, back in the garage in Maryland, slowly rotting.

Mom, I need you.

That's the thing. We're all too busy floundering around in our day-to-day to appreciate things. My mom's Chanel No. 5. Her stack of overstuffed bags bouncing around in the back of her hatchback. The way Calvin looks at Pepper when he's scratching her belly. Easton deep-diving to find me pearls.

What if I never see them again?

What if I never see them again? It sticks in my throat.

I've been a fool.

I love them, all of them. Calvin's told me he loves me. He's said it multiple times. But I've never said it back. And Easton? The day we buried the diamonds, I thought he was going to say it. He loves me. I know he does. My stomach twists. I didn't tell them out of fear. Fear they would disappear into the wind when we got off this island, that they'll leave me like Steven, like my mom, my dad. Like everyone I've ever loved.

It's stupid. So stupid. These guys are nothing like Steven. Not even close.

I drop to my knees in the dust next to the slab Dante uses as a kitchen counter. Penny crawls a few feet closer to me so that her cool nose is pressing against my leg. I sink my hands into the uneven curls on the top of her head. Sam's no dog groomer. It pulls me from a downward spiral of stupidity.

"You're such a good girl." I sink my nose into the fur on the top of her head. "Holy crap, Penny. You need to stop rolling in seaweed."

Penny barks.

"It's true." I hold her head in my hands. Things are totally in the shitter, but I'm feeling a bit better.

She gives me the side-eye.

"Well, you're right." I nod at her. I shouldn't be so stupid about all this. Love isn't hard.

Zane comes around the corner. "What's Penny right about? And were you yelling something, Little Bird?"

"I love you." I burst into tears. Not delicate, elegant, movie star tears. No, the kind where you can't catch your breath, your face goes splotchy for a week, and you end up with a zit on the tip of your nose. My chest heaves up and down, and I'm sure I'm going to hyperventilate and pass out when he pulls me into his arms.

"Of course you do, Little Bird. We know you love us. All of us do. But it's damn nice to hear it from your lips." He presses a quick kiss to my mouth.

I'm shaking, and its more than my insides. Like my hand is vibrating on its own.

"Oh, no." He holds my shoulders, staring into my eyes. His brown eyes sparkle in the dappled jungle light. "Stop thinking that way." He doesn't ask me what I'm thinking, so I guess he can tell that it's not all chocolate and days at the amusement park.

I nod.

Zane grips me hard. "I mean it. I love you. I knew you loved me, and those two are some of the most capable blokes I've ever known. They're okay. I'm sure of it. And they know you love them." He pulls me to his chest, hugging me tightly into his warm inky scent. I focus on my breath while Zane rubs circles on my back. "There you go, Little Bird. You're good. Have you let it all out?" He tips my chin up to his face.

"Yeah, I didn't mean to say it like that . . . I did mean to say it, though. I do love you. I'm sorry I didn't say it before."

"I love you too, Little Bird." But Zane's normal smile is missing. "I do, and I never doubted that you loved me too. Things don't happen at the same rate for everyone. It's great when it does. But sometimes it's better when you have to wait."

I nod, snuggling back into Zane's arms. "I'm such a nincompoop."

"You're not!"

A rustle comes down the path from the ocean. Dante's hands ease around my sides. "Sassy." There's gravel in his voice. He doesn't ask what's wrong.

I lift my head from Zane's chest and turn to him. "I love you, Dante Saffron Jones."

"Right back at you, Sassy. You know they're fine, right? I can feel it. Can't you?"

"I . . ." I don't know if I can, but I nod.

Dante kisses me behind my ear. "Let's get you some pomelo juice. That will make you feel better." He kisses the top of my nose.

"Dante?" Zane says. He massages my shoulders, sticking his thumbs into pressure points with precision. I close my eyes and shut off my ever-funky brain. "We don't—"

"I thought they were all gone, too, but I found them in a tub yesterday." He shrugs, and from under a cloth, Dante pulls two large fruits. "They appeared out of thin air. Happened last week too."

"I don't—"

"They won't keep much longer, Sassy. We'll go soon. But first, a quick break for the girl we all love."

I can't help it—I sniffle and start choking. Zane hands me a cup of water. "Can we just share it as a snack instead of juice?" I suck my lips into my mouth.

"Sure." Dante has the two fruits peeled and quartered. "I can even take some up to Sam if you want me to?" He hands me a coconut bowl with one of the two-prong forks Calvin carved.

I roll the fork between my fingers and try not to cry again. "Please."

"You going someplace, Sassy?" Dante eyes my backpack I packed for going out to find the guys.

"I . . . I know you all want to get camp more defendable, but—"

"You want to go after them?" Zane whispers next to me.

"I do. You're right, Zane, they're capable guys. But the pirates Sam saw had guns. And there's bound to be a lot of them. They were able to tow the Rock Candy off the reef. That's not something one or two guys could do. So yeah. If there's even the slightest possibility that they might be on the other side of the mountain, I want to go after them."

There's noise coming from the top of the tree. We all crane our necks up.

"Yo, Sam. Everything okay up there?" Dante's deep voice fills the camp.

"Yeah, I'm coming down."

I wipe my eyes with the edge of my jacket.

"You look amazing," Zane says and kisses the top of my head.

"I don't need a mirror to know that's a lie." I huff out a half-laugh.

"What's going on? Did you find something out?" Sam's forehead furrows.

"I think Haley did. But that's something she can talk to you about later." Dante has his smirk on. Shit. I love Sam, but I'm not telling him that, not yet. I think it would scare him so far back into his shell we might never see him again. "She wants to go after them."

Sam winces. "You might be right. I really thought they would be back by now." He moves around to the far tree that supports the treehouse, where we've got a rudimentary map of the island. Camp, the cove where the Rock Candy landed, the derelict, the waterfall, and the pomelos. "You two know Chicken Beach better than me. I've never even gone over there. How does it fit in with what Green has drawn here?"

Zane nods and takes the black marker. "It's hard. I've never gone all the way to the pomelos from here or from Chicken Beach. No one but Green has. But the beach curves in. There's a lot of ferns, and I found another stream, but I didn't follow it too far. Just far enough to find another nest before we came back. But from the top of the platform, you can make out how the island bulges out and then narrows back in. It's like a bulb. This area up here, the top of the bluff, is above the cave on top of the mountain. It wasn't possible to climb. Not without ropes and belaying equipment." Zane draws in more of what he knows, adding the ocean cave and spots where Chicken

Beach curves. A small squiggle for the part of the shore they found.

"So the question is, can you get from Chicken Beach to the pomelos and back over the mountain like Calvin did? Or is this whole section of the island inaccessible without ropes?" Sam pokes at the newly drawn section of the map.

"It's really steep. That's one of the reasons we were in the cave instead of yelling down to you from the top of the mountain. The rocks were loose, and the climbing was not easy."

"Right." Sam uses the marker to point to the other side. "But this is where Calvin climbed up over the mountain?"

"Yes, down here is where the trees are. But we haven't taken the time to explore this part thoroughly, or even the area on the side of the mountain between the pomelos and the derelict," Zane says.

"We have rope. Granted, it's not rock-climbing rope, but we've got a line from the Rock Candy. And rock-scrambling was one of the things I did with my dad on the weekends. There are lots of little mountains between Maryland and the Pennsylvanian border." I hated those weekends more and more the older I got. Now I can see my dad was trying to do the best he could. He never really knew how to communicate. My mom never badmouthed him. She'd shrug and say it's hard to have a meaningful conversation if you're the only one talking. I've got more of my dad in me than I'd like to admit.

Sam shakes his head. "I don't know, Haley."

"Any of you rock-climbed before?" I ask.

"I was on a seventy-five-footer that had a rock wall on the back. We had to change out the foot grips every day for the owner to make it challenging for them. But real rocks? No," Zane says.

"So then I climb down and look around. I can do it." I set my jaw.

"Down's the easy part," Dante says.

"Now I know none of you have experience climbing. Down's easy if you're being belayed on a rope. But climbing? No way. It's a lot easier to see your handholds on the way up. On the way down, things disappear until you get used to what to look for."

"It's too bad we don't have one of those harnesses we use for washing the sides of the boat. If you think you can do it, Little Bird, I don't doubt you."

"So we all go. Staying together is always a good idea."

Chapter 6

Dead Weight

Calvin

"**I**'m not leaving you here. That's fucking stupid." I glance at Easton's limp arm. And he angles it away from me.

He said it earlier, and he's right—there's no way we're going to get over the mountain like this. The handholds are too important, and he's barely got one arm, let alone two. He's sitting on the ledge, knees under his chin, shoulders rounded. His head hangs, his focus on his feet or the bottom of the cliff we climbed up.

"Are you going into fucking shock?" I shouldn't have said it. The last thing I need is for him to lose it. We're at least two thousand feet above sea level.

"What? No." Easton jerks his head back, but his no didn't have his normal arrogant force.

"Well then, don't say stupid shit like that. If I leave you on this ledge by yourself and you roll to your death, there are going to be people fucking upset with me."

"Way to make me getting shot about you."

I'm glaring. Seriously, how did we ever have a truce going? I have no fucking idea. He's not good, and he's not going to get better without rest and water. "We stay here and wait it out until morning. We've almost lost light. It's going to get dark quickly. Ten, fifteen minutes, maybe. At least here we've got a ledge."

"Sure, whatever." He's sitting with his legs crossed like some weird yoga guest on a day charter. Rich will do what rich want to do. That's what they say, and it's true.

"Let me see your arm."

"It's here. I'm not getting up to let you glare at it."

"Fine." I ease over to him. The ledge isn't narrow by any means, but we're both big enough that when we sit, we take up most of the room. I lift the edge of the bandage I made from my shorts' fabric and look at it. "There's got to be something we could use to slow the bleeding."

"I'm sure there is, but our resident botanist is on the other side of the island."

"Right, Haley. I keep forgetting that was her major."

Easton's forehead furrows. "How?"

"We don't talk about it."

"Do you even know the girl? You spout 'I love you' to her enough. But where is she from?"

"Florida. No. Fuck." She was talking to Dante about something the other day. Crabbing. "Delaware."

"No."

"New Jersey," I say.

"Are you fucking serious? Maryland."

"There's something about Delaware and New Jersey," I growl at him.

"Her dog is in New Jersey with the ex's mother. And her dad lives in Delaware."

"That doesn't mean I don't know her."

"You forgot she was a botany major."

"So I forgot what she has a degree in."

Easton shakes his head. "She didn't finish it. Her mom died. And she got into yachting. She was going to go back, but she met her ex. Then her grandmother died, and she stayed in yachting."

My stomach is turning into knots. "I still know her." Did I know about her grandmother?

"We've been on this island for five months."

"159 days."

"*That* you know."

"So what? I can love her and not know that."

"So, 159 days. What do you know about the rest of us? Are you that stuck in your own head that you can't be empathetic to anyone but yourself? Fuck, don't answer that, because you don't even have empathy for yourself, do you? How many siblings does Dante have?"

I shake my head.

"One sister, who has"—Easton's picking up and piling pebbles in front of himself—"two kids, twins. What about Zane?"

"A sister."

"Okay, good. But he does mention her a hell of a lot."

"That means nothing. You're being absurd. You don't know anything about me." What in the hell does he think he's getting at, anyway?

"One brother who cheated with your girlfriend. They have two kids. Your parents live on the family farm. You have a degree in archeology, but you prefer motors. You spend your free time taking them apart and secretly want to break the world record for speed putting a small engine back together. You love your parents, but going home is too hard—"

"Shut the fuck up. I'm not—"

"An asshole? No, some of the time you're not."

"Enough. We don't know that the pirates didn't land. I might be an asshole, but what the fuck will it matter if we're both dead?" I stand and close my eyes. "Stay fucking there. Behind that rock. I'm going to get some water for you."

"With what? Your fucking pocketknife? Just sit down and rest. The last thing we need is for you to be flashing your pasty white ass at the pirates."

I look down at my legs. The strip of skin that would have been under the bandage I cut off for him is pasty white. "It will give them a target since you're too fucking slow on land. Just stay put. I'm going to scout up ahead and see if there's a better place to stop for the night. Move behind that rock outcropping on the side. You'll be less likely to be seen."

He inclines his head to me, which I take as a *fuck you*. I make my way back over to the side we were coming up before we stopped on the ledge. I reach and stretch for each foothold before I make it up. I'm hoping the damn pirates gave up on us, because Rockwell's right. I'm a pretty large target when I'm pulling from one handhold to the next. What I'm really hoping for is that this side of the mountain has a cave or two like the other side. But there's nothing so far.

I'm up another ten feet when a small ledge opens up with a path that cuts across the mountain. Fucking hell. The little path is big enough to walk one foot at a time. I turn back, staring at the way I came. Is there any possible way that Rockwell will be able to get up forty vertical feet before the sun goes down?

The sun wavers on the horizon. I've got no time to see where this path leads before I go back and try to haul his ass up. Him staying on the ledge with no water? Sunrise won't bring anything but heat. I fucking kick myself for making the decision to charge up here. Hiding in the underbrush on the other side of the stream—that would have been a much better idea.

Fuck. Second-guessing myself isn't how I operate. Ten feet down the path, twenty. I don't have time to see where it goes, but if it doesn't open out onto something . . . staying where Rockwell is, that's the better plan.

Pebbles skitter down the side of the cliff from where my bare feet are moving quickly. The goat path goes on. I'm going with my gut. The path straight up isn't one a goat could make. They're coming from somewhere. And that somewhere is better than here.

Holding on to the side of the wall, I pivot and make my way back to the sheer cliff. I map out the best holds for coming up as I descend to Rockwell.

When my feet drop down onto the ledge, Easton stands. He's not holding his arm. So maybe we can do this. "What you find? Water?"

"No. The stream's coming down farther north up over the side of the mountain. But I did find a goat path. One that might take us over the side ridge to where the pomelos are."

"I thought you said Chicken Beach and the pomelos don't connect?"

"I didn't think they did. And they might not. But we fucking don't have much daylight left. I'm betting on this goat path taking us to an easier way back to camp. Or at least not here. We haven't seen any goats here. And I didn't see any evidence of them down where we started climbing up. The best thing for us to do is follow the damn trail and see where it goes. It's up higher, though."

"Let's do it."

"You sure you're up for it?"

"Fuck, Green. If you tell me we have to do something to survive . . . I'm not going to lie down like a toddler and beat my one good fist in the dirt like I have to have it my way. You know this shit better than me. If there's anything competition taught me, it's when someone knows more than you and they tell you to do something, just fucking do it."

I give him a nod. I have never, not once, taken someone else's advice without questioning it. But what the hell? "Let's go. I've mapped out a route that I think will be the best to do with one arm. It's going to be hard."

"Anything worthwhile always is."

He's not the typical rich son prick. Some of the time.

I scramble slowly up, pointing out each hold as I go. It's a longer path than the one I zipped up the first time, but this one doesn't have him stretching his body out, letting his feet do most of the work. Still, he's keeping up.

He's right behind me. And from what I can make out, he's following my handholds mostly. "The rest did me good," he says.

We've got another ten feet to go before the little trail. Rockwell's huffing with each reach of his good hand, but he's not slowing or complaining. I'm going at half-speed, letting him catch up with every few holds.

"Yeah, you're looking good." I'm off to the side. A few more feet and I'll be on the goat trail. The fingerholds to get to it are farther apart than the rest of the holds. How the hell is he going to make this one? I scurry up onto the trail, lying on my belly. I turn back, hanging over the edge. It's hard on him; the last two holds to get his feet up high enough are shit far apart.

Easton cocks his head back, glancing briefly up at me.

Blood is smeared over his chest, and fresh blood runs down his arm. "What?"

"Give me your good hand. I'll pull you up." My left foot is braced against a rock, my ass in the air.

"I've got it." Instead of taking my hand, he reaches for a hold. I leave my hand out as an option.

A split second and he totters backward. I lunge forward for his arm and miss. Easton's fingers scratch down the rock wall. Frantically, I stretch as far as I can. My nails brush his hand.

Near his waist, he finds an errant rock and holds on to it like a doorknob. His head snaps up to mine as he settles into a position. "Fuck."

"Take my damn hand." I hold it down to him. "Take it just to get to the next hold."

His fingers clasp around my wrist, and I do the same to him. I give him enough tension to get him up to the last hold before he can move his feet over. I scrunch back, the rocks tearing at my chest, to give him enough space up on the thin ledge. My heartbeats come on top of each other, leaving no space in between.

The shadows are long above Easton's head as he makes his way to beside me. I catch his eyes.

"You've got to be fucking joking." Easton grips the side of the wall.

Now's a shitty time to tell me he's afraid of heights. "What?"

"Hold on."

"What?"

"Behind you—"

Chapter 7

Tethered

Sam

There's no talking her out of it. I've got the gun. We've got all the supplies we might need. And there's nothing we can do about it, but I'm going to have to bring Penny. She's bouncing around the campsite. She always knows when we're going on a trip. No matter what type of trip it is. "Zane, when you're up there, can you grab the L-E-A-S-H?"

"Y-E-S."

"What in the H-E-double-hockey-sticks is going on?" Dante appears from the stream path. The last two water bottles are filled.

Zane scurries down the ladder. "Our blond, four-legged friend isn't fond of bondage." He puts the leash down on the counter, hiding it behind a tub of supplies.

Haley's turning an adorable shade of pink. "I—"

Dante tugs on Haley's braid. "Did you grow an extra two legs, Sassy? Plus, I think you might have a different feeling about bondage." He trails a finger down her neck. "How have we not tried that yet?"

"We—"

"Holding your hands above your head isn't the same thing, Sassy." Dante angles his shoulders at Haley, and she moves in unison with him. I'm sure she doesn't even know she's doing it. And it's damn enticing. Haley sucks in her lips. My dick's getting hard. Which isn't what I need right now, that's for sure.

Dante tips his head back and laughs. "Here, Sam, hold this." He attacks Haley's wrists like a venomous serpent and pulls them above her head. My eyes flick to where their hands join. He's got his lips on her neck.

"Dante!" she says, a playful lilt in her voice. "We need to go."

"Or come."

Her eyes flick to mine. "Some help."

For a second, I contemplate taking Dante up on his command. I reach for her hands and Dante drops his, thinking I'm up for his game. I interlace my fingers with hers, dropping our hands down. "You're ready to go?"

"I've been ready for a long time." She rises on her toes and gives me a quick kiss. "Thank you."

"Any time, Sugar."

"Ah, see, there's some player in you, Sam. Let's get go find the rest of your guys, Sassy." Dante takes the leash from the counter and snaps it onto Penny's collar without so much as a whimper from my so-called best friend. He snags his pack from a stump-chair and walks a few feet down the trail, then turns back to the three of us. "Well, are we going or not?"

Zane, Haley, and I are frozen.

"Let's go, girl. They'll figure out what they're doing and

catch up, eventually." Penny trots next to him, her focus on his face like she understands every last thing Dante says.

I take the pack Haley has next to her legs and throw it on my back.

"Oh, Sam. I've got that."

"It's fine. I can take both." I pick mine up, and it weighs a lot less than hers.

She cocks her head at me, her hand on her hip.

"Fine, take mine. It's lighter." I hand her mine.

She puts it on. Her eyebrows rise.

"I've got everything I need for Penny," I answer her unasked question.

Zane has the best length of rope we have at camp for climbing wrapped diagonally across his body. The path to the waterfall doesn't seem as long as it did the night the boar chased me all those weeks ago.

I reach back and offer a hand to Haley as we head up the side of the mountain near the waterfall. Dante has Penny, who hasn't moaned or stopped and complained about the leash at all.

Zane brings up the rear. I see him looking around, searching the area behind us. I'm doing the same thing. All my senses are on high alert. If the pirates were to come to the middle of the island, we'd only have a few minutes' head start on them. The sooner we know, the better.

Dante and Penny pull ahead. Penny will alert us if she hears someone else. The times I've taken her hiking on isolated trails, she always barks before I see the approaching hiker. I'm just hoping that goes for yacht-stealing pirates as well.

The climb isn't too bad. The rocks here act like stairs.

"This is the trail to the cave that let us find you to begin with." Dante points to a rocky scramble to the south of us.

Up ahead between the trail we're on and where the ocean will be, to the left side of the trail, a tall bluff rises. Our path curves away from the ocean to the right and continues up in spots. It's almost flat, and then it surges upward. The rocks grow larger with the rise in elevation.

"This is as far as I've ever come," Zane says behind me. "It gets steeper up ahead."

And Zane's right.

Haley stops and sits on one of the larger boulders. I slide her pack off my back and hand it to her. She takes out a bottle of water and offers it to me.

"You first." Once she's had a long drink, I have some. "Thank you." I hand it back and replace her pack on my back. Dante shares some of his water with Penny, and she's resting her head on his lap.

Dante pets her ears. "The boulders are getting too tall for Penny. We might need to carry her."

"That's why my pack is so empty. She can make it a while longer, with some help. But when the time comes, I have a way of putting her in my pack. I'll cut some holes in the bottom of it and sling her through it like a baby. I don't want to cut the holes until I have to."

It's been forty minutes since we left camp. The trees are thinning, and the sun's heating up. There's a sheen of sweat on my skin.

"You doing okay?" I run my fingers down the side of Haley's arm.

"Physically, I'm fine. Emotionally?" She shrugs. "Not so much. I'm really worried. The knots were a sign that Calvin got off the ship. But what if Easton's not with him? What if . . ."

"Hey, none of that." I wrap my arms around her and

kiss the top of her head. "We don't know what's going on with them. So let's assume the best."

Haley laughs, and her blue eyes glisten up at me. "You sound like Easton when I was worried about you."

"See, Easton's a smart guy. I turned out just fine. There's no reason that Easton and Calvin won't both be fine."

She sniffles and straightens her shoulders. "You're right. There's no reason to assume the worst. I have a habit of going there. And it doesn't do any good."

"No, it doesn't do any good."

Dante lifts Penny up for the next few boulders, but then it levels out for a while and the last bit of the trek to the top of the mountain isn't bad. We've been on the trail for not quite an hour when we reach the tree line. The summit would be breathtaking in other circumstances. The wind picks up and brings a bit of relief to my sweat-drenched skin.

"It's really beautiful." Her smile lifts my mood.

"It is."

"When we first landed here, I was really scared. Worried . . . about you. About how we could survive. But we worked together and really found a . . ."

"A rhythm," Dante finishes.

"Working together, we built the camp," Zane says.

"Some of us more than others." Haley grabs Zane's hand and locks their ring fingers together. "I longed for home a little less. Then when we found you, Sam, I was so relieved." Haley's face turns up to me. "And part of me started to care a little less about making it home. I was . . . happy. I mean, I *am* happy. This place—until the pirates came—it became a home. And now it's like they've broken my bubble. My bubble of safety. They have to be okay," she says with a firm nod.

"They are." Dante kisses the top of her head. "You're right. This island is a special place. Nowhere else have I ever been more myself." He pivots and points back the way we came. "That over there is where the pomelo trees are, and back toward camp, that's where we found the derelict."

A million or so years ago, this might have been a volcano. But now we can see a good portion of the island. Not the area past the bluff near the alcove the Rock Candy was beached in, though, or the area around Chicken Beach. The top of the trees near the camp rise above the rest, and behind us there's a bulbous part of the island.

"And that over there is Chicken Beach?" Zane asks.

There's a ridge down the side of the island. Intermixed in the trees, I can make out a large rock outcropping.

Dante hands me Penny's leash, and she glares at me. "Yes, damn. Look at how tall some of those rocks are. It's like a fence dividing a quarter of the island from the rest of the island." He takes a drink of water. "That's where they are."

"How are they going to get over that?" Haley leans forward.

"Calvin knows it's there. I'm sure he's got a plan, and if not, we've got the rope. We'll go over and get them." Zane pats the rope on his shoulder.

Chapter 8

Waypoint

Easton

"**W**hat the fuck!" Seriously, I've never been scared of a goat before. But then, I've never met one with long pointy antlers on a six-inch-wide trail. One that has his head bowed in not a respectful *come pet me* way. No, the thing is ready to charge like we're waving a red cape in its face and it's a running bull in Pamplona. "Nice goat, shoo."

Calvin's eyes go wide, and he flicks his head over his shoulder. "Nice goat?"

I shrug. "What the hell do you want me to call it? I don't want to be gored. I've lost enough blood as it is already. I'm leaning into the cliff. If the thing does hit me, I want to at least have a chance of not going flying down into the bottom of the jungle. I've already done that once today, and that was enough. I'm keeping my feet on this damn path."

Calvin puts one massive foot in front of the other and rises all the way up to his full height. Holy hell, he's even bigger than he normally is. Like a yeti rising out of the night.

His hands above his head, he yells. I'm not even sure what. It's German or something. He growls and steps toward the goat. The billy goat lifts its head and takes a step back, and then it flips itself on the path, running away from us.

"How in the hell?" I'm shaking my head, but I'm moving as quickly as he is. The two of us follow the goat down the trail. I don't want to be in awe. Too much of the asshole Green has been on display today. And if there's anything my dad used to say, it's that when there is stress, that's when people show you who they truly are. Granted, Green's used his smarts to get us away from the pirates and I'm not dead yet, but there's a lot of parts of him that I would rather not have to deal with on a daily basis. "What did you even yell?" The thing was guttural and demonic-like.

"It's some of the only Norwegian I know. My grand-mother used to scream it when she stubbed her toe. I think it loosely means 'shit tied up with a pretty blue ribbon.' Or something like that. Used to scare the hell out of me as a kid. I thought it might work on a goat too. You doing okay?"

"Sure, let's go with okay." Shot and almost fell off a damn mountain. But I'm also not dead. So I guess I can go with okay. "It's getting dark. I can keep moving. I'd rather not have to stay the night here." The ledge we came from would have made a better place to rest for the night, but this path has a good feeling about it. Moving. Better than not moving. Every little bit adds up.

Damn, I'm just full of memories of my family. *Every little bit adds up* was something my mother used to say when I was a kid. I adopted it as a mantra for my swimming training. Every second I cut off my time, I'd say it. And it never steered me wrong.

My mom. My real mom. I can't even remember the last time I thought about her. That's horrible.

"Right." Green's already moving. The wind changes as we round the corner where the goat disappeared to. The rock cliff opens up into a slope. "Fuck, this is good."

"What?" I struggle to keep up with Calvin.

"This is the pomelo side. I've been here before. Well, not here. But over there." He points into the distance, past the goats. Into the jungle.

The goats scatter from the path, not far but enough that I don't think I'm going to get gored. I'm watching the damn goats when my heel gets wedged between two rocks and I stumble forward. Out of damn habit, I reach with my right arm, and when I brace myself with it, I scream. It's probably my imagination, but it echoes around the rocks. I clasp my arm to my chest with my good hand. My legs are fine. My feet are torn to shreds, but nothing too bad.

Calvin glares. "You good?" He stands next to me, his hand out to help me up.

"I'm good."

"Then shut the fuck up."

I nod. "You ever think of becoming a surgeon?"

"No, why?"

"Just wondered." I hold my arm close to me. Every last surgeon I worked with during my clinical rounds had the same shitty personality.

"The light's almost gone. I'm aiming to get us to that flat spot over there. Then when the moon rises, we can make our way down the rest of the way and find some water and maybe some fruit."

I don't care what it takes. I'm not going to stumble again. And I'm sure as hell not going to make the mistake of trying to use my arm to stop me from falling. What in the hell was I thinking?

The flat spot against the wall is protected, and there are no goats, boars, or pirates around.

"Get a little sleep," says Calvin once we've settled. "I'll wake you up when the moon is out."

"Or we could both get some rest and stay here until morning."

Even in the almost pitch black, I can sense Calvin glaring at me.

"Whatever." I lean over onto my side and then roll onto my back. There's no way I'll be getting comfortable, no matter how hard I try. Pebbles are digging into the back of my scalp. I brush them away with my good arm.

Instead of focusing on the throb of my arm, I try to think about how we need to get back to camp as quickly as possible. I don't want Haley thinking we've been kidnapped by the pirates or, worse, are dead. She had a hard enough time when we didn't know what had happened to Sam. Closing my eyes, I can see her blond hair on the day we buried the diamonds. And then I see her in the house in Miami. She's floating on a raft in the pool while I make her drinks. But then she's telling me how to make the drink, and I just stand back and laugh.

Fucking hell, did I make a mistake not telling her I love her? I should have told her. The second I see her, I'm going to tell her.

The unicorn float she's on turns into a Jolly Roger. And her bathing suit changes to a ragged, turn-of-the-century, pirate costume—not one with guns but a kind of bad Halloween costume. She turns to me, and it's like a horror movie; her hands are stumps. I drop the glass.

"Wake up, Rockwell. The moon's out. We can make our

way down to water and down the path to the east. I've got an idea. If I can find something, I can make you a better sling for your arm."

I'm shaking and I'm cold, but my eyes are open. I run my hand over my face, half to wake myself up and half to check whether I have a fever. I don't think I do. But what the hell is Calvin talking about? "Like, out of what? Banana leaves?"

"Yeah, maybe? That might be just the thing, banana leaves."

"Sure." The guy's crafty. After all, he came up with the idea for the fish weir. But mostly, I'm thankful the damn dream's gone. I shiver, remembering parts of it. It wasn't bad, more odd and frustrating.

There are moon shadows around me which remind me of Emily. She used to love to get up in the middle of the night to take pictures by the light of the moon. My sister—I don't think she ever had a good night's sleep in her whole life.

My chest weighs heavily as I clamp my arm to it. Emily and Haley. Fuck, I don't seem able to protect either of them. If the pirates rounded the island looking for us and found Haley, I don't know what I'd do. If anything happens to her, I'll pay to have the entire ocean wiped clean of the vermin.

Fuck, it never crossed my mind before that the other raft might have been found by pirates. I keep picturing them safe and sound back home. Emily and Dad.

I shake the rest of the sleep off. "Sorry. Yeah, I'm ready to go. You think you can make a sling? That would help when we climb over to the other side."

"Yup. It's not as steep as what we had to climb from Chicken Beach, but it's not a stroll on the beach either. You want help?" He's offering his hand to me again.

"No." I glance at my feet. There are scabs and scratches all over them. What's a few more? I step through the sharp rocks, following Calvin downward to the jungle floor. Down and down, losing all the elevation I worked so hard for. But he's right. It's fine.

The jungle floor here is a lot like back at camp. There's a small stream and ferns, but after a half hour of stumbling through the night, it slowly changes from ferns to grass and stretches of fruit trees. My forehead furrows. Calvin specifically said he didn't think they had been planted by people. But last time I checked, trees didn't naturally grow in a straight line.

Calvin frowns at me. "Yeah, I told a white lie. You'll see." He trudges through the dry grass. We break through the grass. There's a small cottage. A barn. Or what used to be a barn. It burned down a long time ago. And the cottage's roof is caved in.

I scowl at him. There are white lies, and then there's just outright lying. "Why?"

"I guess you don't have to see for yourself. Wait here."

"Why?" I follow him.

"Trust me. You don't need to be haunted by it too."

My eyes flit from the caved-in roof to the charred barn. Both buildings were small. But big enough. I could imagine living here. The mud brick walls and tin roof are falling in on the house. There's no exact way to figure out how long it's been here. Not without picking around in the house more. But I've got enough things haunting me. I'll stay here for now.

The way things are overgrown, it's been a long time since this was an active farm. Ten years? Maybe more. There's a coconut tree growing in the middle of the shell of the barn that is twenty feet tall. How long does that take? I have no idea.

The house is set back far enough that I can't see the ocean from here, but I can hear it. Calvin said there aren't any people over here, but there's definitely a trail that leads down to the water. Goats maybe?

I inch forward. Something rubs up against my leg. I look down at what has to be one of Pepper's siblings. I sink into the grass and sit with my legs crisscrossed as the cat jumps into my lap. Emily's always watching those reels and YouTube videos of people saving cats from storm drains and junkyards. They're not born liking people. They have to be trained. This one tilts its chin up to me and demands to be petted.

Calvin's gone for a while. I hear him cough. My eyes flick up to him.

"Yeah, I've got some explaining to do."

"You think?"

Chapter 9

Departed the Ship

Dante

"You got her?" I tighten the straps on Sam's shoulders. I would have thought Penny would have put up more of a fight, being stuffed into a backpack and clamped onto Sam's back, but she's got her front paws on Sam's shoulders and her head on his.

Haley hasn't put her backpack on yet, since Sam had to trade it back for his own. I lift it up. "What do you have in here, Sassy? Rocks? There are plenty of rocks on this side of the island." I slip my pack off and hand it to her. "I'll carry this one for you."

"Wait, I want to get something out of the front pocket. For this, I have to turn Zane's phone on. I need a picture of this." She knows right where it is and yanks it out. "Hey, you two cuties, look at me. She takes a thousand pictures as if she's going to put them on Instagram and needs a hundred different shots to choose from. "What?" she asks me.

"Nothing."

"Go ahead and make fun of me."

"I wouldn't dare, Sassy. You're having fun. I like fun." I put my head next to hers, take the phone from her, and take a half dozen shots of the two of us. I turn my head and stick my tongue in her ear.

"Dante!" She laughs and steps next to Zane, then takes a few photos with him before turning the phone off and putting it away in her pack.

I put my hand out. "Let me have it."

"I can—"

"Of course you can, but you don't need to."

"Well, thank you." She hands it over and takes mine, sliding it onto her back. "Ready?" she asks all of us.

"Ready." A chorus of echoes follows her down the mountain.

Zane's got the lead, followed by Haley. Sam and I are bringing up the rear now. It's steep, and for some reason, the same size boulders Penny could jump onto she can't jump off of.

We trudge ahead for an hour, making our way over the boulders. There isn't really a path, but we hold a relative course with the bearing being simply down. Down to the water, down to where we hopefully find a way over to a rock outcropping that divides the two halves of this side of the island.

Zane stops, and we stop in a line behind him. "To get over Chicken Beach, we need to leave this path and head south." He's got a machete out, and he points to the thicket of bamboo that blocks the side near the rocky way.

"Agreed," Sam says.

It's a slog. I've lost track of what time it even is. But I'm taking a turn with the machete again. Then I'll carry Penny while Sam takes a turn. Then Zane again and round and round. The muscles in my arm ache. My skin's pruned from the water shaking off the bamboo. We're all torn up from stumbling over the cut bamboo.

Our chopping is becoming narrower and narrower, just wide enough that we can slip through. I chop through a clump, and there on the other side is the rock outcropping that cuts down the island, racing to the ocean. A former lava line, the soil we're standing on was once as tall as the rocks I'm staring at. But time and erosion have carried it to the sea.

"Stand back. Let me make it a little bigger." I chop and chop. When there's enough room for all four of us, I wave them in.

"Holy fuck." Zane cranes his neck up.

"Yeah," Haley says.

Penny barks.

"We're not getting over that. Not without the right equipment. At least not right here, we're not. We'll have to travel next to it until we find something more hospitable," I say.

Zane reaches up and tries to climb it. He pulls his hand back. "It's like fucking broken glass. I don't know how we're going to get over it here."

Sam grunts. "Two options. Back along the path we came down, where it sounds like Calvin goes to get the pomelos. We try to get around it by the ocean. It has to have been smoothed by the waves. Or we stay our course and cut down the side."

"The bamboo isn't as thick here," Zane says. "There might be someplace to climb over. The wind always blows from this direction. The waves are going to be crazy. Even if the rock is smoother, it's possible it will be too rough and we'll have to come back. Plus, the bamboo isn't as thick next to the rocks. It will be a little faster-moving."

"I agree." I slide between a clump of bamboo and make it thirty feet without having to cut anything.

Penny barks.

"If you let her down, Sam, we'll all be able to fit through the bamboo. Maybe we can bend it and not chop it." Haley runs her hand over Penny's leg.

"We can give it a try." He lets her down and out. She shakes the metal tags on her collar, and the clinking echoes in the overly quiet jungle. She tilts her head back and takes off past Zane. She turns and barks, then runs again.

Haley jumps. "Do you think she can scent them?"

"It's that or stinky seaweed," Zane says.

Sam cups his hands. "Penny. Don't get too far ahead."

Penny barks back and takes off. She darts through the bamboo like they're slalom poles for a skier.

"Penny," Haley calls. "We need to be able to follow you."

Penny yips and waits until we're almost caught up, then she takes off again. It's a rinse and repeat. Over and over, but now with bamboo not as thick, we're making much better progress. Even though the outcropping isn't anything we'll be able to climb over, I'm starting to think we might not need to. Not with the way that Penny is taking off. Though it might be before we get to the ocean.

The ocean's getting louder, but Penny tears through the bamboo, away from the westerly trail we were taking.

When we break through the bamboo, it drops us into an ethereal world. Straight lines of fruit trees with waving dried grass underneath them. Rows and rows. Some healthy, some dead, all of them overgrown. I pick a pomelo from the ground and toss it back. There are branches of another fruit tree hanging heavy up ahead.

"But Calvin said there wasn't any sign of humans on this side, just lots of trees." Haley's fingertips touch the tree.

"Last time I checked, Sassy, trees don't grow naturally in straight lines."

"Why would he lie to us?"

I shake my head. "I don't know." The same thing rolls around in the back of my brain. "I'm sure he had his reasons."

"They better be damn good," Sam growls.

Damn. Good.

But my stomach turns. Something's not right.

Calvin

It's midday. Almost afternoon. And I'm thinking I might have to leave Easton here and trudge back to camp. Get Zane and some medical supplies. And have Zane help me pull Easton back over the mountain.

The hole in his arm isn't looking good. It's red around the edges, and getting him to wake up is one thing, but getting him to stay awake is something completely different.

I kneel down next to him. "Here, drink some water." I didn't want to, but I've brought him into the corner of the best of the three mud huts. This one has a little more roof left. It also only had one corpse in it. Whereas the others? I spent the morning digging a grave for this one. I've been doing one or two graves each time I come. And I've snuck over here many mornings.

Easton eyes the cup.

"I've washed it." He was furious when I told him. But

then I showed him the second mud house. Not because I wanted to but because he wouldn't shut up about it.

He rolls over on the mat of palm fronds I've made him. He touches the wall, his finger inside one of the holes. "Bullet hole," he says.

I don't know if it's a question or a statement. Doesn't matter, I suppose. "Yes. Now drink some water and eat some more of this. Whatever it is." The last time I was here, I dug three graves and brought back as many pomelos as I could. But there are a lot more graves to dig for the other huts down the beach.

It's taken everything in me to keep the others from coming here. It didn't change anything about this island for me. I've never imagined us getting off it. Not from the moment we landed. But the others? The others, they've had hope, and seeing the bones of three families long gone? That isn't going to make the others have hope. There's nothing here we need. The fabric from their clothes is rotten. A few cups? We had coconut bowls. We had a pot from the derelict. Better to leave this as their graveyard and keep Haley's hope alive.

"Drink, Rockwell."

He lifts his head and takes a sip. "What's that?"

"I don't hear anything."

"I hear a dog barking." Easton lifts his neck.

I put my hand on his forehead. "I'm going to get you some water for your forehead."

"We need to talk." His blue eyes hold mine before he lets his head sink.

"Yeah, I'll be right back."

I grab one of the non-rotten sleeves of a shirt I found in the last house and make my way over to where the stream rolls to the ocean. That's when I hear it too. It's a dog barking. Pepper's brothers and sisters take off for the far cottage, the one they spend most of their time in.

Penny comes racing down the beach and jumps at me.

I drop the cloth and catch her. "Hey girl. You're not alone, are you?" For a second, my mind races to how she could have gotten here. And then I see them coming out of the orchard.

Zane first, Sam, and then Haley, who races for me. "Calvin." Penny's jumping around my feet, but I manage to grab Haley and bring her into my arms. "I love you. You're alive. I love you." She kisses me and then pulls her head back and whispers, "Easton?"

"He's over in that mud hut." I call it what it is. It's a little hard to deny it now. "He's injured. It's not good. He's not good . . ."

She cocks her head. "Injured?" She runs to the second hut, and a brown cat follows her. They've gotten used to me bringing them fish jerky. "There's a cat . . ." She turns back for a second but then races to Easton.

I've got three angry-looking men staring at me. "What do you want to know first?"

"Easton," Sam says. "Pirates, then this shit."

Zane crosses his arms over his chest. "Agreed."

Penny nuzzles up against my leg. At least I still have one ally.

I run my fingers through the hair on the top of her head. "Easton and the pirates are the same conversation. We saw and heard the pirates coming from far enough away that we had time to move. It was late, but we were still up . . . fuck . . . I'll get to that part later. We were up and we hid in between the crew mess and the toy hauler while they were running around the top of the Rock Candy, getting into the liquor. Before anyone came down to the engine room, we were able to slide into the water and swim for the cave. It took them all night, but they managed to get the yacht pulled out. It was almost high tide when they left. We thought the coast was clear. I tied the knots so you would know—"

"Yes, that was a good idea," Sam says.

"High tide, we needed to get out of the cave. And it sounded like they were completely gone. We took the WaveRunner to Chicken Beach."

"Away from camp, smart." Dante shows up with his arms full of the fruit I've been feeding Easton.

"But they weren't gone. They chased us, and Easton got hit. Tell me you have a first aid kit in one of those bags."

"Yes." Zane pulls one out from the pack Dante had on.

"He's going to need all the antibiotics we can get him. I'm not sure. Fuck." I'm not going to cry. I don't cry. But honestly, I'm not sure he's going to make it.

Chapter 10

Patching the Hull

Haley

I race for the dilapidated structure. The exhaustion from the trek over the mountain and through slashing the bamboo vanishes. Easton's alive! And for once, I'm going to be positive. I'm going to push what Calvin just said about Easton out of my head. Easton has to be okay. He will be okay. I'm not going to allow anything but him being okay.

This isn't like my mom. This isn't the John Hopkins cancer ward. I push away the thought, because Easton would be a lot better off if it was. My mom was too. It just wasn't the outcome we wanted.

The tall surrounding grass scratches at my legs as I push through it. The hut's not much more than a mound of dried, crumbling earth. Rotten wood lies next to the entrance. The roof's mostly gone, and I duck under a beam that's jutting out of the wall at an angle. It's cooler in here even without the breeze from the ocean.

It takes me a second to spot Easton to the left. I'm

relieved and horrified at the same time. He's lying on a bed of green palm fronds. So pale. A shiver runs through me, and the image of my mom under layers of blankets bombards me.

Easton's eyes are closed. The little patch of remaining ceiling gives him some shade. His chest is bare, and around his arm is a part of Calvin's shorts and another fabric I don't recognize tied to his arm with a vine, and there's a small clay cup next to him.

"Easton." I drop to my knees next to him. Cautiously, I touch his leg. He's warm and clammy.

"Hey." His eyes open to little slits. "There you are, my Firefly, shining in the middle of the day."

I press my lips to his forehead. I'm not sure if I should say it now, but I have to. I can't hold it back. "I love you. I was so worried about you."

"I love you too." His eyes open a bit wider. He tilts his head up. "Can I kiss you?"

My hand shakes, and I lean over him with care. His lips are cool, but my heart is soaring. I cut the kiss short.

"Hey, that's all I get when I'm the wounded one here?" He flashes a quick smile. And I give him another quick kiss. "I suppose that's enough. I'm calling a rain check, though."

His head drops back onto the fronds. His eyes are red, but the surrounding skin has a ghostly sheen. I press a kiss to his forehead, the way my mother used to when she was checking for a fever. He's hot but not scarily so. The hair rises on the back of my neck. I'm worried. "I'll make a note of it."

"Hmm, I'm going to hold you to it, even though you didn't write it down in your notebook."

I hold his hand, but I'm staring at the leaves and vines on his arm.

"I'm not as bad as I look, Haley. Calvin's been looking at me like he's trying to figure out how big a hole to dig. You didn't happen to bring the first aid kit?" He pushes up on the elbow of his good arm. "Tarzan did the best he could. It's scary how much is tucked away in that huge head of his. Did you know coconut water has an antiseptic quality to it?" His voice trails off as he says it. He's putting on a good front for me.

I shake my head. "Really?"

"I mean, he said so. But then he said that there were no signs of anyone living over here, too. He could just be shitting me to get me to stop moaning." He drops his head. "But the vine was pretty smart." He nods to the green vine around his arm. "It's slowed the bleeding a lot, that and the moss. As ingenious as it is, I'd prefer a nice clean gauze bandage and a shit ton of alcohol for the wound." He's awkwardly propped up with his uninjured arm.

"I'll go get it. Stay still. Sam had my backpack. We brought the big kit." I should have grabbed it before I came in.

"Is everyone here? Everyone okay?" He winces, his eyes shutting and slowly opening again.

"Everyone's fine. We're all fine." I'm repeating myself, but then maybe I'll start to believe it if I say it enough. "I'll be right back." My eyes trail over the rest of the former hut. Everything has fallen apart or rotted. There's a small tree growing out of the corner and a smashed sleeping platform. I take a few small backward steps to the door.

"Okay, hurry, I'm planning to go out for a light jog in a few minutes." He rests his head on the palm fronds.

I take off my jacket, ball it up and place it under his head. "You've still got your sense of humor. I'll make sure to take the shovel away from Calvin."

"I appreciate that," he says, a smile on his lips as he closes his eyes again.

I blink, coming back out into the sun. The series of holes in the side of the building makes my stomach clench. The walls are thick, old and crumbling, but it's not hard to figure out how they got there. This was someone's home. A family. A *large* family. A little village. There are more ruined buildings poking out of the growing palm trees leading in the opposite direction from the orchard.

The guys are a few yards away from the rubble cottage. Dante's holding Penny on the leash. But even with her on the leash, there are cats poking their heads out from under discarded boards and large clumps of ferns. Most of them are copies of Pepper.

"Can I have the first aid kit?" My backpack's on the ground between Sam and Dante.

"I've got it out already," Sam says. "I wanted to give you a minute with him. I'll be right in. We'll need to stitch him up. After we get the bullet wound cleaned out."

"Where's Calvin and Zane?" I'm relieved Calvin's not injured, but at the same time there's a growing anger in my gut. I'm going to examine it later when Easton's feeling better. How could he not have told us about this village? How long did he think he could keep us from coming over here? Well, I guess a long time, since we've been here five months and no one but him has stepped foot near it.

"They've gone to refill the water bottles." Dante's holding on tightly to Penny's leash. Her head spins in all directions at once. Dante drops to a crouch. "They're just cats, Penny. Like Pepper. Pepper's clan. I'm sure her mom and dad are here somewhere." It doesn't settle Penny. Dante scratches her behind her ears. "I'll keep Penny out here. No need to add to the chaos."

"Which way is the stream?" I ask, looking around.

Dante points away from where we came out of the old orchard. "They'll be back soon, Sassy."

I nod. "I'm not squeamish, but I've never done stitches before. Have you?"

"For a gunshot wound, no. But I've taped the hell out of my hands back in my day charter fishing days. And taken hooks out of guests from every part of the body," Sam says.

I hug the kit to my stomach and make my way back to Easton. This side of the island's a lot warmer. Or maybe it's just that the rainy season is almost over. And I'm worried. So worried. "I'm back."

I watch his chest rise and fall for a beat as I enter. He's putting on a good show for me, trying to make me relieved that he's not doing bad. But his labored breathing says it is acting—not reality. "I've got the kit and Sam."

"Hey, Easton. I'm damn glad to see you."

"Same to you, Captain."

Now I know he's putting on an act. None of the guys have been calling Sam "Captain." Not since we've been together.

Sam kneels by Easton. "Mind if I take a look?"

"Uh, I thought Haley was going to . . . Do you have any experience?"

I crouch by Easton's head. "More than I do, I'm sure. But I can do it if you want me to." More than anything, I want Sam to be the one to clean the wound out. The idea of hurting Easton more sends a wave of fear over me.

"No, it's okay, Haley. Sam can do it." Easton drops his head. And I run my fingers through his soft brown hair, smoothing it away from his forehead. It's getting so long. When we found the Rock Candy, we did a day of "salon and barber shop."

But then the repairs on the boat took over, and with the endless rain, we were on our own hamster wheel of never-ending work. Like being back on the mainland. Or when Zane was trying to get the shelter built. It's an easy cycle to slip into, I suppose.

Easton takes in a big breath, and I bring my hand back quickly. "Am I hurting you?"

"No, the opposite. Please keep petting me. It feels good. Don't stop."

Sam's working in the kit. He's found a sterile pad and has it open. Easton's the one who stocked both of the kits. There are little bottles of vodka in them. Sam holds one up to the light. "How's the pain right now?"

"It's okay."

"You don't have to be a hero, Easton." Sam's voice drops. "You should have some of these, anyway. It will help with the swelling." Sam holds out two tablets and a bottle of water we brought from camp in his gloved hands.

"Open up," I say. I take the pills from Sam and put them in Easton's mouth. I hold his head up while I help him sip some water. Then I go back to petting his hair. I'm doing the best I can to distract Easton from Sam. Sam's unwinding the tourniquet of vines and removing Calvin's shorts and the leaves. But he hisses when Sam pulls the last bit away.

"I'm going to wash it out with some alcohol. This is going to hurt like hell," Sam says.

"It's fine. I know it's necessary. It's already pink around the edges. And if my fever has anything to do with it, we need to beat down the impending infection." Easton lays his head back on my legs. His skin is more than pink. It's bright red with streaks going out from it.

"Hold his other shoulder, Haley," Sam says.

My eyes flick to Sam's. His forehead is furrowed. I'm

doing my best to not look. I'm not squeamish. But bullet holes are a lot scarier than a foot ripped apart by coral. Or maybe it's that Easton is the one with the most medical experience and I just trusted him.

"He's going to be okay." Sam nods at me. "Now hold on tight because this isn't going to be pleasant."

"I'm not going to flop around. Just do it." Easton's got his head cocked to his arm. "See the spot toward my elbow where it's really pink? Make sure you get that section." He nods to Sam and drops his head back to my legs. "Do it." Easton's eyes are tightly closed. There's a tick in his jaw.

Sam's got gauze, antiseptic spray and bandages set on a clean pad ready to go. I'm holding on to Easton's hand, my arm wrapped around his side, ready to put downward pressure on him when Sam pours the alcohol, in case he can't stay in place.

"One, two . . ."

Chapter 11

Baren

Zane

There's a loud scream from the mud huts where we left the rest of the group. It's sharp and clear but stops as quickly as it started. I'm pivoting to go back when Calvin grips my arm.

"They're cleaning him up," Calvin says without stopping his pace into the jungle. "As long as we hear nothing else, we should get the water. The sooner we can get him back to camp, the better off everyone will be. This side of the island is better off left for the ghosts."

I'm glaring at the backside of the knuckle-nut's head. Seriously. "Or this side of the island has goats, chickens, and—"

"—a fuck-ton of cats. And there's no chicken. If there had been chickens, I would have brought one back. And what are we going to do with a goat? You think Haley would let us eat one? And keeping them for their milk? Too much work. Plus, I told you there were goats."

I stop on the narrow trail. "But you could have told us that this was over here." I'm steamed.

"I was planning on it. But I wanted to . . . I wanted to bury the dead first. Then we found the Rock Candy and I thought . . ." He's not stopping, so I have to quickstep to catch up with him.

"You thought what?"

"I had fucking hoped, okay? For the first time in a long time, I had hope. With enough man hours, we could have gotten the thing started and then, with what we found last night, I thought we could make it out of here."

"You mean you found the pirates?" I jog to keep up with him.

"It doesn't matter. The stream's up ahead. Let's just get the water."

"What the bloody hell, mate? You need to get your shit in order. No more secrets." I push back a branch and there in front of us is a large bay. It's rocky, but under other circumstances I'd be shocked by the beauty of the place.

"The freshwater stream's up there. It's a bit of a scramble. You ready?"

I'm scowling at him, but it's more than a scramble to get over the giant boulders. I'm using all the air in my lungs to keep up with him, which might be his plan to keep me from yelling at him. The serious fucker. I want to smack him into next week. "How many times have you come over here without us knowing?" I shout into the waves.

He turns around and gives me that silent stare. "It's up here. You need a hand?" He stops, standing on a tall boulder, and reaches down to me.

"Nah, I've got it." I'm not short by any means, and in a lot of ways, I'm a lot nimbler than the damn Viking.

I can smell the fresh water before I see it. There's a

small waterfall where the freshwater makes its way into the ocean. There's a rainbow in the spray as the water crashes over the rocks. I stop next to it and pull the water bottles out of my pack.

"Give them to me. I'll climb up there and get it from the stream. There's bound to be salt in this section from the ocean spray."

"No, I'll climb up. You can wait here."

Calvin shrugs. "We can both go up." He grabs handholds with the swiftness of someone who's been here many times. And in the end, he's standing on the edge next to the waterfall before I can get there.

It's flat, and the jungle is thin here. Off in the distance is another structure. Compared to the ones on the other beach, this one appears whole.

"What's that?"

"I haven't . . . Listen, there are things that the rest of you don't need to carry. Okay? Please." Calvin runs his hand over his face.

I've got my chin jutted out, and I take a few steps down the stream. It splits a hundred feet up ahead and goes back the way of the other huts. "Any reason that we couldn't have just gone the other way? Any bloody reason we couldn't have come around the back of the huts and gone there?"

"Yeah, about ten."

"Calvin?" I hold my hands in the air.

"There's ten bodies in a pool that empties out into an underground stream. They dumped them there. They, whoever did it. They're bones but . . . this water should be cleaner. I hadn't gotten to . . ." A tear runs down the side of his face. "I wanted to put them all to rest first. That's all . . . I should have told you."

"Fucker, you should have. I would have helped you. You

don't have to do everything yourself. You know that, right?" I want to wrap the big lug in a hug, but . . . but I'm not sure that's what he wants. Instead, I squat and fill up the stack of water bottles I have. I pack them in my rucksack and put it on. When I turn back to Calvin, he hasn't moved. "You okay, mate?" I step up to him.

"You would have helped me? Not told Haley?"

"Fuck man, I'm pissed that you would even have to ask that. There's no way I would have told Little Bird about a bloody massacre. I would have helped you. Fuck, don't take this to heart, but I would probably help you bury a fresh body. You're my friend. Don't go and muck that up."

Calvin winces.

And I realize what I've said. "You really think Easton's not going to make it?"

"I don't know. I think it's just this place. It makes me go dark inside."

"I can see why. It's too beautiful to think that something so horrific happened here."

We're both standing staring back over the bluff at the ocean. There's a nice breeze, and it's more protected. I'm locked in, mesmerized by the way the water crashes against the rocks below with the stream running over them. "I bet the people who lived here really liked it. And they were happy."

"Happy?"

"Yeah, how could they not be? Getting to look at that all day—they had it all."

"Until they didn't," Calvin says. His hands rest on his hips as he glances back at the more intact structure.

"But there comes a time when we all leave this world. There aren't a lot of people who leave this world without pain." I grip my sides. Because I think of my dad whenever I think about death. But if ever there was a man on the planet who thought daily about how to live life, it was my dad. And there's no way he'd want me to think about how he died and not how he lived it. With purpose. He was the best at what he did, living.

"No, I suppose you're right," he says. But Calvin doesn't get it. Not yet. Maybe he never will.

"You ready to go back to the others? When Easton's good, we can come back and take care of the rest of those who need to be buried."

"Thank you."

The way back to the other huts is a lot faster than the way over. A universal truth, but this time I'm in the lead. And I keep turning back to check on Calvin. He's keeping up but lagging. We break through the jungle into the overgrown clearing by the huts. Dante's sitting on a pile of rocks, looking at a mound of earth, Penny at his feet.

"You okay?" I ask.

"This was an oven." Dante's poking at the surrounding crumbled mud bricks and grass with a long stick.

"How's Easton?" We were gone less than an hour.

"He's not going to die, if that's what you're asking." Dante sits upright. "You didn't need to scare Sassy that way, Calvin."

"I—"

"Don't, we're pissed. And that's not the royal 'we.' That's all of us. But good job getting the two of you out of there," Dante growls.

And Penny barks.

"I know." Calvin drops to his knees.

"Damn. I—"

"There's more to all this." I wave my hands around the ghost farm, just as two cats, a white one and a brown one, come running over to Calvin. The white one rubs itself on Calvin's thighs. And the other one pushes its head between Calvin's knees until Calvin drops down to the ground and the other cat curls up in his lap. Calvin scratches the cats behind their ears as his head hangs low.

"Yeah, I'm guessing that. But we didn't need to be kept in the dark. There's no military clearance needed. Not here. That's only going to bring us more problems." Dante hands me Penny's leash and sits in the dirt next to Calvin.

Calvin lifts his head. "How is he really?"

Dante glances at the hut. "It's going to hurt like hell when we take him over the mountain. Not just for him, but for us too."

"I'll do it," Calvin says.

I really want to smack him. "Like Little Bird says, we're a family, Calvin. We'll all do it together. You're not the only one here with muscles. Brothers help each other."

Calvin scoffs.

"Well, good brothers do. And I aim to be a good brother," I say.

"I know you do, Zane. There's not a bad cell in your body."

I laugh. "I wouldn't go that far." I touch Calvin and Dante each on the head. "I'm going to check on them." I shrug my rucksack off and take a fresh water bottle with me.

It's dark and stale in the mud hut. But Calvin's right, this place has a sadness to it. The type of sadness that leaches into your soul. Easton's sleeping, and Haley's sitting on Sam's lap, her head resting against his chest.

"Hey," I say softly. Easton opens his eyes, and Haley sits up. "How are you doing?"

"Better now that Sam's not pouring acid on me. I'd like to get the hell out of here."

Haley slides off Sam's lap and sits next to Easton. "I think you should rest more."

"I don't want to stay here, not overnight, not again."

I glance at Sam, and he gives me a sideways cock of his head. "You think you can walk?"

"Through the bamboo?" Haley asks. "Oh, no. We won't have to go through the bamboo, since we're not trying to get to Chicken Beach."

"It's not as bad coming down the other path." Calvin's in the doorway. "Even if you think you can walk, we should make a pallet to put you on in case that changes."

"Agreed. We'll be right back." I kiss Haley's cheek and nod at Easton and Sam. "Bamboo?" I ask Calvin.

"There's plenty of it around."

Carrying Easton down past the waterfall on our side of the mountain is a hell of a lot easier than the way up the other side, where every step I worried about him tumbling off the stretcher. "You doing okay?" I've got his head and Calvin's got his feet, and most of the weight.

"I'd do better if you let me walk."

"Calvin, I think we can let him try to walk," I call ahead.

Sam has taken the lead with Penny on his back again, and Dante and Haley are behind us.

I've been watching the expressions on Easton's face almost as much as where I step. The rocking of the pallet, with the difference in pacing between Calvin and me, causes him to grimace as his body is torqued.

"We're almost there," Calvin says.

"Calvin?" Haley calls. "Stop." And he does.

"You want to walk?" Calvin lowers the stretcher to the ground, and I follow suit.

"I do." Easton swings his legs around and I help him up.

"Let me know if you get tired." I'm ready to grab him around the waist if I need to.

"I'm good." Easton stumbles a half-step, and I reach out to grab him, but he rights himself before I have to. "It will be good to be home." He laughs.

"Yeah, it will." Home. It's where your family is.

Chapter 12

Broken Mast

Calvin

"**A**t least he accepted help to get up to the sleeping platform." I glance back up at where Easton rests.

Dante grunts at me. He lit the fire and went to town on some sort of fish stew. It smells amazing. But he's not criticizing or talking smack, and it feels really wrong. Like *really* wrong.

Pepper jumps into my lap and rubs herself all over me. The same way she always does when I come back from the other side. Like she has to reclaim me as her own, away from her old clan.

Dante glances over. "You know, I always wondered why she did that after you disappeared for a while. I thought she just missed you. Hmph."

"Yeah."

"You planted Pepper, carried her back from the other side?" Dante asks.

Easton and Haley are up on the sleeping platform, but I

don't know where Sam and Zane are. They aren't around, though.

My voice is soft as that day months ago comes tumbling back. "I'd gone off exploring. I was frustrated about something that I can't even remember now. And I wanted to see what else was on the island. Understanding our resources was important. It's still important, and there's more we should know about this place, since we're definitely stuck here for the rest of our lives. The section between the stream and the coastline to the derelict—I have no idea what's there. Did anyone live there? But anyway, I'd been frustrated. I'd taken a water bottle, my knife, and a sack from the raft. It's the only way I made it work. Up and over the mountain like we'd just done. I found the orchard first, and then I stumbled upon the cats with just one litter. The mother had left them for the day. Gone off hunting, or most likely was trying to give them space as she weaned them. I'd seen it plenty of times with the barn cats. Five little ferocious bundles of fur and claws. Pepper let me pick her up. She wasn't happy about it. I left the bag of pomelos and found the huts. After I went to each of them, I sat with her on my lap and cried. She let me pet her, like she is now. She didn't purr, but she didn't bite me. After the third hut, I made the decision that I couldn't tell anyone. Not until I took care of things."

Pepper looks back at me, purring.

"Yes, the massacre happened a long time ago. But when I looked at what was left of them, I could see it all playing out in my head like some kind of sick film. I didn't want that for Haley. I didn't want that for any of you guys either."

"You know you're a fuckhead. A really good guy, but a fuckhead." Dante stirs his stew.

"So I've been told." I pet Pepper for a while and look up at Dante. "I'm going to—"

"No, you're not. Just sit there and pet that damn cat until you feel better. And when you feel better, then go take a fucking nap. You're not doing a damn thing today. Or maybe for the rest of the week."

"We need to—"

"What? Get ready to be attacked by asshats with automatic rifles who like to slaughter innocent families? Just go take a nap, Calvin. They've got a yacht to play with. They're not coming back for us, not anytime soon."

I spend a good twenty minutes with Pepper before I put her on the ground and head up to the sleep platform. Haley's there, lying next to Easton, awake.

"You need anything?" I ask.

She reaches out to me, and I crawl onto the mattress with her and pull her in tight. My nose in her hair, I fall asleep.

Pivoting on the observation platform, I turn to the mountain. There are no goats visible today. There haven't been any for weeks. I've watched the water and the mountains. There's nothing out there. Not yet. When we first got back, Dante said to me the pirates have a ship to play with. But at some point, they're going to figure out who the ship belongs to and wonder if they could make even more money by selling Rockwell. Or not. Maybe they'll want us for target practice.

Even the plastic of the binoculars is warm today. I make another pass with them. It's important to stay focused, but soon enough I start wondering if Zane really will help me finish up on the other side. It's the right thing to do. I shake off that thought and scan again.

We've all been on edge since Easton got shot. Walking on eggshells, watching him, waiting to see if the pink line coming from the bullet was going to turn brighter red or fade away. It took longer than any of us wanted. And we all held our breath, watching, waiting. He's okay, or as okay as he ever is.

"Hey!" Zane yells up. "I'm going to take a turn on the observation platform. You want to come down?"

"Sure." I take one long slow pass with the binoculars. There's nothing, same as the last three weeks. Ocean, a whale, no pirates, no cargo ships. Nothing. I'm quick with my steps, jumping the last few feet to the living room platform. I hand Zane the binoculars. "How are things down here?"

"More of the same." He puts the strap around his neck. "Dante made lunch, Sam's washing laundry, and Haley's collecting plants."

"By herself? We're getting too complacent."

"She took Penny. I doubt any boar would nose up to her after it smells Penny. She's been rolling in seaweed again."

"It's better than alone, but . . ."

"Haley needs to live too. You can't protect her all the time. As much as I would like to wrap her up in bloody bubble wrap, that's not healthy." He slaps me on my back, and I wander into the kitchen.

"You hungry?" Dante asks, handing me a bowl.

"Thanks." It's good. There's fruit in it from the other side. We don't know what it's called, so we're calling it Pepperfruit. Which is kind of confusing, but whatever. I eat it in silence and place my bowl in the container. "I'll go wash these."

"No, I've got it," Dante says.

It's like he's going out of his way to keep me from doing anything productive lately. But whatever. "Which way did Haley go?"

"Toward the waterfall." He inclines his head.

Away from camp, I'm jogging, not because I have to but because I'm getting antsy. Idle hands are the things that work, or one of those weird things my grandmother used to say. Growing up on the farm, there wasn't a minute I didn't have to do something. Then with football, every minute was work out, study plays, school. Then, being an engineer, there's always something to do. Free time sits on my chest.

Fuck. I miss my books. I didn't think to bring my e-reader from the ship.

Each step pounds on the path. Ferns swash by my thighs. I'm not even looking for Haley anymore, just running through the jungle scaring birds from their branches into the sky. The waterfall is in front of me before I realize it. I skid to a stop, staring out over it.

Memories flutter at me. Haley. I breathe in, and it's like I can smell her coconut shampoo on the wind. I pivot, expecting her to be there. The jungle greets me, bamboo swaying.

I step off the trail and head down the logical path for her to take. There's a clearing where a bunch of plants grow that Dante's been making tea from. I'm a hundred yards down the path before I find signs of her walking this way. A broken leaf, a scuff in the open dirt.

When I reach the clearing, she's there, as I expected. Bent over, her black leggings covering her divine ass. The last time I was alone with Haley, fuck, it was on the Rock

Candy. And I'm panting inside. I need her so much. I don't see Penny. Where did the damn dog go?

I'm stalking Haley, each step carefully placed. And with each silent footfall, I'm getting harder. I'm salivating at the thought of touching her. It's torture. I should run to her side, grab her, and swing her onto my back. But this is better. The expectation of a gift can be so much better than the actual thing. Unless it's Haley. She's the best present I could ever ask for.

And I've been a silent ogre, ignoring her. Stuck inside myself.

Another step around a clump of ferns. She moves forward. I'm not sure what she's even picking. But the closer I get without her noticing, the more I'm salivating, and I'm getting mad. How does she not hear me? I'm good, but I'm not that good.

She ducks her head, reaching for another plant.

I freeze.

But then she picks up her basket and darts off like a quick little rabbit. She shimmies through a small space in between the trees. Her almost blond hair flows behind her, her laughter in the wind.

Fuck me.

She glances back but then picks up speed. She rounds the trail, going back on the side to shoot to the waterfall, her basket in her hand. Either she's gotten faster or I'm getting slower. She's pulling away from me. Each step, she takes with a sure footing. And the damn giggle joins the wind.

It's fucking hard to run with a hard dick. Stopping isn't an option, not when she's loving this as much as I am. We're past the halfway point back to camp when she slows.

"I'm going to get you."

"No, you're not. You're too slow, Green." She finds

another gear somewhere. Her heels pushing into the path, a cloud of dust and pebbles kicking up behind her.

Deep in my gut, I'm rooting for her, and I laugh. With each huff, I slow, and she does it—she beats me into camp.

"Sassy, what's going on? Is it a boar? I got worried when Penny showed up." Dante's standing, his hands at his sides.

Haley drops her basket on the ground and races for the treehouse. I'm at her waist as she's halfway up. I reach for her, but what am I thinking?

"Not a boar, but a bore," Zane says from the living room platform.

Haley zips past him, a giggle on her lips.

"Damn. Well, alright then." He follows her up to the sleeping room.

"Sam, get down here," Dante yells up to the observation tower.

"What's wrong?" Sam hits the bottom at the same time I reach the room.

"Nothing," Dante tosses over his shoulder. "Find Rock-well and get your asses in here."

Haley has her hands on either side of Zane's face. He's got his fingers tugging down her leggings.

"Arms up," I command, and I pull off her T-shirt. Under her leggings, Haley has on a pair of underwear from her suitcase. The place we all are delighted to see when she opens it up. It's been too long. Fucking hell.

I'm not wasting a spare second on deciding whether that's my fault or not. Whatever cracks I drove through the lot of us, now's not the time for reflection.

"Damn, Sugar. Those look good on you, but they're going to look better off." Sam's through the door with Easton at his side.

Haley has her hands above her head.

"You're ready to play, Sam?" Dante's got his clothes off already. "It's about fucking time."

"I don't play," Sam says. His clothes are off in a flash.

Haley's tongue is in Zane's mouth. And when she tips her head back, it hits my chest. Her amazing tits stick out, and Zane's on his knees, his mouth clamped around her nipple.

My fingers skim along the sides of her waist, goosebumps trailing behind them. "You like being chased, don't you, Bunny?"

"Bunny?" Dante's lying down under Haley.

"She's quick like a rabbit, aren't you, Chiefie?"

"Two nicknames? Move over, Green." Sam sidesteps into me.

But I've got my right hand firmly around Haley's waist, and my lips are positioned in that hollow behind her ear. The one that turns her into a puddle. Her head tips back. Zane has to move quickly to keep her breast in his mouth.

Sam's neck is bent, his lips under her ear.

Easton's beside me. "Here, I took this from the suitcase." He hands me a lube-coated butt plug.

"You know the combination?" Zane pops off her breast to ask.

"Yes, of course. It's not hard," Easton says.

Haley turns to him. Her lips hit his. She tugs on Easton; it's the first time she's touched him without treating him with fragility, since . . .

Easton lines up in front of her. Zane's all smiles as he steps to the side. "That's it, Rockwell."

Haley's moaning into his mouth as my fingers part her cheeks. Sam's hand slides in next to mine. He drops to his knees and pushes his index finger on her rosebud. Damn, today's going to be a fucking good day.

Chapter 13

Commander

Sam

I've had enough of standing back. I want this girl. I want her in ways I didn't think were possible. And if I have to rub more than elbows with the rest of the group, fuck it, that's what it is. But I'm taking what I want and giving her everything she deserves. That's it.

It's as if the last three weeks we've all been walking around like zombies.

I heard her coming into camp—her infectious laughter—and was already on my way down the ladder when Dante called. This girl. I push one finger into her tight ass, but there's no room for a second one. Not with an ass as tight as she has.

Dante's got his head between Easton and her stomach. She vibrates from his tongue working away on her clit. And from the resistance I'm feeling, he's got a finger or two working inside her pussy as well. She's grinding against Dante's face and pushing back on my fingers at the same time.

"Relax, Sugar, you need to let me in." I'm holding on to her hip with my free hand, clamping more than holding.

Her ribs shift, and the sinew of her thighs twitch. But I'm able to push a second finger in before I replace it with the plug from Green.

I skim my free hand down from her hip to her knee. Damn. Watching Dante go down on her from this angle makes my cock jump. Calvin's leg bumps into my back. He's holding her around her waist, holding her up. It's a vertical game of twister. He might be the one holding her now, but . . .

"Don't get too comfortable there, Green." I kiss back up the side of her, stopping at the underside of her knees. And she buckles more into Green. Fuck, there're spots all over her body that turn her to lava. Behind the ear, behind the knee . . . I'm a man on a mission to locate them all, over and over again.

I stand, letting myself get close enough to Green that our sides are touching. Of course, the fool hasn't taken his clothes off yet.

"Do you want to lie down, Sugar?" I growl in her ear.

A mew comes from her.

"Clothes off, and lie down, Rockwell," I bark. And he does, his lips leaving hers. "Straddle him." Her long golden legs do. I tap her ivory ass. "Ass in the air, Sugar. Take her hands and hold them above her head, Morris."

"He's giving orders?" Easton reaches up and holds onto her waist. Yet a second ago he took my order without complaining.

"Shut up, Swimmer Boy, it's fucking hot." Dante rolls onto his side, his eyes wide.

But I don't care about what he thinks is hot or not. I want to control this. I want to make this the best I can for her. She's tried so hard. Her breaking point came when she thought we'd lost Green and Rockwell. She wants us to be a fucking family.

Fucking family. Yeah, I hear it. But not now.

"Calvin, kiss her."

He does. Their mouths collide while I'm moving behind her. Damn, I love her. I want the best for her. I love her. Fuck. If this is what she wants, then I want it too. My fingers circle around the rounded muscles of her ass cheeks. I slap each one. The vibration shakes her. She's hovering over Easton. I grip her waist above Easton. I can feel he's pulling her down.

"I said not yet, Rockwell. I'm sure Dante wouldn't mind sliding in there instead."

"Fuck, no," Zane says. "His cock isn't allowed to play with double entry."

"Who said anything about double entry?" I flick my eyes to Zane.

I might never have done anything like this, but my not-so-innocent brother Charlie is far from the good boy image he puts out there. And with a few beers in him, with friends he trusts, he has stories. Stories and things that make what we're doing here beginner stuff.

"But you're right. The big guy's going to have to wait. Or not. Stand up, Jones. Kiss Haley, Rockwell." I take her hands from Zane. Because I've got a much better idea. Haley kisses him, and when she pulls back and flicks her eyes to me, I lift her off him and hold her to my chest. "Do you trust me?" I stare into her blue eyes.

Fuck, I'm not one to be poetic anymore. My ex wiped all that out of me . . . or maybe she didn't, because I see my future in Haley. With her, whatever that means. Not that the future here is guaranteed. But then it's not back at home either. That makes it even more important.

"Yes." She swallows.

"Good. And you'll tell me if I take this too far?"

She nods. I bring her in for a kiss. Her swollen lips linger on mine for only a second before I flip her around and point her at the others.

"Lay down again, Green," I bark at him. He's slow to move. The canyon-sized furrows on his forehead give me pause, but then he sinks to his knees, his head aiming in the same direction as Easton's. "Not that way. Turn around, your feet toward Rockwell."

I let Haley slide down the front of my chest until the plug in her ass grinds against my jumping cock. Damn, this better fucking work.

Calvin's the first one to not jump to my commands. Dante clears his throat, and Calvin moves, lying on the mattress the same direction as Easton. Calvin's feet are near Easton's head.

"You're going to have to be more specific, Captain." There's a lilt to Dante's voice. The damn chef likes this a lot. But I don't care either way. This is for her, not us.

"Closer, Calvin. Scissor your legs with Easton."

Calvin's jaw visibly ticks, and he glares. I stare back. He snaps and moves his legs, one over and one under Easton's. Haley looks back at me as she sinks to her knees beside them. Like I've given her a present. Their damn dicks are like twins. She takes one in each hand.

"If you're doing this, you need to tighten up the rope," Zane says behind me.

"What?" Easton twists.

"Get closer," Dante laughs. He's playing with the lock on the suitcase. It clicks open. "You want this, Cap?"

So it's Cap now. I take the vibrator from his hand. "No, use that massive equipment you have to loosen her up and stretch her out. We don't want Sugar feeling anything but the pleasure she deserves, the pleasure she's earned."

I kneel next to her, moving her hair out of the way. I kiss along the side of her neck as she works them separately. I nibble along her hairline, and when she's joined her hands together, making one dick out of the two of them, licking around the heads, I whisper into her ear. It's not fucking romantic. It's a need. Waiting another second, another hour, another day might be the right thing to do. Find the right time, but I can't. It's my needs I'm going after now.

"I love you," I whisper.

She hears it. The bob of her head freezes for a second. Her mouth's full. I don't want her to say it back. Fuck, I hope she doesn't, not right now. This moment isn't about me, not any more than I've made it by saying it now. I move back to the spot behind her ear and suck hard.

Her hips buck next to me. When I glance back, it might not be from me but rather from Dante's massive cock impaling her.

The buzz of the vibrator sets the high notes of the music that Green and Rockwell are filling with "Fuck" and "shit" as she sucks them into her mouth.

Zane's working her clit while Dante's holding on to her hips, slamming into her. "You feel so good, Sassy. You think that the two of them are going to fill you this well?"

She pulls her neck away from me. One arm's holding her up, the other hand's wrapped around the two of them, but her head snaps to Dante.

"You don't like it when I point out that my cock is the best. Got it, Sassy. It will be our huge secret."

Her head flicks back, and she all but growls at him.

He momentarily lifts his hands in submission.

"You can be replaced," Zane says from the other side of her.

"Indeed," I agree.

Haley drops her head and takes the two of them into her mouth again. They're clawing at the mattress and blankets beneath them.

"Damn, Bunny."

"Oh fuck, Haley," Rockwell adds.

It might be their words or Haley's humming and choking as she sucks them down, but Dante's thrust turns ferocious, and shit, my cock is leaking watching all of it. My eyes catch Zane, and he gives me one of his smiles, only these say everything I can't. How fucking lucky I am to be here, with a woman who will do this, and do it so amazingly well.

Dante screams his release, and Haley gasps for breath as she moans over Calvin and Easton. She's close but hasn't gone over the edge yet, and that's even better.

Zane's there, lifting her up. "Legs this way, Haley." He places her over the top of Easton, facing Calvin.

Dante lifts his head from where he's lying on the mat. "Catch." He tosses a tube of lube to Calvin. "Use a lot."

Green nods and puts some on himself.

"Damn, Green," Dante huffs out a tired breath. He rolls to the side, his eyes wide open like he's pulled an all-nighter but needs to read just one more chapter.

Green nods and hands it to Haley. She applies more to Rockwell.

"You ready?" Zane asks.

"Yes," her voice comes out raspy. But in the dim light of the twinkle lights, she gives me a sly smile. I lean in and take her lips. I'm going to take a lot more of her in a second.

"Hold yourselves together," Dante conducts from his reclining pose. He's moved a few feet for a better view, I suppose.

It's Easton who reaches through her legs and holds Calvin and himself together. While Zane and I help her into them.

"Go slow, Little Bird. Only move when you are ready. Not until then."

She grunts. Zane and I are on our knees. Holding her sides.

"You good?" I ask her, searching her face for the truth.

"Yess," she hisses out.

"Go up a little," I say. I wiggle my hand between her legs and slide my pinky slowly inside her. Calvin and Easton are there, but I'm not thinking about it. Her skin's taut.

"Here." Zane squirts lube on my finger, and I work it around her. Haley wraps her arms around my neck. Her forehead drops to my shoulder.

"I've got you. Relax, a deep breath in." I incline my head to Zane, and he pulls the butt plug out some. I work a second finger on rubbing the lube where I can reach.

She takes a deep breath. Her teeth scrape along my collarbone. "Better." She lifts her head.

"Good. I believe in you." I want this, but I'm not going to let her get hurt. "Chest to Calvin."

"Come here, Chiefie." Calvin leans up on his elbows and kisses her, but when I push her hips slowly down, seating her all the way, he hisses, his head bouncing on the mattress.

I straddle Easton and pick the lube up and put a good dollop in my palm. I pull out the plug. Haley moans as I do.

I place it to the side, and I lube my cock and her bud. I grip her hips. Her pale skin shines in the dim light.

I open my mouth to say something, but Zane cuts me off. "You ready, Haley? Sam first." He's rubbing his hard cock near her head.

"Yes." She reaches out to grab him by the base.

"Sam first, Little Bird. One step at a time."

Her head shakes.

"I want your voice, Sugar."

"Yes, please. Now move. I can't move. Make us come, Sam."

I give half a laugh. It's not the right thing to do, but I can't help it. What a weird family. But we are—we can get through anything.

I place my cock on her bud. Inching it in slowly, stretching her a little at a time. She's quiet. Too quiet. For as quiet as she's being, Calvin and Easton are swearing and grunting.

"You good, Sassy?" Dante's on the opposite side from Zane.

"Yes."

"What are you waiting for, Cap? The wheel is yours," Dante says.

Easton groans behind me, and I have to agree. But then I push the rest of the way in and she's so tight. And with each stroke I take, that's what I'm doing. I'm not controlling just my orgasm and hers but the rest of them too. Haley's got her lips around Zane's cock.

I roar with my thrust. "You're mine. You're ours." And damn if I don't want this to last forever.

Chapter 14

Small Fish

Haley

My body has no end. There's a carnival of sensations going on around me. I'm on fire in every sense. I'm stretched more than I've ever been, but with each thrust Sam takes, I love it more. I'm becoming addicted to it. I'm addicted to all of them, more than I ever thought.

Then Sam whispered he loves me and I left my body. How could I ever be so lucky? There's no way I deserve any of this. But I'm taking it; I'm going to take all of it. Fake it until you make it, right? I moan again. My soul hovers outside of my body.

I dart my tongue out around the tip of Zane's cock. I want to taste him fully at the base of my throat. But it's hard when I'm . . . so full. My eyes dart up to his brown pools. Can love shine from eyes? It can because that's what his do.

"You're so fucking gorgeous. Look at you taking all of us. You're such a love, Little Bird." His cock moves from my mouth, and I reach for him. But his neck dips and he sucks in my lips, then kisses around my neck to my ear. "I love you, Haley Brewster."

"I love you too."

"Good, because I'm going to come on your tits now." He pulls my left breast out between Calvin and me. His hand shakes on his cock until thick streams fly from it, coating me. Sam slows his pace. The second Zane's done, Sam's grip on my hips tightens.

"Haley." It's an affirmation, question, and statement, Sam says.

"It's so good. More, please. More."

Dante chuckles from the side. He's hard again, his hand on his cock. Zane was right. This isn't something I'll ever do with Dante. There's not enough lube in the world. Sam's a piston sending Calvin and Easton deeper into me with each thrust. I ease my hand between Calvin's chiseled abs and my stomach, and I swear I can feel them under my ribs.

"Let me do that." Dante pulls my hand out and pushes his in instead of mine. His fingers find my clit. He contrasts Sam's motions, rubbing when there's space, and I'm gone. Rational and irrational thoughts vanish. My senses are gone. I have no idea of anything. Only a velvety night with stars that grow behind my eyes.

I'm coming harder than I ever have. My stomach flutters, convulses, with my hips matching Sam's. Shouts fill the jungle. It's a melody of love and sex. I'm bouncing on Calvin's chest. Aftershocks wrack me. Fingers grasp at me, pouring over my skin. So many hands, each of them different. I'd know each one of them without a speck of light or any clues.

"How you doing?" Sam's commanding touch runs down my spine.

"I can't move."

Dante laughs, but there's a moment rustling from the rest of them.

"I'm just a limp poodle." There's chuckling around me. I meant noodle, but I don't have enough strength to correct myself.

"Well, I don't normally like limp poodles or noodles, but in this case, I'll allow it." Dante kisses the top of my head. "I'm going to go get a tub of cool water to give you a sponge bath."

I shiver. I'm not sure I can—

"A light-handed sponge bath, and then we're going to tuck you into your softest pajamas and tuck you into a clean bed, Sassy."

I lift my head from Calvin's chest. Or at least I think I do.

Sam pulls away first. I both love it and hate it. Then Easton wiggles out from underneath the pile. He hisses under his breath. And I spin. In the throes of it all, I forgot about his arm. It's been three weeks, but I see him stretching it at odd angles when he thinks no one's watching.

"I'm good, Firefly." Easton places kisses on the top of my head. "I'll be right back."

My hand flings to my clammy chest; my heart won't stop thundering behind my ribs.

"Come here, Little Bird." Zane cocks his head at me. I don't want to move. But Calvin's got to want to get cleaned up. I push to sit up, letting him have his freedom.

"Don't move." His head cocks to Zane.

"She's good. You can go help Dante with the water if you want. It's a hardship I can bear."

Zane holds his hands out to me again.

"I've got her," Calvin's tone clips deep.

"Okay, okay." Zane stands. "You want something to eat?"

"Is there any Pepperfruit left?"

"You know, Dante's got some squirreled away just for you."

"Thanks." My head drops to Calvin. And it's only then I feel him twitch inside of me. "You sure you don't want to—"

"I'm good." His arms lock around my back just as I start to shiver.

"Are you cold, Haley?" Sam drops a blanket over our legs, not waiting for my response,

Calvin moves, spreading out and smoothing it over my back. My eyes flick from Sam to Calvin. Tonight has changed everything. We're in this all together. And I'm not the only one who's realized it. Sam took charge, and we did things that wouldn't have happened without him taking the lead. Not even with Dante hinting at them before. Yeah, there's going to be a hell of a lot of awkwardness. Maybe.

I push to slide a few inches up Calvin's chest. "Hey."

But he doesn't look at me.

I grab his chin. "Hey, I love you."

"I love you too." Calvin kisses the top of my nose. He moves me to the crook of his arm. His cock slides out of me.

I gaze up at Sam, standing at the side of the mattress. "I love you." The memory of his words comes back, warming me up.

He crouches next to my legs. "I love you." But he grabs me around the back of my neck and kisses me until sharp sparks zip around my groin and I have to clench my legs together. I interlace my fingers with his as the kiss wanes. I place my other hand on Calvin's chest.

"This, this isn't a competition," I say. If this spirals into a testosterone-fueled feud, who can fuck me better . . . No, I don't want that.

"Of course," Sam says, bringing my knuckles to his lips for a kiss.

"That was a lot of teamwork." Calvin kisses the side of my cheek.

"A team—that's what I really want us to be. One where we share things," I say.

"I'd say we've got the sharing thing down pretty well," Dante says as he hits the top step. He's brought a large bin of water up.

"Oh, I should have just gone down and gotten cleaned —" I move my legs from Calvin's side and sit up, but nope. I'm not climbing down that ladder, not tonight.

Dante laughs.

"What?" My hair is stuck under Calvin, and I have to give it a yank.

"You should see the look on your beautiful face. You need to stay here." He lays a clean sheet down. "Bring her over here, will you, Sam?"

And I'm airborne. Over in Dante's washroom.

"Zane," Dante calls out.

"Yo?" Zane's hand reaches up with a bowl in it. "Take this. I want to get some other things."

Dante puts the bowl on a stool Zane made. "Hey, you need to make us a washroom addition."

"I'll get right on that," Zane calls up.

"A bathroom?" I laugh.

"A washroom. We'll figure it out tomorrow," Dante says.

I reach for the cloth, but Dante doesn't let me wash myself. He's efficient, and the cool water on my skin breathes life into me. Moving has me groaning.

"Be still. Let me do this, Sassy." Dante slaps my hand away when I try to take the cloth.

And I let my arms go limp at my side. I'm a noodle, *be the noodle.* "Thank you." I bite my lip.

Calvin and Sam strip the sheets off the mattress. "And don't you even try to do the laundry tomorrow. Or I'll have to punish you." Dante dries me off. "Hands up."

I hold my arms up, and Dante slips my pajamas onto me even as my eyes drift closed. He picks me up and holds me to his chest. I breathe him in. It should be illegal for anyone to smell as good as he constantly does.

The light's bright and full-force when I wake up. "Holy crap." I no longer reach for a phone or even a watch to tell what time it is. I don't need to anymore. The shadows streaming across the floor let me know it's got to be close to three.

Pepper's lying on my feet, and Penny has her head on the mattress.

"Hey there." I rub Pepper behind her ears first and then move to Penny. But I don't hear anyone else bustling around below.

I stretch my legs. I'm sore and covered in bruises. There are two on my hips, another on my thigh, and one on my breast. There's also a wicked smile on my face when I remember everything that happened.

"Where is everyone?" I ask Penny as I gingerly get up and slowly move to hunt through my cubby for something to wear.

Penny follows at my heels and drops to the floor when I stop to put on my clothes. She's got the most expressive eyes. It's almost like she's saying they're off doing dumb boy shit again. I climb down the ladder to the first platform. Penny jumps the four feet and heads down the ramp on the far side of the tree that Zane made her. You can tell she doesn't like it. And if Calvin's anywhere near, she'll whine until he picks her up.

I cup my hands and tilt my head up to the observation tower. "Hello."

There's no answer, so I head down to the kitchen area. Pepper and Penny are already waiting for me. "Where are they? Did you two get breakfast? Heck, lunch?"

Penny's tail wags in double time. But I'm not falling for it. I know they fed her already.

Pepper strolls off to the beach. Which may or may not be her answer, or it could be her being her sassy self. I stop by the kitchen. Under a covered bowl, I find a breakfast of coconut grits mixed with some of Pepper's fruit. I stare through the thinning jungle to the beach as I eat. But I can't hear anyone. They wouldn't have left me alone. I chomp on the toasted coconut. I would have thought I would be sick of it by now, but with the rainy season gone, it's good, and things are crisp instead of soggy.

I head out to the beach, taking the zigzag path behind the new blind that the guys have been working on. Dante's out at the fish weir. It's low tide. But something's different. And it takes me a good second to pick out what it is.

"Where's the tender?" My stomach flips, and I want to lose my breakfast.

"Sassy!" Dante says, his voice full of his normal sunshine.

"Don't you Sassy me. Where are they?"

"They went to see if the WaveRunner is still there."

"And . . ." Because I can definitely see there's an "and" going on here.

"And they went back to the Pomelo village to bury the rest of the villagers."

My mother used to say, *"It's a good thing you're not a cartoon because there would be steam pouring out of your ears."* It's one of the reasons why I learned to control my emotions in front of guests. But it's true. The guys are family now, and I'm not hiding my true self anymore.

"Hey, they'll be back soon."

"But they didn't need to go at all."

"Sassy . . . this has been festering in Calvin for a long time."

I cross my arms over my chest. "I'm not heartless. It's a really noble thing he wants to do. But they're dead. He's putting not only his life in danger but Zane, Sam, and Easton's too."

"Sam wants to know if the pirates came back to take the WaveRunner. And Zane . . . Zane wants—"

"Chickens."

"Yeah, but don't tell him I told you. He wants it to be a surprise."

"And Easton?"

"I think Easton wants—"

"Closure." I drop my arms. It's easy to tell that he's not been himself since he was shot. He hasn't even tried to swim yet.

"Closure? You think? I think he just wants to make sure the lot of them don't get hurt and upset you." Dante tosses a fish into the basket.

"Oh . . . sure, that's probably it." I nod at Dante and sink down onto the big rock next to the fish weir.

Dante's got the weir mostly cleared out. I watch a small fish swimming around in the shallow water. It's small enough to fit through the bars, but it can't find its way out of the prison. And suddenly I feel a lot like a small fish.

Chapter 15

Motley Crew

Easton

The waves are choppy as we round the cove to where the Rock Candy used to sit. It's fucking weird seeing the full wall of the bluff without the yacht there. I'm not sure why I've even fucking come. But talking them out of going didn't seem like it was going to happen.

Last night, that . . . yeah. Last night was one of the craziest things—if not the craziest thing—I've ever done. And I've done some shit. Most of it while drunk and out of my mind after a big team meet. But nothing like that. Yeah, I'm still processing.

We should all be back at camp, not on this damn tender, but here we are on our little four-man journey, not processing what went down. And we're not there with Haley this morning because we have to do this now. Now—when the WaveRunner has been sitting there for the last three weeks and those poor people have been there for a long time. Yeah, but the waves bounce us up.

"We've got enough fuel?" I shout into the wind at Zane. He's got his hand on the tiller of the outboard motor.

"Yeah, we got a shit ton for this trip and more stored back at camp. That was Dante's idea. Scary brilliant, that bloke is," Zane says. His eyes flick to mine and then back at the horizon. Zane's deep in thought too. His Britishness always goes up by ten factors when he's thinking too hard.

Calvin and Sam sit in the row in front of me, searching the cove. We took the binoculars. That was the most discussion we had after Sam unilaterally declared we should be searching for it and then Zane added his little side quest. He spent all morning making a crate out of one of the storage containers, carefully replacing the lid with one made from bamboo he'd woven together. It's tied down next to two spare plastic fuel containers.

I don't know if Zane's ever tried to catch a chicken. It's not as simple as walking up to one and grabbing it. And that's with ones used to people. But then, Zane will probably just flash his gleaming smile and the chicken will jump into the container and pull the lid shut itself.

I laugh, thinking about a ten-year-old Emily chasing chickens. Every time she caught one, it would flutter from her hands, squawking and jumping. More than once, we spent the night on the neighbor's farm in Maine. I had to help with the chores. I think it was Susan's way of trying to teach me responsibility.

I told her I hated it, but I fucking loved it. That's probably the only reason I was allowed to continue to go. That, and Emily and I were on our own. I'd have taken shoveling shit for weeks on end to not have to listen to the sound of Susan's voice. I think she finally figured out how much we loved it, so we weren't allowed to go anymore.

Frustration rises up from my toes. This whole thing is

tied to Dad and money, of course. It's always about money. At least with my family. Damn, my dad has horrible taste in women.

I try to think of my mother, but I can't even remember what she sounded like, only a faint memory of her smell and that she loved Christmas. The house was alive. We had money back then, fucking wealthy compared to everyone else in the area, but nothing near what Dad has now. That was back before he made a new company with Harding. Back when everything was only Rockwell Tire, no Rockwell-Harding financial.

I blink into the sun. I'm searching the coastline and the horizon of the ocean. But there's nothing here. Nothing at all but water, surf, and rock. It's bright and hot.

"Hey!" Zane yells forward to Sam and Calvin. They turn. "I'm going to keep going if you two are okay with it."

Sam waves back. "Yeah, let's go. The less fuel we use, the better."

"On it." Zane steers carefully past the cave where we'd tied up the WaveRunner. It's a large cave when it's low tide. Sam and Calvin have their heads down, watching the vanishing reef below the boat as Zane pulls us out deeper into the ocean.

We run next to the bluff. And my stomach hardens. The last time I was here, we were outrunning the pirates on the WaveRunner, praying they didn't see us. My hand reflexively goes to my arm and my shoulder. The bullet went through my bicep. But most days I've got a deep ache in the back of my shoulder.

I change positions and lean back, stretching my arm out. The damn neuropathy sends tingles through the fingers of my right hand. I shake it out, swallowing down the urge to swear into the tender's spray. The rock wall towers up next to us. I crane my neck back. It's fucking impossible to think that I ever thought I could climb up there with a useless arm. But we're here, alive. And that's how we're going to stay.

The boat skips on the waves. I'm gripping with my good hand, and I send the fingers of my other hand through my hair, smoothing it back. Chicken Beach emerges from behind the cliff. The WaveRunner is there, lying on its side. And relief crests over me.

"It's there," Zane shouts, but he sounds a little upset.

There's two schools of thought: Calvin and Zane were hoping it was still there. But Sam and I were both hoping it was gone. If it was gone, it meant the pirates came back, searched for it, didn't find us, and got the hell out of here with it. I don't think it's a good idea if we take it now.

It's low tide, but there's no reef to speak of around the long sandy spit. Zane pulls up as close as he can get. Calvin jumps off the front, and Sam slides into the water. The outboard motor tilted up, we pull up onto the sand, high enough that the boat won't move with the tide. And then we're standing around the WaveRunner, staring at it like we're doing a damn autopsy.

"It wasn't hit. At least, not what's visible," Calvin states after brushing the sand off the sides. It's sunk a few feet into the beach.

I grab the shovel out of the tender and start digging. Each shovel has my shoulder crying out.

"Let me do it," Zane says.

I ignore his hand. "I've got it." I dig out the front, then stand up, my shoulders still hunched. I've made a dent, but the other side still needs to come out.

I take a breath, but Calvin's hand lands over mine. "Give me the damn shovel," he says.

I let go and stand back and watch. Zane's on his knees digging with his hands. Sam grabs the handlebars and Zane the back of the seat. We push it out onto the compact sand.

It's a mess. The key is rusted into its slot.

"Is it worth it?" I stand back.

Calvin glares like I've said to pull the plug on his grandmother's life support. "If we can get this working, we can use it to get fruit, fish, eggs. It uses a hell of a lot less fuel."

I shrug. Because I still think we should leave it be. Let the pirates think we died.

"Shut up." Calvin crouches.

I throw my hands up. "I didn't say anything."

"You said enough back at camp. Them coming back is going to happen. It won't matter if this is here or not."

"Your opinion, and I disagree."

Sam stands back, his hands on his hips. "I don't think it's going to matter. This has got more sand in it than Penny's fur at the end of the day. No way it's going to run."

"That sounds like a challenge." Calvin smirks up at him.

"Fine, you play with it. Help me find some chickens." Zane cocks his head to the jungle.

"Sure." I follow Zane up the beach as it rises to the jungle. How much time are we going to spend here? I just want to get back to Haley. It's got to be at least one—I check the sun as we dip into the jungle. We fight through thick vegetation. The memory of that morning surges back at me. "Where did you find the eggs before?"

"This way." Zane turns the opposite direction to where Calvin and I ran.

It's coming back in waves. The thud of our steps, the tearing of my skin. The bile rising up my throat.

This side of the island must not get the same breeze as

back at camp. It's damn humid, and bugs are buzzing around my ears. I swat at my neck, and my shoulder cries out, on fire. "Fuck."

"You good, mate?"

"Peachy."

"I don't see any signs of the chickens yet."

"Yeah." I clench my eyes tightly closed. It isn't helping anything. We need to find some damn birds and get the hell out of here. "They can be tough to spot. Look low."

Zane shoots me a *no shit* look.

"You found them before. We can find them again."

"That's the spirit." He gives me a verbal slap on the back.

We move through the jungle, and it's at least ten minutes before I realize that neither Zane or I are making any noise. There in the underbrush beneath some ferns, I spot some dark red and brown feathers. I point and make hand signals that seven months ago would have had me scoffing. Zane follows my instructions, circling around the side.

I dart my hand under the fern and snag the leg of a hen. I pull her out upside down. She's squawking, batting her wings against my legs. I do like the farmer used to do and tuck her under my arm. Her neck cranes up to me.

That's when I see it. She's sitting not on a nest of eggs but a nest of chicks. Ten or more scramble out around my feet, missing the warmth of their mother.

"Shit, shit." Zane's eyes are wide. "You did it."

"Yeah. Take your shirt off, tie one end shut, and get all the chicks into it," I say.

Zane does, dropping flat to the ground and filling his shirt. "They're so cute." He pivots on the path, going back the way we came.

"Wait." There's peeping coming from a few steps away. "Fuck, there's another nest."

I've got a hen under each arm. Zane's cradling his shirt as we come out onto the beach.

"What the hell have you guys been doing?" Calvin yells.

"Wanking off," I say, sounding more like Zane than myself. "What the hell does it look like we've been doing?"

"Hold this. Don't drop it." Zane passes the chick bag to Sam. "It's chicks," Zane answers before Sam asks. Zane grabs the bin from the tender and pulls the lid off it. He takes the chicks out of the shirt one at a time, carefully placing them in the tub.

"Get the lid ready. I'm going to drop the hens in together." As long as I've kept pressure on the birds, they've been mostly quiet.

"No, wait, give me one." Calvin takes the one from my bad arm. He flips it over. Holding its wings and back with one hand, he draws a line from the beak down with the other. The chicken closes its eyes in a trance. Calvin lays it down in the bin of chicks. The little balls of fuzz gather around it. Calvin takes the second one and does the same thing. Zane affixes the lid.

"We got what we came for," I say. "How's this hunk of junk?" I point to the WaveRunner.

"Well, we're not going to be running it anytime soon. But I can fix it," Calvin says.

"A man of many talents—chicken and motor whisperer." Zane laughs.

I want to say not everything is worth fixing, but then that kind of wrecks Calvin's entire personality. And I'm still not sure how I feel about him. Even after last night. Which I'm fucking confused about.

Chapter 16

Rouge Wave

Zane

Calvin's sitting next to me, and we're pulling away from the beach. The WaveRunner's almost floating and tied up to a tree. The tide will lift it off the sand in the next hour. When we swing back around, we'll be able to grab it and tow it back to camp.

I glance over at Calvin. Sam and Easton are in the front of the tender. And damn, I know he wants to do this, but it's getting later in the afternoon, three, maybe. And the sun will start to set in a few hours. Five, five-thirty. It's light a little longer than it would be back home.

December. I'm trying not to think about it. My mom and sister are all alone for Christmas. It's December tenth, if we haven't lost track of any days. And I don't think we have. It's been a long time. But it feels longer.

And I get it. I get why Calvin wants to bury what's left of the people over at the pomelo beach. But we need to get back home.

Fuck. Home. But that's what it is.

"It's like three," I say.

"Three-thirty," Calvin counters like he's got some atomic clock in his back pocket.

I cock my head at him.

"It's just a guess. But yeah, it's getting late. Tides for this kind of trip will never be perfect." His head bows.

And I'm feeling like a fucking asshole.

"We can do it some other time, another day, another year—I suppose it doesn't matter." He looks out at the rocky shoreline that follows Chicken Beach, then back to the bin of clucking chickens. "It's not right to keep them from water and bugs either. Plus, we're going to need to build some kind of enclosure. At least at first, until they just start hanging out near us."

"You sure?" My heart soars.

"Yeah, we should at least poke out around the end of the island and see what we can see."

"Hell, yeah." I shouldn't, but I push the throttle down. It gives us a little more speed.

Sam's head snaps back to me. "What's that for?"

"We're going up a bit and then turning back to camp," I say.

"That's a fucking good idea." Sam gives a single nod and pivots back to the front of the boat.

The coast undulates in and out for a good clip. And when we edge out to the ocean, it's just as rough as I expect.

"Hold on," I shout. And fucking hell, we catch a rogue wave and bounce. Most of the things are tied down—everything but me.

My feet fly out of the boat, and my hand leaves the tiller. Calvin screams. I'm arching my body as far away from the motor as possible, and when the waves hit and it's just water—not the searing pain of a blade chopping through my body—I've got to say I'm relieved.

I'm not wearing a life jacket. Because, well, complacency happens. That's what flashes through my mind as I'm sinking down. Fuck, how easy it would be to not even try.

And then I see Haley's blue eyes shining at me. Her smile, her calm demeanor.

I'm pulling at the water, rising up as I do. It's ten seconds, maybe less. When I gasp through the surface, the tender's over a hundred feet away. I raise my hand up like I've got a question. I bob for a few seconds, sputtering out the saltwater from my lungs. And then I head straight for the raft. Well, not that straight—my line is more of a crooked path. But Calvin's got the tender pointed at me.

I glance up every few strokes and make sure I'm not heading off in the wrong direction, but then the raft is there and Easton and Sam are yanking me from the water.

I'm searching for something light-hearted to say, but I've got nothing when Calvin smirks at me. "If you were getting too warm, you could have just spoken up."

Sam's glaring at me. "Damn, Zane, that scared the shit out of me."

"Me too." I sit in the middle row of seats and look over at the chick and hens.

Easton sits down next to me and leans over, too. "They're fine. Maybe a little confused as to why the ground is shaking."

"Chickens? They're too fucking stupid to know that the ground isn't supposed to shake," Calvin says.

"Right, well, no more shaking." My attention is caught by a flash to the side. The sun's beating down on a long white sand beach around the corner.

Calvin slows the boat. "Damn, that's pretty." He

glances over at Sam and then to me. "You want to take a look or head back to camp?"

"I think we're pushing our luck," Sam says.

But I counter with, "Sure, I'm good, and now we know the current around the edge of the island makes for some crazy waves." It's something I should already have thought of.

Is it weird I'm just as happy knowing that the little chicks didn't die as myself? I'll have to figure it out. But then no. That's something I can do with Haley later. With my head in her lap, her fingers caressing my ear. A wave—no, no more waves—a sensation of calmness fills me.

"You sure?" Calvin holds my eyes. I know for certain he wants to check it out. He always wants to explore.

"Down a little and back?" I suggest. The sun's hanging lower.

We all turn to Sam, and he shrugs and points to the beach. "Ten minutes and then we go back and get the WaveRunner." Sam tosses me a life jacket.

I put it on without comment. The trip to the beach has the sun in our eyes but the wind at our backs.

"Damn." Calvin's voice trails out behind us. "I think that's more orchard."

"It's the effing motherload." Easton points.

We're off the tender and have it tied up to a solid post of what must have been a dock a long time ago. And it goes without saying that with so much food available and visible from the shoreline, the pirates must either have access to a port or an island rich enough in food that they don't give a hoot about what's here. Because bloody hell?

"Ten minutes. Let's take as much as we can but no more than what can last." Sam's got the machete in his hand.

I grab the shovel. I'm going to play whack-a-mole with some low-hanging coconuts.

We end up with one huge bunch of bananas the size of Calvin's torso, and the bottom of the tender is littered with coconuts. There's a bunch of Pepper's fruit here too and even a few mangos and papayas—we haven't seen any papayas on the island before. I fill my shirt with them.

Easton's approaching the boat with his arms loaded down with more mangos.

"That's got to be it. Any more and we're going to be overweight," I say.

"Agreed," Sam says. He holds the line, waiting for the rest of us to gingerly hop in.

Calvin takes it slow around the corner, and I'm not a fool—I hold on for my life this time. I'm not ready for another dunk.

It takes longer than any of us like getting the Wave-Runner hooked to the back of the tender, and when we slowly pull into the home beach, the sun isn't going down—it's down. We pull in with twilight at our backs.

Penny's the first to greet us, then Haley runs out onto the beach. Her arms are crossed over her breast, her stew face firmly in place. Dante's behind her, and she drops her arms, her mask too. She runs toward the boat.

And when she comes closer, I can see it. Her face is puffy and her eyes are red. And my heart sinks. We did her wrong. So wrong. I don't have anyone to blame. This morning was awkward, and I think we all wanted to run away. Run away with our excuses instead of facing the things we need to.

"Oh, Little Bird." I hop out of the tender. Calvin's still motoring it in, but I don't give a fuck. I pick her up and hold her head to my chest. "We shouldn't have gone and made you worry."

"No, you shouldn't have. And . . ."

I let her lean back. I can see it in her face—under all the worry is a good solid layer of mad. "You're angry. You have every right to be."

Her brows furrow and her lips purse for a second. "I—"

"Have every right to be mad. I apologize too, Sugar." Sam takes her hand and kisses it.

Her eyes float over to Easton.

"I went to keep them out of trouble," he says. "But yeah, we shouldn't have gone."

"I'm the fucking idiot who almost got Zane killed," Calvin growls.

"What?"

"He's exaggerating. But damn, I'm bloody glad to see you." I pull her in for another tight hug, as tight as the life-jacket will let me.

"Exaggeration or not, that's not good," Haley says. Penny jumps in the surf at the side of the tender, which is something she never does. "What's she so excited about?"

"That's our surprise. Let's get the tender tied up." I take the rope from where Easton tosses it, and Sam, Easton, Haley, and I pull and yank the tender up onto the sand. It's a hell of a lot heavier with the WaveRunner and the load of fruit, and maybe Calvin being on it might have something to do with the weight too.

Dante's showed up at some point. Pepper's at his ankles. "Damn." He peers into the tender. "Merry Christmas to us. What's in the box?"

"It's a surprise," I say.

"Does it say cluck, cluck?" Dante grinds his hips in a poor imitation of my unforgettable lap dance.

"Yes, and no. Now don't ruin the surprise for Haley." I point my finger at him.

"Didn't your mum tell you it's not polite to point?" His head tilts back as he laughs.

"Don't get too excited." Easton stops at Haley's side and kisses her cheek. "I really am sorry," he whispers into her ear.

"It's not a 55-million-dollar diamond. No, it's better." I take her hand and lead her up to the beach. "Sit here. I'll bring it to you." I jog back to the tender and take the bin out. It's not that heavy, more awkward. I set it down, and through an opening big enough for my fist, I pull out a baby chick and set it on her lap.

"Oh, it's the cutest thing."

"How many more are there?" Dante asks.

"You're not killing it."

"Haley, you're not a vegetarian," Dante laughs. "Where do you think chicken nuggets come from?"

"Not Violet." Haley runs her finger over the fluffball's head.

"Fine, but if there's a Gus and Mike in there, when they grow up—" Dante stops at Haley's stare. "We can talk about it later." Dante throws his hands in the air and heads over to the tender to help the others unload the fruit.

"You got the WaveRunner too." Haley's looking more at the chick than the other guys or me.

"We did."

"What happened? How did you almost . . ."

"Die? I didn't. Or at least now I didn't. But if that had happened six months ago?" I shrug. "Rogue wave when the current shifted around the side of the island. I was going too fast. Everyone else was hanging on, the supplies and chickens tied down. I flew off the back. But between you and Easton taking the time to show me how to swim, I was fine afterwards. There was a second when I thought I might not be when I was sinking, though. And all I could think of was you. I don't want to live without you. I know I've said I love you. But I need you to understand what you mean to me. You calm my soul. You make things right." I pause because I've been saying *when we get back* before but now it's a lot harder. "When we get back, I don't want there to be a time in my life when we're not together."

She nods.

"No, Haley, I mean it. Fuck, at any other time this would be where a guy drops to his knees and begs the best most amazing girl on the planet to marry him. But it's a little different for us. For you. Whatever the equivalent of marriage is in this sort of situation. That's what I want. Picket fence. House full of little Haleys. I want you. I want you always. I choose you."

She's crying, and damn, my stomach twists because I've gone and overwhelmed her. I should have given it a minute. Let her have some space. She needs space.

"I want that too." The tears are full-on coming down her cheeks.

"Fuck, yes!" I jump up and punch the sky. But this isn't some sort of alternate universe of a Brat Pack movie. There's no credits running with us huddled behind that white picket fence. There's a tender full of fruit and a Wave-Runner that needs to be hauled onto the shore and hidden with brown palm fronds.

But I don't care. I pick Haley up and twirl her around. Her shoes go flying, and her arms are scrunched below my life vest. I gaze down at her. My girl. She's mine. And that's how I always want it to be. This moment will live frozen in time for me. "I love you, Haley Brewster."

"I love you too."

A peep comes from between us, and I pull back. "Oh, shit."

"Violet's good." She holds the chick up and then gently places it back with the others.

"Well, alright then. We should have a 'welcome to the family' party. When's Thanksgiving, anyway?"

Chapter 17

Recruit

Haley

"I forgot about Thanksgiving. And Halloween! We forgot about Halloween?"

The little chicks' peeps are louder than the waves. And it brings me back to when Steven brought Ginger home for the first time. She was such a little ball of fur. I was in love—with more than the puppy. At least, I thought I was. I thought he was too.

I glance back at Zane. His big brown eyes are glowing at me. Glowing with love. The chicks aren't puppies, and he's not Steven.

I'm going to have to trust that each of them are telling me the truth. Bring it back into my broken heart. Hell, I should know better than the average person that nothing is guaranteed. Not time, people, or money. We have it all right now. And it's amazing. My life right now can be amazing if I want it to be.

Yes, the Rock Candy being gone is horrible. But three

weeks, a month, have gone by and there's no sign of us being in more danger. There's no sign that we need to panic.

I glance over at the guys hauling fruit out of the bottom of the tender. We've got enough food for weeks, and sure, eventually we'll run out of gas to use the tender or the WaveRunner, but if we use the path and avoid the bamboo, it's not so bad to hike to the other side of the island. It's . . . gut-wrenching and sad. But the people who lived there would want us to use what they planted. I would at least want to know that I'd helped people survive.

"How could I have forgotten about Halloween?" I say.

Zane's taken off his life vest. He leans over me and kisses me. "We were busy?" He shrugs. "We'll talk more about this later. I should help." He cocks his thumb at the tender.

"I should too." I reach for my shoes that fell off when he spun me around.

"Do you mind watching our new charges? I don't want Penny or Pepper getting too nosy with them." He squeezes my hand.

I'm nodding with wild abandon. Zane's good. I'm good. He's fine. I'm fine. We're good. The little peeps hammer into my brain. "Oh, yes. I think I can manage that."

I'm getting spoiled with letting them do all the physical work. But then, there's five of them and only one of me. There's also a lot of stomping going on, and there are sand flies around Calvin's ankles.

They've got to be done with the fruit. I take a step away from the box and the chicks, and the peeping gets louder. There's a few clucks thrown in too. I pick it up but then quickly put it down. It's heavy. Instead, I drag it a few feet back to a rock to sit on.

"You guys doing okay?" I put my hand into the box. A chick runs over and plops down on my palm. I hold her up to my face. Her white eyelids close.

"Last one." Easton tosses a fruit over to Sam and jumps out of the tender.

Sam makes a detour from carrying a bin of fruit, heading over to me. "What did you say a little bit ago, Sugar?"

It does something to me when he calls me Sugar. As much as yesterday was, I'm ready to go again. I hold Violet the chick up for him to see. Sam winks at me, kisses the top of my head, and then plants a kiss on top of Violet's little head too.

My mouth dries, and there's a twitch in my nether regions. "I said we forgot about Thanksgiving and Halloween."

"We had a lot going on then." Sam holds up a Pepper-fruit to Violet. She pecks at the lemon-colored skin. It's driving me crazy that I don't know the real name of the tree or fruit. Would I have known it if I'd finished my last year of school? Probably not. Maybe. It doesn't make the fruit taste any different.

"That's a lot of fruit," I say. Dante's got a large container and is heading up the trail. He wiggles his eyebrows at me.

Sam sits on the log next to me. The mama hens are quiet, but the babies are chirping.

"I'm still . . ." I search for the right word because mad isn't quite right.

"Yeah, I get it. This morning—it was intense. There wasn't a hell of a lot of eye contact. Well, maybe from Dante. And I guess Zane. But then, he lives in his own happy little bubble. Honestly, I don't even know how the whole thing happened. One second we were eating grilled coconut in silence, and the next we were in the tender speeding away from camp." Sam shakes his head and runs his fingers over the stubble on his chin.

"It's not a good excuse, but I understand how it happened."

"Well, I'm glad. And when you figure it out, you can explain it to me. It's like I blacked out for the entire thing. The only one who was acting normal this morning was Dante."

"And Zane?" I pull Violet back out of the cage.

"No, he was going on about chickens and how great it would be to have eggs again. And when someone said something about going, he started vibrating."

"Vibrating?"

"Yeah, you know when he gets all smiles and then it's like the air starts vibrating with positivity?"

I know exactly what he's talking about, but I guess I never thought that any of the guys would see Zane the same way as I do. "Yes."

"It broke the tension, and then we all started talking about things we could do with the tender. We weren't running away from you."

"I know. Last night was a lot." I'm staring at Violet, and when I look up at him, his blue eyes are searching my face. "In a good way."

He nods, and I see the relief on his face.

I hold Violet out for him to take. She looks even smaller sleeping on his palm.

"Things snapped for me last night."

A rush of adrenaline zings through me. "Snapped?"

"Yeah, not broke. Snapped as it fell into place. It was like I didn't really know I had that in me until last night."

I can only imagine how wide my eyes are.

"Fuck, Haley. I've never wanted anyone as much as I want you. And it scares the shit out of me."

I want to tell him how I feel about him. The words that I've told the other guys linger on my tongue. They roll around my mouth, but I can't get them out. I fear that if I tell him everything in my heart, he'll pull away. He was in charge last night, but he's still broken.

I rest my hand on his knee. "I want you too. Last night was a lot of fun." It's the wrong word, and I inwardly cringe as I say it because it wasn't fun. Well, it was fun. But it was more than amazing sex. We were a group, working together. And he was fully committed to it. When I close my eyes, I can hear the way he growled the orders. He got us to do things that I didn't even know were possible. It's more than crazy.

"Fun. Yes." His eyes question me.

"Wait, Sam. It was more."

"It was, wasn't it?" He takes my hand from his knee and holds it by the tips of my fingers. The kiss he brushes to my knuckles is a whisper that I can barely feel.

My smile catches his, and we're suspended in time like that until a curse from Dante pulls the moment away.

Sam turns. "What's up?" He's jumped up and taken three steps before Dante's done with his ranting and cursing. I wanted to tell Sam I love him.

"I just stubbed my toe. It's nothing; carry on with your canoodling. No, wait until I get back."

I'm shaking my head.

"Work first, canoodling later." Sam takes the tub from Dante and winks back at me.

"Let me see your toe." It's not bleeding, but there's a red spot on the side. "Does this hurt?" I drop to my knees.

"Hmm." His forehead furrows. "Maybe a little higher."

I skim my fingers over the top of his foot.

"Higher, Sassy."

I cock my neck back and hold his eyes. "You're horrible. Work first, canoodle later." I run my hand the rest of the way up his leg to the growing massive bulge on the front of his shorts. I stroke him twice through the cloth as I stand. Then I toss my ponytail over my shoulder as I pivot away. My hair's getting long. Maybe I should let one of the guys cut it?

"Sassy?" Dante says.

"Are you going to help with the work, Dante?"

"I'm going to need a minute."

I laugh as Easton comes over to the box of chickens. "Hey, Firefly . . . I'm sorry. I should have woken you up. Want some help moving these to camp?"

"Yes, and yes."

He cocks his head at me.

"Yes, you should have woken me up. And yes, I would like some help moving them. They're crowded in there." I place Violet back in the box, and she sleepily huddles under a mamma hen.

Easton picks up the box. "I actually went back to the sleeping platform and thought about it. But then you were snoring so peacefully."

"Snoring?" I know I snore. Steven used to tell me all the time how loud I was. Every cabin mate I've ever had said it's more heavy breathing than snoring. He was a walking red flag. If I had a time machine, I'd go back and slap his phone number out of my hand.

He's making good time up the path, but then he stops. "Cute snores, not like the Blue Angels taking off over Pensacola—"

"—like Calvin," we both say together.

I chuckle.

"It's good to hear you laugh. I was nervous about how angry you were going to be. And then when Zane fell off the boat . . . I was worried about him. About how hurt you were going to be if something happened to him when I could have prevented it."

I nod and wait for him to take the chickens to camp. Penny's lost interest in what the other guys are doing on the tender and is jumping at his side. Which attracts Pepper. Easton sets them down next to the big tree. And Pepper jumps up on the ladder and gazes down into the box.

"They're our friends, Pepper."

She mews. So polite.

"We're going to have to figure out how to keep them safe from their new friends," Easton says.

I put my hands on his shoulder. "Hey."

"Hey back at you."

"You know you're not responsible for anyone but yourself?" I hold his blue eyes.

He shakes, trying to laugh it off. "I'm serious. What they do or don't do is up to them." He blinks at me. "But the same can be said for you, too, Firefly. Right? Not everything that happens here is your responsibility."

I wince because he's called me out. And he's not wrong. For a long time, I've taken every little thing that goes wrong onto my shoulders. It's one of the reasons why I like being chief stew. It's not the being in charge part, it's the fixing part. It goes way back.

But then there are times when you can't . . . when you can't fix things. I couldn't fix my mom. I couldn't fix my parents' marriage. I couldn't fix Steven being an asshole. I couldn't fix . . . I . . . My chest is heavy, and I can't breathe. I can't even look Easton in the face. Tears erupt from my eyes, water falling down my cheeks.

"Haley," Easton says on an inhale.

And I bend at the waist. I can't make this better. I can't get us home. I can't fix them. And now what? I've given my soul to them. And there's no making it better.

Chapter 18

Trailblazing

Easton

I catch her as she goes down. She crumples into my arms. "Whoa, whoa." I'm holding her by her waist; her head dangles between her legs.

Her words burst out between hiccups. "I'm . . . stopping . . . myself from . . . hyperventilating."

"Haley," I say softly, rubbing her back with my bad arm while my good one is anchored around her waist. She's still gasping for breath, her hair dangling over the box of chickens. "You're good. It's okay. Let it out if that's what you need to do."

The rhythmic rasping slows enough for me to pull her upright into my chest. Her tears run down my back. And fuck it—stupid bad arm be damned. I sweep her feet off the ground and hug her the rest of the way to my chest. Pain ratchets through my bicep and down my spine. I grit my molars and move to the ladder for the sleeping platform. Fuck me, after last night she should sleep for a week. Not be worrying about our stupid asses.

"What the hell?" Calvin storms through camp and Haley is ripped from my arms. "What are you doing?" Punching him while he's holding Haley isn't a good idea. But it doesn't stop me from thinking about it. His blue eyes are unreadable, and I shake it off in favor of smoothing Haley's hair away from her face.

"He didn't do"—she hiccups—"any"—hiccup—"thing."

"Other than almost drop you. His arm's still fucking useless." Calvin glares at me over Haley's head. "Why are you crying?" It's less of a question and more of a demand.

"I . . . Put me down, Calvin, I'm fine."

He lets her feet slowly sink to the ground. Which frankly shocks me.

"What's going on?" Sam growls.

Dante, Sam, and Zane bound around the corner, with Penny behind them. When I turn around, who said it doesn't matter—they all have the same look on their faces. They're pissed. At me or Calvin—it doesn't matter.

Zane's the first to move. "What is it, Little Bird?"

"Nothing. It's all good." She blinks. "Shit, I hate crying. Really, it's nothing. I'm good." With the back of her hand, she wipes away an errant tear.

We're not idiots—well, at least I'm not. There's more going on. But I don't blame her for not wanting to go into it with all of us staring at her. Shit, I spent two years in therapy as a kid, just staring at the therapist. Some nice older lady in Maine with cool puzzles in her office. The only other thing I remember about the whole experience was wondering if she'd like my mother's old shoes. Because hers were so dirty and my mother, well, she was dead. So yeah, cheery.

"You want to go to sleep, Firefly?" I take her hand.

She nods.

I spent most of the night staring at the rafters of our roof—worrying about Haley. We're a silent bunch eating on our coconut. We need to push through this. I cock my head at Zane, but damn, I can comfort her, too, without looking for support from the shiny-smiley guy. "We should have a party," I say softly into the wind.

"Party, Rockwell?" Calvin asks, like I've grown a third head.

"Yeah, a fucking party. I overheard Haley talking about Thanksgiving and Halloween while we were unloading the tender." I clear my throat, and the words come with more authority now.

Dante's stacking fruit in a tub. "A party, though?"

And I figured he'd be the one I could count on to back me up on a party.

"Thanksgiving and Halloween are over." The red ring around her blue eyes makes them pop even more.

"Christmas is weeks away," Sam says.

"We don't need a holiday for a party, but we could make one. Thanks-o-weenie." It just pops out of me.

I scan the group. They're all stunned, I suppose. No one says a word.

Until Haley laughs. "Thanks-o-weenie? That sounds like something Dante would come up with."

"It does, doesn't it, Sassy? Guess I'm improving all of you. It sounds like a fucking great idea for a holiday."

"And what exactly does one do on Thanks-o-wee—"

"Come on there, Sam, Thanks-o-weenie? It's in the name!" Dante slaps his leg.

"Or—hear me out—we could have Island Festival Day. A celebration of living the way we want to live." Zane nods and does a move with his hand that reminds me of a model in one of the game shows that my mom used to watch when I was really little.

"Or we have Thanks-o-weenie, drink a couple bottles of the wine we have left, and fuck." Dante shrugs at Haley. "What do you think, Sassy?"

"Why not both?" She holds her hands out to the side.

"Oh, it's like one of those long holiday weekends where one holiday runs into the other. The neighbors at my dad's house in Miami are from Bangladesh, and they have a huge party around Diwali and a holiday that is right after it," I say.

"Like Christmas and New Year's," Sam says.

"It's Govardhan Puja," Zane adds.

"Impressive. But what do you think, Sassy?"

"Again I say, why not both?" She holds her hands out to the side again. "Both. I like the idea of celebrating each other. And thanking the island and the ocean for feeding us."

"Well, to be technical, I'm the one who has been feeding us." Dante saunters over to Haley and pulls on her ponytail.

"You know what I mean. Maybe we can tie it in with a ceremony on the other side of the island." Haley turns around and stares at Calvin.

"Not now, Chiefie. It's a nice idea, but we should wait until we need food again."

"I suppose that's practical." Haley holds his gaze.

I'm watching him. Not taking care of the farmers on the other side of the island is gnawing at him. I saw the relief on his face when he thought we were going over today. Then to not even get there? Yeah, it makes it worse, I'm sure. It's like training for a meet and then having it canceled a few hours before. Meets are never something I wanted to do, but I was always glad I had done it when it was over.

"Practical is what we need to be to survive as long as we can," Calvin says.

Zane groans. "Stop with the doom, Green. We've made it a long time. No one wants the shirty uncle who ruins Christmas around."

Dante's moving around in the kitchen area and shouts, "This isn't Christmas. This is Island Festival and Thanks-o-weenie. Sassy, come here—I'm going to need your brains to figure out the perfect meals for our new holidays."

She smiles, and a pang of jealousy hits me. I want to always be the one to make her smile. But as long as she's smiling, that's what really counts.

"Oh, I don't know. I think you're the smartest here. But I'll help."

"No one comes around the other side of the other tree until I say so." Zane stops. "Wait, Sam, you want to help me?"

"With what?"

"It's a surprise. Just come on," Zane says.

Sam shrugs and follows Zane. Penny and Pepper follow him, and soon it's just Green and me standing under the living room platform. I look over at the kitchen. Dante has Haley sitting on the counter, and she's laughing, their heads inches apart.

"That's good!" She giggles. It's soul-filling music.

Calvin has his hands on his hips. "Come on, then."

I look around. He's talking to me.

"What? Maybe I have something else I need to do." I lift my chin to him.

"You don't, and Zane's not working on a new home for these guys." He points at the chickens. "We'll need to do it."

I glance back to Haley, who's oblivious and coming out of her funk. "Fine. What are we doing?"

"We'll need to give them a home base that they like. Free food. And then we can give them more freedom. Let them spread their wings. We had chicken tractors on the farm. Huge things we pulled with the tractor."

"We don't have a tractor."

His eyebrows rise. "We also don't have a thousand birds."

"Right. Where do you want to start?" I'm wishing I'd spoken up earlier and helped Zane. But then, avoiding Green isn't going to be possible. And we should talk about what happened. Or not—I'm sure that's what Green was planning on doing.

Yesterday was weird. Not the Haley part. That was fucking amazing. Being inside of her when she broke apart completely . . . Damn, thinking about it makes me want to do it again.

I'm not into guys—I don't think I'm even bi—but the whole thing turned me fucking hard. I can't imagine getting it on with just Calvin. Fuck, the thought of having to deal with Green on a daily basis without Haley makes me want to puke. Not bi then, but also not *not* bi.

Whatever, I've had plenty of chances with guys before, and I never wanted to take them. I still don't, but yeah, yesterday has left me a little scrambled. And I should talk to him about it. I'm all in with Haley. If the grumpy Viking walks away from her, from this, when we're back on the mainland, I won't be the one chasing after him.

"We need more bamboo and vines. Get them some water and food scraps while I get the pack ready."

"Aye-Aye."

Green glares at me, and I pivot away from him. "Hey, the admiral wants me to feed the chickens. What do we have?" I ask Dante.

Dante moves around the kitchen space without taking his eyes from Haley, gathering bits of things in a tub he's been using for waste.

"How's the festivities prep going?" I place my hand on Haley's back.

She turns her blue eyes to me, full of light now. "Really good. Thank you for this. It's exactly what I needed."

My heart soars at her recognition. When did I become so needy and thirsty for attention? "Oh, it's going to be fun." I plant a kiss behind her ear. "You sure you two don't need any help with the food?"

Dante thrusts the bucket at me. "Absolutely. You take care of cranky pants. And here's a couple of our older coconut bowls for water for the chickens, Swimmer Boy." He drops them into the bucket.

"Can't fault a guy for trying." I take the supplies and quickly get the chickens set up before Green comes around the corner.

"Here." He holds out a spare pack for me.

"How far are we going?"

"The vines I want grow above the waterfall."

"There's vines by the derelict."

"Not the thin bendable kind that the chickens won't think of as food."

"True. But are we going to have enough time? To get back for the parties?"

His forehead furrows. "Island Festival Day is tomorrow and Hallo-o-givings is the next day," he declares loudly to the camp.

There's a chorus of, "Okay" and "Works for me" from behind the tree. From the kitchen Dante says, "Thanks-o-weenie."

Calvin's eyes crinkle. He fucking knows what it's called.

We take off at a pace that's just short of a hell run. My college coach took the team on one when he found out we'd had a party the night before a big meet. I didn't mean to, but somehow I ended up in the middle of what I thought would be the craziest night of sex in my life. Thinking back on it, it looks like a ten-year-old's birthday party now.

"What are you smiling about?"

"Nothing. Is that as fast as you can walk?" I push around him and take off at a jog. We've got a few hours of daylight left.

Soon after, he's got a bunch of vines looped in his hand like a cowboy's lasso. My pack is full, and there's sweat running down the sides of my face.

"Sure, we need to cut less bamboo from our side," I say, "but the shit grows fast. Let's get it from the patch near camp."

"No, we need to be responsible."

"Fine," I say.

"Indeed." He zips up his pack, the vines shoved deep inside.

"Good talk." I take the volcanic rock steps down the side of the hill faster than a mountain goat I hope I never run into again.

I'm down the other side of the mountain and into the field of bamboo when Calvin screams, "Fucking hell!"

Chapter 19

Mudflats

Calvin

My legs are sinking into the mud. Not sinking—disappearing. The bamboo next to me is thick, so I reach for a stem, but the damn thing snaps off in my hand. I reach with my other hand, but of fucking course that hand's got the machete and it goes tumbling out. It lands point-down in the mud six feet away, vibrating like some damn sword in the stone that only the righteous can pull out.

I'm certainly fucked. The more I try to pull my left leg out, the more I sink. It's down to my knee. Like thick paste. My right isn't down that far yet. I can still see the laces of my shoes.

Rockwell's thundering through the jungle.

"Stop!" I yell. "Don't come any closer."

"What is it, a goat?" Rockwell's voice shakes.

"A goat? Fuck no. It's some sort of soul-sucking mud. Don't come any—" I close my eyes because the damn fool is standing right behind me.

"It's mud."

"No shit, Sherlock."

"Damn. I can't pull my foot up," Rockwell says. But there's hard ground right behind him.

"That would be why I told you not to come any fucking closer."

"Right. Okay. It's like a mud bath the dinosaurs would get stuck in."

"What the hell are you talking about?"

"You know all the fossils they've found of dinosaurs being trapped in mud?"

I want to stab him and every wannabe-paleontologist in their damn dinosaur-obsessed heart. An archeologist trapped in fucking mud doesn't want to hear about shitty cold-blooded reptiles.

I look back at him, and he's almost smiling. No, it's just him. I want to stab him. But my machete is having its own King Arthur moment right now. I narrow my eyes at him. Because moving will only sink me deeper into this muck.

"Right. Well, cut some bamboo and use it to disperse our weight and inch out of here."

I point like a hunting dog at the flap of the blade that is slowly sinking down.

"Damn. Okay, can you reach that cluster of bamboo?"

I hold up the snapped-off bit in my hand to show him. Because I'm gripping it. At least it's keeping me from forming a fist and risking sinking even deeper.

"Right, can you grab a bunch at one time?"

"No. And shut the hell up so I can think." There's a thud and then a splatter behind me. I crane my neck around. Rockwell's lying on the ground on his back. His arms are splayed out at his side. He's moving like a snow angel, swimming backwards a millimeter at a time.

"You need to drop and disperse your mammoth size, or you're going to end up like, well, a mammoth." Rockwell's close enough to the edge of the dry jungle that he rolls to his side and shimmies up into the dried leaves. He spits mud out of his mouth when he stands and opens his pack. "You're farther in. But lie down and I'll help pull you out."

"We need to get the machete." My eyes are focused on it. It hasn't sunk any deeper, so at least there's that.

"We need to get you the fuck out of there. You're smart enough to know that. Let the damn blade go." His voice smacks me.

We're fucked without the machete. We've got a saw, but how long will we last without the blade? We've got my utility tool, and Zane has his knife from the Rock Candy too. But without the machete?

I brought as much as I thought we could to camp. Did I think that pirates were going to steal the ship? Fuck no. I thought a storm was going to push her sideways onto the reef and crack her in half, filling her with water. So hell, I brought as much to the shore as I thought we could.

I'm inching down deeper into the mud. I've known I need to disperse my weight from the second I got in here. But which way? I lie down, my head facing the machete. There are a few spears of bamboo growing around it.

"What the hell are you doing? You can't move that way."

"I've got to get the machete."

"For the love of . . . You are the most infuriating person on the damn planet."

"So I've been told." I'm staring up at the darkening sky. I reach over my head and grab a rotten stump. It breaks apart in my hand, but it does give me enough leverage so I can inch forward to the machete.

"You blockhead, turn the fuck around." Rockwell's voice is moving. It's less at my feet and more to the side now.

Another reach and pull of mud, another fraction of an inch. But my toes are free. And I fucking still have my shoes.

"Would you just listen to me for a change? Can you listen to anyone?"

"That machete is our life. We won't make it another rainy season here without it."

"We can go through the huts. They must have had one. The big house that Zane mentioned he saw when you went for water."

"We're not going in there."

"We are, if it means getting a damn machete. Or something else we might need."

In my peripheral, I find another medium-sized stump. This one holds, and I move three feet.

"Fucking hell, you're going to actually do it. You've got another three feet, and you should be able to reach it with your left hand. I'm making my way over there. There's a big clump of bamboo. I should be able to get close enough to throw you a vine through the trunks," Easton says.

"Bamboo doesn't have a trunk. They're all stems."

"Now you want to get into fucking semantics. Just get the fuck out of there, Green."

"I'm working on it." I turn my head, looking for another tree to grab, and get a splatter of mud in my left eye. I get a strong grip on another stump and drag myself another foot.

"Here, I'll toss you a vine. Hold your right hand up."

I put it up, and there's a smack of mud near my head.

"Too short. Hold on."

That continues two or three times, and then I catch the

fucking vine. The vines we picked are narrow and more suited to being bound into a rope. I don't have much hope that a single one is going to work. But I wrap a length of it around my wrist because when I get closer to the machete, whatever hasn't broken off could come in handy.

"Give me some more slack." I hold on to the vine with both hands. And fuck if he doesn't move me two feet before it snaps. But he's also pulled me away from the blade. I flutter, wiggling in the mud, getting myself close enough to throw the vine around the handle. It takes more than a half dozen tries before I loop it and pull it close enough to bring it to my body.

"You want me to throw you more vine? I've got it doubled up this time."

"Do it."

This time he does it with no warning and it smacks me across my face.

"Fuck." It stings, but it was more the shock of it.

"You good?" Rockwell asks as I wrap it around my wrists.

"Yeah."

He pulls me directly into a clump of bamboo that smacks the top of my head. "That's as far as I can get."

"I'm good." I wiggle between the bamboo, holding on to the machete with one hand and pulling myself along. When the ground feels firmer, I test planting my feet down. This feels different. There's mud between my toes. I glance back out at my right shoe. "Here." I hand the machete over my head to Rockwell.

"Got it."

I pull off my one shoe and hand it to him. Holding on to the end of the doubled twine, I plunge back into the mud.

"What the fuck, Green?"

I repeat the whole damn thing. Only this time, the mud is stirred up and everything takes twice as long. It's fucking horrible. Going out to get my shoe, there's nothing to hold on to.

When he pulls me back up and I stand next to him, my mud-soaked shoe in hand, he's livid.

"You could have told me my shoe fell off."

He doesn't stop walking. We take the long way around the bamboo, taking each step with care. Being barefoot, I do it doubly so. Rockwell hasn't said anything since he tossed me the rope.

The more we walk, the angrier I get. "If you'd told me my shoe had fallen off, we could have saved an hour."

"You are a complete ass." Each word is its own threat.

I've been threatened before, by a lot scarier and bigger guys. "Yeah, so? You didn't know that before."

"I did. And I'm not gay or bi or bi-curious."

I'm gobsmacked. I have no idea where the hell that came from. I look him up and down. My forehead's furrowed. And I know I must look like my grandad after he fell into the pigpen, back when I was five. "Okay. What does it matter? I'm not either."

"Exactly," Rockwell says and stomps into the jungle, drying mud sloughing off his back.

Oh—it fucking dawns on me. The other night. "Wait. Rockwell, Easton." I take a muddy step, holding on to my shoes, and catch up to him. "Hold up." I grab his arm. "The other night, damn. That felt good. That doesn't make you gay or bi. It doesn't make you not bi or gay either. You know what I mean?"

He glares at me.

"I'll take that as a no." I run my hand over my beard, sending a spray of mud to the ground. "We're in this thing with Haley. It's not something that any of us—well, besides Dante—have ever done before. And things get blurred, if that makes sense. I think of you as my brother."

He cocks his head at me.

"My brother before he fucking betrayed me."

Easton nods.

"I love Haley, but I'm never going to love any of you guys like I love her. But that doesn't mean I don't . . .Fuck. I mean, what is love? That kind of love. I enjoy being around all of you. You all drive me fucking batty. Some of you more than others. But I like all of you. Even Dante. I wouldn't be able to do this thing with Haley if I didn't. And I want to keep you all fucking safe. Her, you, all of you—mentally and physically." I hold the machete up. "It's one of the reasons I didn't tell you or the others about the Pomelo Beach. The place haunts me, and I don't want—I *didn't* want—them to see it. Not until I fixed it. But I can't fix it now, not for them. For the ones who lived here before us . . . I suppose I can't fix it for them either. But I can at least give them some respect."

"We're not your responsibility." Easton wipes his hands on the little bit of clean fabric on the front of his shirt. "No, I take that back. We're each other's responsibility. I want to keep everyone safe too. But I don't have the same skill sets as you. Although at least I fucking knew you're supposed to lie down in quicksand—quick-mud. That's cartoon lesson number one."

"I knew I had to lie down. I was just deciding if we could make it without the machete or not."

Rockwell's eye twitches. Which isn't good. Because he's really not going to like the next thing I tell him.

Chapter 20

Fair Winds

Dante

"The theme . . ." Haley laughs. "I sound like a stew. 'Theme.' I'll just call the provisioner and have them send over . . . what? A case of champagne? Something environmentally-friendly, don't you think?" She has her notebook out, her pen on the paper.

"I don't know; I hear these guests really like to party, Sassy. You think a case will be enough?"

"You're right. I'll make it two." She puts her hand to her face like a cellphone. "Oh no, they're not picking up."

"Guess we'll have to punt. You're good at your job—you'll figure something out. So yeah, the theme. What ya got, Sassy?"

"Island Festival Day. Part Thanksgiving, part thanking the island for what it gives us. What if we set up garlands around camp and then after dinner we go down to the waterfall—"

"Now you're talking, Sassy." I grin because I know she's not talking about sex. Although why not, I'm not sure. We should always talk about sex. I push a tendril of her hair away from her cheek.

"Dante! And launch a small float into the water."

I cock my head to the side. "A small float? Like a Viking burial? I think Calvin might object to being set on fire. But I'm not going to yuck his yum. We can ask him."

She playfully slaps my arm. "No, something small." She grabs a coconut. "Like this, we can put a candle in it. Or better, lard—we don't have many candles—and set it on fire. After we all say something we respect or like about the island or each other."

"I like it. I'll use only things from the island for the food." That's not going to be hard. Sure, there are still some cans left from the Rock Candy, and spices, but I've been using them sparingly. And making sure they are the star of the meal.

Honestly, we're damn lucky with the amount of food that's around. And knowing about the pomelo farm and the extent of the food on the other side? It's a blessing. Even if we can't keep taking the tender over, we can hike over.

I've been distracting Haley for the last three hours. We've made a crateload of decorations for tomorrow. Garlands of elephant leaves. I have no idea what they're called. They look like an elephant's ear. I wish we had some flowers. I know there are some orchids growing down by the waterfall, but I don't want to pick them.

"Oh, Sassy." I take her hand in mine and interlace our fingers. Fuck, I love holding her hand. It fits mine so perfectly. "Come with me."

"Where are we going?" She turns back to the pile of leaves we've gathered. I should have thought of this before.

"You'll see."

"Don't look," Zane shouts from behind the tree.

"Just passing through. We're not looking," I holler back. I hold my hand loosely over Sassy's eyes, but a few steps later, my hand slips down over her mouth and she licks the inside of my palm.

"Sassy. Are you being a naughty girl?" My cock thickens as her blue eyes flick to mine.

"Where are we going?"

"I want to show you what I found the other day. But now I'm going to show you even more." My heart thumps against my chest. She's going to love this. Have I been keeping it a secret? Yes, sure. A little bit. But it's not a magical waterfall or a farm of fruit. Still, I know that she's going to love it. And when I found it, things weren't blooming fully, but that was a few days ago, so they should be now. I step off the path through the thick ferns.

"Where are we going?" Sassy repeats.

"Calvin's not the only one who does a little exploring. This way. It's not far up ahead." I've got her hand locked into mine. The ferns are thick, but there's no thorny underbrush, so that's a plus.

It's farther than I remember. But then it opens up to a large clump of Birds of Paradise. The broad-leafed plants surprise even me. They've grown taller since I was here. A good portion of them reach my shoulders. Vivid flowers perch atop the stalk-like stems, tall and thin like banana leaves.

"Oh, Dante! There's so many. It's breathtaking." She shimmies around the clump. "They've been growing here for a long time for there to be so many." Her mouth hangs open.

"Come here. There's a little rise and a group of rocks we can stand up on and see all of them."

"You've been holding out on us."

"Not really. They weren't blooming until recently. I wanted you to get the full effect." I lift her up onto a three-foot rock.

"It's stunning."

"Yes, it is."

"You're not looking at the flowers."

"I'm looking at the loveliest of flowers."

"Oh, that's . . ."

"I can be cheesy, Sassy. I'm the chef." I bite my lip and take a step into her, wrapping my arms around her waist. With a quick tug, I have her swim shorts down and off one leg, the rest ringing her left leg. Her pussy's at my chin, and I don't waste any time digging into dessert. I stroke down the center of her with a finger as my tongue flicks around her clit. She's salty and tangy, a delicacy that I want to feast on for the rest of my life.

Have I thought about that before? The rest of my fucking life. The rest of my life.

I heard some of what Zane and Haley were talking about on the beach. I'm going to have to do the same.

I pull back and glance up at her. Her head is bent, her eyes closed.

"Dante?"

I go back to my meal. She's so responsive she's dripping already. I pull her hips tighter to my face with my free hand and lean into the lava rock. Its sharp prongs grind into my knees just as Sassy grinds onto my face.

Her hands are in my hair, and she's holding on to the thin branch of a tree meekly growing out of a crack in the rocks. The leaves rattle in her grasp. "Oh, Dante. Don't stop. It's too good."

I'd love to flip her over and pound into her from behind, but my girl needs a little break. An orgasm to stave off her sex hangover. A little hair of the dog. If I thought I could take her softly, I'd do it. But she drives me crazy, and there's no way she can take it. I'm not going to break her. No, I will never hurt her. It's a promise I've made only to the women I'm related to.

Her fingers twist and pull my hair. And fuck if the twinge of pain doesn't make me harder. I curve my fingers and hit that spot inside of her at the same time I suck on her clit. She cracks around me.

"Dante."

Damn, I love my name on the air. A bird takes off, flapping its wings into the sky that's verging on twilight. I pull my finger out of her. I'm holding her up. Her skin shines in the low rays.

"How are you doing up there, Sassy?"

She breathes out. "That was amazing. It really is beautiful here."

"It is." I smile up at her and help her right her pants. "You want to get cutting and take some of them back to camp?"

"Oh, no." She holds her hands out, and I try to help her down. "No, you come up."

I do, and I grab the back of her neck, pulling her into a long kiss. Until I have to stop or risk going back on my promise and fucking her until she's nothing but a stain on this lava rock.

"Look, Dante." She points out the massive clump of flowers. "Look how perfect it is, the Birds of Paradise with the ferns growing and then the trees hitting the blue sky. I don't want to ruin it."

"They'll grow back, Sassy. You're not going to clear cut them."

"I know. But they belong here." She pauses. "I'll take just one and we can use it for the float on the water."

"I think that's a great idea."

It takes us the next twenty minutes to find the perfect flower before we head back to camp. She glances back at me. "Thank you. That was a really nice surprise."

"Any time, Sassy."

When we reach the camp, I'm surprised that Easton and Calvin aren't back. But I've got a quick meal to toss together; they'll be back in time to eat. Haley finds a place to keep her flower safe up on the living room platform.

I get lost in cooking, but next thing I know, Haley's pacing underneath the treehouse. "Where are they?" Her voice cracks with tension.

Easton and Calvin haven't come back. Then again, I'm still waiting for the two of them to either fuck or kill each other. And I'm a little disappointed that one or the other hasn't happened yet. Maybe neither will. Whatever.

I hand her a bowl of coconut fish curry. "Sam, Zane! Dinner's on," I project past the treehouse.

They come stumbling around the corner with weird smiles on their faces.

Haley drops onto a stool. "This is delicious, thank you." She holds her spoon up in a toast. "But where are they?"

"Knowing Calvin, he's got enough bamboo to build three chicken tractors." Zane takes his bowl and inclines his head to me.

I sit down next to Haley. "They'll be back soon. He said they were getting—"

"If you'd quit trying to spear me with your bamboo, we'd have been here an hour ago." Calvin's deep voice echoes through camp.

I glance up at Zane, who's already finished his meal

and is holding a chick on his lap. He's laughing. But when they round the corner caked in dried mud, we all stop laughing.

"What happened?" Haley's on them, her hands in Rockwell's muddy hair and then on the side of Calvin's cracked cheek.

"You know when you were a kid and you worried about quicksand?" Rockwell scrunches his face, and dried mud falls to the ground.

"Yeah, I mean, nightmares for years." Haley runs her hands over his arm.

Rockwell puts down a good dozen bamboo poles. Green has twice as many.

"Well, think quicksand but mud."

"Oh no." Haley smooths dried and cracked mud from Rockwell's neck. "It's like you had a mud bath at a really bad spa."

"A horrific spa." Rockwell kisses the tip of Haley's nose, leaving specks of dirt on her face.

"Why would anyone want to dip themselves in mud?" Green growls.

"It's good for the skin. Opens the pores and all," I say. "I went to a mud bath house in Indonesia that . . ." Haley's blue eyes are wide. She doesn't need to hear this story. But damn, it was a good time.

Rockwell's not letting Haley move. His cracked-mud fingers hold her wrist, but his glare lingers on Calvin. "It wouldn't have been that big of a deal, but Green dropped the machete. And he wasn't willing to call it a loss."

"Fuck, without the machete we'd be . . . yeah," Sam says. "I'm glad you're both okay." He picks up the bamboo Easton dropped and moves it over out of the way.

"I'm taking a swim." Easton peels off his shirt. "Come

with me, Firefly?" He tugs at her hand. She looks back to Calvin, and his bamboo clatters next to Easton's.

"I'm fine," Calvin says. Haley nods and walks with Easton down the zigzag trail to the water. We all watch them go. Haley's black swim shorts and her not-so-white shirt vanish behind the pond fronds.

I point to the decent-sized pile. "Let me guess, you cut the bamboo after you fell in the mud?" Because it's just like Green to complete a job even when you're in pain. Fucker needs a smack to the side of his head.

"We were there. And it was the whole reason why we went. We can't cut all the bamboo around here for the chicken tractor. He wanted to stop at the waterfall to get cleaned off, but on the way out I saw boar tracks. We need to do something about them." He peels his shirt off and drops it with a thud on the log stool next to him. It's something I would throw away if we were back in the States. But we're not.

"We can do it after the holidays." Odd—we only decided upon them this morning, but they're ingrained in me already. And I want this to be big for Haley. No, I want this to be big for all of us.

When the ship was taken, it was like a balloon popped. For most of us. Everyone but damn Green. It was like he expected this to happen all along. But then seeing what he saw in the huts . . . I suppose his sense of doom is logical.

Fuck that, I'm going to live. And as much as I was hyped up for Thanks-o-weenie, I'm even more excited for Island Festival Day tomorrow.

Haley's back. And the three of us stop and stare. "I want to get some towels."

Zane tosses her one. Lucky for us, Rocky only bought the best for the boat, because they're getting a beating.

"Thanks." She turns to go back to the beach.

"Wait, Haley, you want me to start putting up your garland?" I ask.

"Yeah, that would be great." She waves over her shoulder on the way the way to the trail.

Calvin takes off with long steps, his large frame rattling the palm fronds as he pushes out into the evening sun, following Haley.

Chapter 21

Breaststroke

Haley

"Hold up." Calvin's calling to me.

I don't know if I want to hold up. He keeps doing these things that put himself and others in danger.

His elbow rubs up against mine. "Haley."

"You went back into the quicksand to get your shoe? It's a shoe!" I'm furious at him. Easton gave me the quick version of what happened while he was scrubbing himself in the surf.

"It was mud." He runs his fingers along his ear, and clumps drop off.

"Mud, sand. Doesn't matter what it is if you get sucked under." I gaze out at the water. Easton's paddling out past the breakers, and I just want to get back to him.

"It wasn't going to suck me under."

"Easton said you were sunk in up to your knees." I peel off my shirt; my bikini's on beneath it. I'm going to go in and be with Easton. He's upset. He says he's not, but it's rolling off him.

"I was. But I wasn't stuck. I was contemplating what to do, and he overreacted."

I cock my head to the side. That's the thing with Calvin: any sign of emotion is overreacting. "Was he? Or was he just being kind and worried that you might fucking kill yourself over a shoe or a machete?"

I push on his arm, but he doesn't move. He just stares at the spot where I touched him. "I don't want to lose you. Okay? We can figure out how to make shoes. Heck, I'm sure there are plans for a forge and a smelting operation up in there." I mean to touch the side of his head gently, but I end up giving it a good smack. "Oh, sorry, I didn't mean to." I shake my head as my hair flies in the wind. "It's just that you . . . you make me so gosh darn frustrated. I keep telling you that you don't have to take care of everyone, that we can take care of you, too. But you don't believe me, do you?"

"I do," he says, his low voice floating off into the wind.

"Do you REALLY, Calvin?" I say. "Because I need you to know, understand, how much you mean to me, and if something happens to you, it would just completely gut me."

He tilts his chin up to the sky. When he looks back at me in the twilight, his blue eyes shimmer. There's almost a tear. It's like he can't possibly believe that anyone could truly care for him.

"I told you I love you, and I mean it. Please don't do things like that anymore. Just because you don't believe that we're gonna get out of here doesn't make it true. We could still find a way home, even without the Rock Candy."

He is quiet, his jaw firmly tilted to the sky. He shakes his head. "I love you, Haley . . . But forget it. We can enjoy what we have now. That's what this whole Festival Island Day is about, right? Enjoying what we have, thanking nature and this hunk of rock for letting us live?"

I blink at him. "I suppose you're right. That is what we're supposed to be celebrating tomorrow. But it's more than that. I just . . . I know you can't make someone have hope, Calvin. I know you aren't gonna change just because I snap my fingers. I don't want that. I don't want you to change. I love you for who you are. You're empathetic. You're kind. You're smart. You're intuitive and a wizard with motors. But you're careless. You're careless with your own self, and that hurts those of us who care about you. You mean something to us. What would you have done if I had gone back into the mud for a shoe?"

His neck bends, his head facing the sand, but he glares at me. "I would have gone in and gotten you, ripped you out of the mud, and let myself drown in it instead."

"Yeah, that's exactly what I'm talking about. You can't do that. You're just as important as we are." I point back to camp and out at Easton in the water. "You need to understand how much we care about you. Love you. Not just me. All of us here need you. You're important."

He glares at me, his hands on his waist.

"You are an integral part of all of us, Calvin." I stand on my tiptoes and run my hand over his beard. Bits of dirt and leaves fall out. I run my hand down his arm and interlock my fingers with his.

He takes my other hand, pulls me against his chest, and I take him in. He's so tall and big, and being surrounded by him is like nothing else. Normally, it makes me secure. But right now . . . not so much. I tilt my head up. "Let's get you cleaned up."

He sweeps me off my feet and we're into the waves in

two steps. The water's up to his shoulders when I wiggle out of his arms and swim over to Easton. Calvin doesn't spend time scrubbing his skin with sand. Instead, he swims out with me.

"Hey." I wave. Being here has done lots of things for me. It's changed both my insides and my outsides. I'm down a few clothing sizes, but I don't even care about that. I'm fitter than I've ever been. Fitter than when I was in high school, back when I was a benchwarmer for the girls' lacrosse team. I swim out to Easton.

Easton smiles at me. "Your stroke is getting better."

"Thanks." I bob next to him. "I'm trying to follow what you said."

"I can tell."

Calvin's a good ten feet away, floating.

"How are you doing there? You look like a leopard," I call over the waves. His skin is tinted with mud all over his arms and back.

"More like a house cat," Easton says.

"A house cat?" I ask.

"Yeah, they do what they want and don't come when called."

I'm floating next to him on his right side. The spot where he was shot isn't as red as it was before, but it's puckered and shiny. I touch his elbow below the spot. "How is it?"

He paddles around me, turning his left side to me. I don't think he even knows he's doing it. Hiding a wound that can't be hidden.

"Stiff. But fine."

"You've got some mud in your hair still, right there." I brush over his ear, and he cocks his head, letting me wash it away. "Stiff?"

"Always, when you're around." A wiry smile slips onto his lips.

"You're sounding more and more like Dante. Want me to scrub your scalp?"

"Yes, please." Easton lies back, and I try and figure out how I'm going to do what I offered without drowning.

But I manage. Dirt loosens and drifts away in the waves. He's making noises like a German Shepherd being petted. Little grunts and groans. He closes his eyes, and for a moment, I think he might have fallen asleep. I lean over him and gently kiss his forehead.

Easton grabs my shoulders and twists me around into his arms, and I wrap my legs around his waist.

"Is this okay?" I lean back and use my arms to help keep us afloat.

"More than okay." Easton's naked, and I can feel his cock pushing against my shorts.

"I think I got it all out."

"You, sure? You could check for more." He tilts his head to me, and I laugh.

"I'm sure. We should get out. You must be hungry."

"I'm hungry, all right."

"You really are turning into Dante." I rest my hand on his chest. "I've eaten already, but I'm hungry again." And now I'm not sure if I'm talking about Dante's meal or what I did with him by the clump of flowers standing on the rock. I've done a lot of crazy things since being on this island, but that was one of the most . . . When the orgasm took me, it was like I was the bird flying out into the sky.

"It's getting late." Calvin's snuck up behind us. His fingers skate down my shoulder and back. His lips pause on my shoulder blade.

The three of us float for a while. Their hands roam over

my skin. Until Easton tosses me on his back and takes off, swimming the butterfly. It's like I'm riding a dolphin. His powerful strokes take us along the shoreline before he turns and heads for the beach. Up and down, his breaths blowing out with every few arm motions. I'm holding on, my legs clamped around his waist. It's exhilarating, how fast he's going, and I want more.

I'm laughing so hard that when a wave hits us from the side and water slides down my throat, I'm coughing, but I'm still laughing as he dives, taking me under with him. The tweak of his ribs gives me a nanosecond of warning that he's going to dive under the water. I get my mouth closed before I become a water balloon. A few good strokes and we're close enough to shore that he can stand. He cinches me up with his right arm, but it gives way and I fall back into the water.

"Chiefie." Calvin high-steps through the water.

I spit and cough a bit when I stand on fawn legs. The waves crash against the back of my legs, but a few steps and I'm free on the hard-packed sand of the tidal line. Calvin reaches me first. I'm bent over and coughing.

"I'm good. No worries," I say into the sand.

He frowns and stares over me at Easton coming out of the waves.

"My arm locked up. Shit. I haven't done the butterfly stroke since—"

"Since you were fucking shot. I told you to be more careful." Calvin growls.

"Right." I put one hand on Calvin's chest and the other on Easton's. It's like a flashback to the first day on the beach when I got in between the two of them when they were getting ready to fight and my ankle ended up twisted.

It's a lot different now. Things are a lot-lot different.

Then I was going to flash them. Now I have more powerful weapons in my arsenal.

"Don't." I point at Calvin.

Easton's naked, so he's the easier target. I drop to my knees in a fluid motion. I don't just suck his cock—I inhale it. Taking him quickly to the base of my throat, I cup his balls with one hand and the other, I'm not sure who the hell I'm becoming. I thrust it in my swim shorts. My thumb easily finds my clit. It's still enlarged from the round with Dante. Calvin hoists my hips up, pulling my shorts down with a quick tug. I hold on to Easton. Calvin's hand replaces mine, his cock nestled between my butt cheeks. He grips my left hip and, with his other hand, his fingers rub my clit. He thrusts into me. I moan around Easton. Calvin thrusts into me from behind, but I keep my focus on Easton, who's now holding my head still as I suck him off.

The waves crash against my ankles. Calvin's trembling thighs and the way Easton grips my hair send me higher.

"Haley," Calvin groans, and I explode around him. My head jerks back, and it sets off Easton's release. His toes grip the sand, and he loosens his grip in my hair. I swallow the last bit of him. Easton's blue eyes twinkle in the low light.

"Love you," I say up to Easton. Calvin's grip of my hips loosens, and he slides out. I flick my head to Calvin. "Love you too."

"Love you," the two of them reply back. Easton helps me to my feet and cradles me in his arms, back into the water to clean up, again.

Chapter 22

Signal Flags

Zane

"**M**ove." Sam's got his captain's tone out.

"No. Let them be." Dante sits on a stump next to the zigzag path to the beach. He's just come back from a short trip to wash dishes. Though I notice he didn't bring the dishes back with him.

"What happened to us being all in this together?" Sam's gruff.

"We are. But right now, we're not. Let them be." Dante drops his leg, letting Sam make the decision for himself.

It's not something he makes quickly either. Sam turns and looks back at me. I shrug because Dante's right. He's got this weird empathic sense about him. Like he's a witch or something. Touch wood. And that makes me smirk. Because Dante is frequently touching wood.

"What are you laughing about?" Sam pushes on my shoulder.

"No reason." I'm back to looking at the code in the planner. It's not a simple cipher, where numbers equal letters.

I've got a knackered notebook. One I used on my last boat. I've got a dozen pages left, but I'm using them sparingly.

"You're still at it." Sam pushes at the planner.

I've got the clue box on the counter. I haven't taken most of the evidence out of the box. Just the planner with its infuriating code. The two halves of the torn paper are in there. The rings are gone. Easton took them a while back. The sticker and the washers from the door are in the box too.

Sam picks up one of the photos. His fingers go over the photo. He holds it up to the light and then back to me. I let him be, going back to the code.

I'm still at it an hour later when Easton comes back.

"Where's Haley and Green?" Dante asks.

"They're finishing up the dishes." Easton flops next to me. "You're still at it? Honestly, maybe my dad was just scribbling numbers?"

My stomach twists. Because there's no way. "There's a pattern to it. I just can't figure it out."

"It's something to do with one of the two companies being sold. Although, the last I knew, Rockwell-Harding had an evaluation of more than six billion. And Rockwell Tire was worth only two and a half billion." Easton holds the two cards together.

"Only," Sam says.

"Money is a figment," Easton retorts. "It's something my mom used to say. After a point, it doesn't bring any more happiness. I think that was her point." Easton places the cards back in the box, the one from the tuxedo reading $R.\ T.\ To\ H$ $3.1B$ and the other side from the agenda reading $R\ H\ 5.2b$.

I stare at the cards. I've tried using them as a key, but Easton's right. These aren't in Rocky's code—they're evaluations. But was Rocky trying to sell his shares to Harding or his family company to Harding or both companies to someone else? And why didn't he talk to Easton about it? And why rip the card in half?

It makes sense to sell the company. Neither of his children want it. He was marrying Candy. I shudder. Why anyone would ever want to marry her is crazy. She wasn't going to have any children. Another shudder runs through me at the thought of someone that selfish having children. She would have been a horrible mother.

Now, Haley? She'd be a fantastic mother. My brain takes off on its own. Thinking about Haley getting pregnant makes me long to see her being a mom. But not here. Not now. This is no place to raise a child.

Easton picks up the photo of the girl on the cot. "There's just something about her."

"What do you mean?"

"Like, she doesn't look happy." Easton swings his legs around toward me.

"She doesn't look unhappy," Dante says over his shoulder.

"But where is this?" He shakes the photo.

"What, that's where you went to school?" Dante says.

"Ha, ha. No, it's not like Haley's science building. That's the thing. Look at the wall."

"What?" Sam takes the photo from him, shrugs, and hands it to me.

"It's plaster," I say. And then I look at the crease by the ceiling. "It's old. Like, older than America. This has got to be in Europe."

"It's a college in Europe, then?" Sam takes it back from me.

Now I'm squinting. "No, I don't think so. Weird cot and a cross on the wall."

"She's got dark hair, high cheekbones, and an olive shade of skin. Or at least I think so. It's hard to tell with a black-and-white photograph."

"Are we playing 'who is she related to?'" Dante picks the photo up, his eyebrows raised.

"Why not?" I turn my notebook to the list of people on the other raft. "While people can have relatives that look like anything, it's not Cruz. He's—"

"A hundred and twenty percent California," Easton says.

I cock my head at him.

"What? We talked about surfing when I was working out and he was wiping down the side of the boat. He wanted to know what exercise to do to be a better swimmer."

"Fair, that sounds like something Cruz would do." I put another negative sign next to his name. I'd already ruled him out, but I'm glad to have someone else do it too.

"Waldo has red hair," Sam says.

"But he was born in France." I tap my pen by his name.

"There are a lot of churches in France."

Sam's holding the photograph upside down. "What's this?" He hands it to me. "Look at the bottom of her ankle. She's got a tattoo."

"Yeah, it's like a cartoon. How did we not see it before?" I hand it to Easton.

"It's a lot brighter outside, and it's awfully small. Easy to miss," Easton says. "Weird tattoo. Is that a tri-corner hat on a cartoon character?"

"Hey." Haley and Calvin come around the blind. Calvin's carrying the tub of dishes. She sits next to me and wraps her arm around my shoulder. "What's a weird tattoo?"

"The girl on the creepy bed. She's got a tattoo on her ankle." Easton hands it to Haley.

"I mean, that's Sir CC. I suppose it's weird. But then I'm a Washington Wizards fan."

I stare at her. But then I realize the other guys are too.

"What, none of you watch basketball?" Her mouth is open, her eyes wide.

"Football," Sam, Dante, and Calvin say.

"I didn't have time for anything else but swimming."

"Football, the real kind." I cock my head at her.

"Well, that's Sir CC. He's the mascot for the Cleveland Cavaliers." Haley holds it close to her face and then puts it down on the bench. Everyone picks it up again, but hell if I'd know a Sir CC from a Sir Zed.

I read down the list of details I have on each of the guys from the other raft. "Cleveland is in Ohio, and the photo of the other girl is from Pittsburgh, both of which are close to Youngstown and Erie right?" I look up at Calvin.

"Doesn't mean that he's the one who did it. But it certainly looks suspicious."

"Fucker. Mitch. He knew more than his CV led on. But why?"

I lift the ripped index card. "Money."

"It doesn't matter." Calvin glares at the card and picks up the photo.

"Oh, it matters," Easton growls. "There's something weird with these photos. Being the owner might not prove he's guilty, but it feels like he is. If he is, he's going to pay."

"And how exactly is he going to pay? In coconuts?" Calvin drops the photo.

"I'd prefer mangos. We don't have enough of them."

Dante moves between Easton and Calvin. "Better yet, some wagyu beef."

"When we get home, we'll give the evidence to the police." Haley takes the picture and puts it in the box.

Calvin grunts.

"We can get it sorted when we're back on the mainland. And until then, I'm going to keep working on the code," I say and close the agenda. In less than a month, it will be out of days. Well, almost—there's a January page too. When we found it, I really never imagined we wouldn't be going home. We had the ship, and while getting the crank to turn felt difficult, it wasn't impossible.

"That's exactly the right thing to do." Haley kisses me on the side of my cheek. "Now, tomorrow's Island Festival Day and I have something else I need to make."

"Can I help you, Little Bird?"

"You know, I think you could. Are you done with whatever you two were working on?" She leans to the right, as if she can see behind the tree to where Sam and I set up a workshop.

I glance up at Sam. "Done enough. But you'll see it tomorrow."

"Not now?"

"No, not now. Have some patience, Little Bird." I grab her around her waist and pull her onto my lap. "How can I help you?"

"Not here. You're not the only one who likes surprises." She takes my hand and tugs me away from the other guys. Fuck if I don't like it. I'd make her anything, just to see that smile on her face.

She grabs a small box from the corner of Dante's kitchen slab and runs up to the living room platform with a small sack, then comes back again.

"What are we making?"

She holds a finger up to her lips and walks us down the path to the beach. "A little float."

I'm awake early. There's no rooster, at least not yet. One of the little chicks is bound to be a bloke. Then we'll have a built-in alarm clock for sure.

I lift my head. When we were on the boat, I woke up early. But then, so did most of the crew.

I blink, but it's really early. I'm shocked at how empty the platform is. Only Calvin's asleep across from me. Not surprising—he was still up when I went to sleep. And down the path toward the derelict back where Sam and I made our surprise, I can see the evidence of what he was working on. There's a pen made of bamboo and vines, and our chickens are happily scratching away at the dirt.

"Morning, Zane." Haley pulls me into a hug.

The area around camp is completely transformed. She's hung garlands around the kitchen area. Leaves of different colors and sizes hang around the camp, waving in the breeze like banners around the pitch for a special game.

"It looks amazing here."

"Thanks." She jumps a little.

"You ready?" Sam peers at us from around the base of the treehouse.

"You want to give it to her now?"

He nods. "It looks good."

There's a clear spot behind Dante's counter. "Sure, let's do it."

"Do it?" Dante appears out of nowhere. "Count me in."

Sam groans. "Just cover her eyes and don't let her peek."

"But who's going to cover my eyes?" Dante's laughing.

"I will." Haley has her hands on his face, and Dante does the same.

Sam grabs my arm. "Let's hurry before he starts pulling her clothes off."

"Right." I hustle behind Sam and grab the end.

Chapter 23

Run the Gauntlet

Sam

I'm walking backwards, lifting my feet so I don't trip. When we made it, I didn't think it would end up this heavy.

"Stop there, Sam," Zane says.

"Can I open my eyes?" Haley asks.

Dante already has his eyes open, and his mouth is hanging slack.

"Go ahead, Sugar." I'm smiling so wide my face hurts.

Dante drops his hands from Haley's eyes, pulling her back to his front. His hands settle on her hips.

Haley blinks. "Holy moly." She and Dante move together. "You made a dining room table. Like an honest-to-goodness table."

"Every family should have a table. Zane designed it," I say.

"Sam found the wood."

Haley runs her hand over the top. "It's so smooth."

"Coconut oil," Zane says.

"It really does look nice." Dante ducks his head under the bottom, inspecting it. "This is going to make eating . . ." He stands and turns away.

"Bloody hell. I think we made the heartless bastard cry."

"I'm not crying." Dante blinks up at me from his crouched position.

It's been a long time since I've been able to work with my hands on wood. I knew Haley would like it, but I didn't think we'd bring the chef to tears.

Family. It's something Haley said that has had my head spinning. I thought that's what a crew was, but not like this. I really would give my life for any of them.

I grip Dante's shoulder. "Nothing wrong with tears."

"Thank you. This is . . ."

Zane clears his throat. "Let's get it into position."

When it's centered, Haley bustles around getting the top of it decorated like the stews always do on the yacht. But hers is even more beautiful. In the middle of the table, she places something covered with a piece of burlap.

Calvin's back from the beach—he never naps long. Not with the WaveRunner to work on. I've helped some. He's taken it apart. I'm not sure it's ever going to go back together.

Easton appears from down the trail. "Wow. This looks fantastic." He pulls Haley in for a hug. "Happy IFD."

"IFD? Oh, Island Festival Day." She gives him a quick kiss. "Happy IFD to you too!"

She goes right down the line, kisses and wishes. It's not a competition, but we're making it one. Zane dips her, and when she comes upright, she wobbles.

"Happy Island Festival Day, Sam."

"Happy IFD, Sugar." I chuckle and take her warm and smooth lips with mine. I hold her waist and deepen the kiss.

Fuck, I turn into a teenager whenever I get my hands on her. I could kiss her all day long.

"Enough, Miller." Calvin taps my shoulder.

I shouldn't be an ass, but it makes me turn her away from him. I want to growl out *mine*, toss her over my shoulder, and run into the jungle. She moans into my mouth, and I let her go. Her blue eyes hold mine for a moment.

Calvin kisses Haley, but he doesn't play along and wish her a happy Island Festival Day. When their lips part, he cocks half a smile at her. "Are we ready?"

"Ready for what? We're not going to eat until later. And—"

"Come with me." Calvin grabs her hand. "The rest of you too."

There's bamboo hurdles set up on the beach, and out in the water, there are clusters of coconuts floating like buoys.

"It's the Island Festival Games," Calvin decrees.

"Oh, like the Olympics?" Haley claps. We do this sort of thing for guests all the time. Setting up relays or hula hoops. But those are things the deck hands pull out of the toy hauler room. Everything on the beach, Calvin's made. And he made the chicken coop yesterday.

"When did you sleep?" Zane places his hand on Calvin's shoulder.

"Full moon. Didn't need to sleep."

"Of course you need to sleep. But this is wonderful. What game are we going to play first?" Haley's holding on to Calvin's arm.

Calvin nods. "You can decide that. Hurdles, soccer, and the triathlon."

"Don't we need bikes for a triathlon?" she asks.

"Not if one person has to carry the other person," Calvin says.

"I pick Haley." Zane's quick to grab Haley's hand.

"Nope. Rocks." Calvin pulls six rocks out of his pocket. Three matching sets: black, white, and sandy brown. He cups them in two hands and shakes them around. "Pick a rock but don't show it." He holds it above his head. "Haley first."

"Okay, this is fun." She grips the stone in her fist.

I'm the last to pick before Calvin. He moves one stone into each hand and holds them out in front of his chest.

"Can I say it?" Haley's smiling.

"Sure," Calvin says.

We all have our fists in the circle.

"Reveal." Haley giggles. And I'm all smiles. The ebony black rock in her hand matches the one in mine.

"Trade you?" Dante asks.

"No way. I've got the best partner." I wrap my arm around Haley's shoulder.

Zane and Easton both have brown rocks. Leaving Calvin and Dante as a pair.

"Fine. Don't worry, Viking. I can carry you."

That's when I see Easton staring at the water. I cock my head to Haley, who picks up what I'm saying wordlessly as she moves over to Easton. She kisses his cheek. I'm fucking expecting him to go sit on the log and not participate. I haven't seen him in the water since he came back. Maybe he was in yesterday.

"Let's get moving." Calvin points out the markers he's placed for the course. "Okay, on my mark—"

Haley jumps at Calvin. "Wait! We need a minute to come up with a strategy."

"You better be fast, Haley. The Viking judge doesn't put up with time delays." Dante laughs.

"One minute," Calvin barks. He turns to Dante. "I'm carrying you. Don't even try to carry me."

Dante throws his hands up.

"What's our strategy?" she whispers in my ear.

"Are we playing to win?"

She furrows her brow at me. "Of course."

"Against a giant and a gold medalist?"

"Yes . . . We can do our best."

I suck in my lower lip because I can't believe I'm going to suggest . . . "Or we cheat."

"Sam." She playfully smacks the side of my arm.

I shrug back.

"How?"

"A little distraction?"

She tugs on the bottom of her shirt and pulls it over her head. She's wearing her bikini top underneath it. With a quick tug on the strap, it drops around her waist. Damn, her breasts are perfect. I'm not going to let her run with her top off. No, but I know for a fact running while you're hard . . . there are easier things in life.

"Whoa, whoa, the Russian team is going to need to be disqualified for distracting the other contestants," Dante yells.

"I'll allow it," Calvin says.

"Fine." Dante strips off his pants. "Ready." His massive dick hangs like another leg. How the hell is he going to swim with it there? "Put your top back on, Sassy. We don't want the girls getting damaged."

"Her strap was loose." I help her tie her top up, but Dante doesn't pull his pants back on.

Calvin's at the strip of bamboo that marks the start. "Ready?"

There are nods all around. Zane gives a "Bloody hell, yes."

Calvin raises his arm. "Go."

We take off running. I thought with Calvin's size, I might be able to beat him. But the guy has some pep. Zane hits the water first. And when I say hits I mean *hits*. He high-steps into the waves and belly flops into the water.

Haley's behind him. I had no idea she could run that fast. It's impressive. Calvin and Easton are behind them. Dante's a few paces behind me.

Things change as soon as we get through the breakers. Calvin's strokes have him keeping up with Easton. Haley and I are evenly pacing. Dante and Zane pull up the rear. But holy hell, it's a lot farther than I thought. Running is one thing, but swimming it? My lungs are burning, but Haley's next to me, and for a second her eyes twinkle at mine in the sunlight.

I'm gasping for air as we head out onto the beach. There's a line of palm fronds where we're supposed to change to carrying. Zane and Dante are just rounding the corner, coming out of the water. Calvin and Easton are waiting for them.

"Ready?" I ask Haley.

"Yes." She jumps onto my back. We have to run down to the spot where we entered the water.

I'm half a dozen steps down the beach before Calvin has Dante on his back and Zane and Easton are having a standoff about who's carrying who. We pace three strides for every two of Calvin's but we're not losing ground. Haley's holding on tightly to my shoulders. I'm not sure what Dante's doing to Calvin, but he's grunting at him. Easton and Zane have figured it out.

"Easton is carrying Zane, and they're catching us,"

Haley squeals. And it pushes me to pick up the pace. "You've got this, Sam."

We're close to the finish line, but Easton and Zane are right on our heels. But we're over the line first.

I swing Haley around to my chest and kiss her. Her wet hair's plastered to the side of her head. We're both covered in sand from it kicking up at us. I let her slide to the sand.

"We won." She jumps up and gives me another hug.

"We did."

"We're all winners with you, Sassy." Dante's sitting on the sand, his legs caked in it.

"No, they are the winners," Easton says. And I can't read what he's thinking.

Haley collapses down next to him. "Are you okay?"

He laughs. "The earth didn't open up and swallow me whole?"

Haley furrows her forehead.

"That's the first race I've lost in ten years. Of any kind." He lies back in the sand.

"It was just for fun." Haley's hand lands on his chest.

"I know." He lifts his head and takes her hand in his. "But a loss is a loss. You won it." He kisses her. "Good game, Sam." He shakes my hand.

"Thanks." I nod at him. "I had a good teammate."

"You did," Easton says.

"Hey, I was a good teammate. I could barely swim before I started boating. Shit, I wasn't any good at it six months ago," Zane says.

"You did great, Zane." Easton stands up and pats Zane's back. "We'll get them next time. I can teach you how to improve your strokes and do something about your scissor kicks."

"Your shoulder and arm are okay?" Haley smooths sand

from Easton's back. It's something she does for all of us. Taking care of us, making every day a little better.

"Yeah, Firefly. I'm good. Now we need to get you your medal." Easton cranes his neck like he's trying to find something for her to have.

"I've got that taken care of, Rockwell." Calvin jogs to where his shirt and towel sit on the big rock. From a bag, he pulls two circles of wood on a vine cord. "I've got the hardware." Calvin places one over Haley's neck and then one over mine.

I'm too busy looking at Haley smiling up at Calvin to examine the wood hanging around my neck.

"You've carved a map of the island." Her mouth falls into an O as she gawks at Calvin.

"Shit, if I'd known this was the prize, I would have found another gear." Dante laughs.

"We've got two more events," Calvin says. He points to the hurdles and the nets down the beach.

Zane and Easton each have two medals around their necks by the time we settle down at the table.

Zane drops his head to the polished wood. "I'm knackered."

"Well, you didn't have to score all the goals." Haley places a bowl in front of him.

"Yes, I did," he says, head held high and smiling broadly. "I didn't realize how much I missed being out on the pitch, playing footy."

"You did great." Haley drops a kiss on his neck.

"Thanks, Little Bird. You did, too." Zane lightly tugs on

her wooden medal and gives her another kiss. "You're not a loser." He tosses a fallen leaf from the banner at Dante.

"Careful. It's not smart to piss off the cook." Dante raises his eyebrows at Zane.

Penny barks, short barks, but not her *I'm playing* bark. Three more in succession.

"Where is she?" Haley steps away from the table.

Pepper runs past, her hackles up as she races down the path away from camp. There's a thundering snort coming from down the path, and the ferns are vibrating. My stomach twists, and time freezes as we all stare at where the noise is coming from.

Chapter 24

Broadsided

Easton

"What the hell?" I stand from the table, grabbing one of the sharpened sticks that are all around camp in piles of twos or threes.

Calvin puts his hand out, and I toss him one. We've all gone silent. Penny barks again. It's drawn out, not her cute *I'm barking for fun*—it's a distress bark. The get-the-fuck-out-of-my-home bark you never want to hear.

Calvin points at us to fan out and for Haley to climb up into the treehouse. Thank fuck she doesn't balk but heads right up the ladder to the living room platform. His beefy finger points again, and she goes the rest of the way up to the sleeping area.

The gun is up there. Not that I want her to get it. We haven't taken it out; they brought it over when they came to search for Calvin and me. And it can stay in its box, but if she needs it, I want her to have it.

Penny's barks are coming from the ferns now. Not a pirate, then? But then Penny comes crashing down the path with a boar on her tail. The damn thing is focused on her. They both run right through the middle of camp, past us.

Sam throws his spear, and it grazes the side of the beast but crashes to the ground, bouncing off the path. I throw mine nearly at the same time, but it doesn't go far, not with my arm. Fuck, it barely makes it past the table. My arm is shit after the swim.

My heart races. Until the island, I never fully understood how large boars are. Its head reaches past my waist. This one is bigger than any of the others we've seen.

Zane and Calvin take off after it. It's chasing Penny, and the tusks on it could really hurt her. I scoop up my spear and head after them. Sam's at my side. We charge off after it, but damn, Penny and the boar are moving fast. We fly around the bend; I have to quickly stop to keep from running into Zane.

"I can't see either of them," he says.

"Me, either." I close my eyes and listen—something Calvin taught me to do a few months back. And I hear it off to the side. My eyes fly open, and I spot a broken twig and what looks like tracks? "This way," I yell at Calvin's back. He's a hundred yards up the path already.

Now I'm in the lead. Me and my screaming shoulder and arm. I plow forward. Sam's behind me with Zane.

This part of the island we've gone over many times, and it shows. There are crisscrossed paths through the ferns.

A hundred feet in, I lose the trail. "Fuck." I crane my neck around, looking for any signs that could help me find it. Off to the side, I see an area that looks like it could be a new disturbance, and I go that way, stopping after a few feet to listen again.

There's a rustle to the left, and I change course toward it. Here, the land dips down before it goes out to a rocky outcropping that joins up with the beach. Penny has jumped up onto a large boulder, and the boar is snorting beneath her.

But the second it sees us, it turns and charges straight at me. My heart thunders as it does. The tusks seem to glisten in the air, catching the afternoon's dappled sunlight. I hold my spear up, Zane on one side of me, Sam on the other. Calvin is nowhere to be seen.

Instinctively, I hold the spear as long as I can, wanting to get off a true shot even with my bum arm and then be ready to jump out of the way.

Twenty feet. Fifteen feet. Ten feet.

I throw my spear. Zane and Sam do as well. One goes into the beast's right front leg. The others bounce off. I don't know who's made contact, but the boar comes forward at full tilt. I scramble to the right, my eyes scanning the low scrub jungle, searching for a tree to climb.

There's a shot, and the boar comes skidding to a halt right where I had been standing. Dante's here, the gun in hand. The limp corpse makes a sound I don't want to think about.

Calvin skitters to a stop. He's circled back around, and his eyes land on the pig first, then us, then Dante.

Dante blows on the end of the muzzle, shrugs, and then goes over to the pig. He shakes his head and says, "I don't want to be associated with anyone who takes joy in killing an animal. Now, eating an animal, that's a different story. Don't mess with friends, pig." He closes the pig's eyes. "What?" he says. "Didn't anyone ever tell you not to bring a spear to a bar fight? A spear to a boar fight." He laughs.

Sam takes Penny back to camp and fills Haley in on

what happened. It takes the six of us two hours to drag that boar to the beach, where we've set up smoking racks.

Calvin's far into butchering it when we realize we still haven't eaten dinner. Not only that, but we haven't finished our Island Festival Day. We're all moving.

It's well past sunset by the time we've got everything cleaned up and are back at the table. Penny's up on the platform, Pepper at her side. I'm not sure either one of them is ever going to come down again.

"They really have become friends," Haley says and heads to her cubby in the kitchen, Zane's phone in hand. She points it at the unlikely best friends.

Penny puts her leg around Pepper's back and cocks her head to the right, like she's a paid actress. Haley takes the shot, but Penny changes positions. Damn, that dog should have its own show.

"You're such a ham." She turns, her beautiful face twisted up.

"Good one, Sassy. Here you go, Penny." Dante tosses her a treat. "Now you really have the ham."

Groans circle the table. Dante managed to whip up a fresh meal. Once our Pepperfruit dessert is devoured, I just want to crawl up into bed and sleep for a hundred years, but Zane and I gather the bowls and put them in one of the tubs.

"With the lid on, the dishes will keep until tomorrow, right?" I say.

Zane snaps the lid in place, and we both ignore the stares from Dante. I'm two steps away from heading to the sleeping platform when Haley stands up and takes the centerpiece in her hand. "Are we ready?" she asks.

"I can hardly wait, Sassy," Dante says, but I have no idea what she's talking about.

"Ready for bed?" I ask hopefully.

"No, I have something planned for us down at the waterfall. Unless everyone's too tired? We can do it tomorrow."

Sam and Calvin stand up immediately.

"Not like that, blokes. This is going to be nice," Zane says.

Calvin turns to Sam. "I thought what we normally did at the waterfall was nice."

"Agreed," Sam says.

"Today is Island Festival Day. Tomorrow is Thanks-o-weenie. Geez, get it straight," I say.

I glance back at the treehouse, but everyone else has gathered towels and the rechargeable flashlights. Haley's vibrating with excitement. I would reincarnate for this girl, so I need to get my shit together. If I thought things were acting up before with my arm, I had no idea. Swimming, soccer, and then throwing a spear? Yeah, I'm ready for twenty hours of sleep. But something has Haley bubbling with a second round of energy, so I'm in. Anything that makes Firefly happy, I'll give her.

"You okay, Rockwell?" Sam puts his hand on my shoulder. He's got a small pack on his back.

"Yeah, I'm good." Fuck, old habits of never admitting weakness are hard to get over. "Arm's sore."

"Damn, I'm sorry. I'm in the best shape of my life. Odd enough to say. But today I'm feeling it, too."

"We can do this tomorrow. It's fine." Haley has snuck up behind the two of us. She still has the cloth-covered package under her arm.

"I'm good to go, if the old guy here is." I smirk at Sam.

"Let's do it," Sam says. Guess I'm not the only one who's tired.

I take long steps and catch up to Haley. "What's under the cloth, Haley?" When we first sat down at dinner, I tried to lift the cover and see it, but she grabbed my hand. That was a heck of a long time ago, though.

"You'll see." She gives me a kiss on the cheek.

The waterfall feels especially far away tonight. It's dark, but the moon has come out and there's a glow around the pool. A light breeze sways the palm trees, and I'd really like to strip my clothes off and go for not a swim but a soak.

Haley places her package on the big rock near our feet. "Today has been . . . a perfect example of this island. We had so much fun: the beach games, the table—"

"The decorations," I add.

Haley smiles. "Everything and then the boar. It was scary. For all of us. Pepper, Penny. But we handled it. You guys handled it, but as a team. This place has become home, and I want to thank it." She removes the cloth from a wreath with a bird of paradise flower in it. Dante lights the wick in the middle of it, and Haley gently places it in the water. She gives a clap as it floats to the middle of the pool. "I'd like it if we can each say something we're grateful for."

"Are we doing the no repeating rule?" Dante asks.

"The what?" Zane cocks his head.

"My family had a no repeating rule for things like this. You have to come up with something original."

"Oh, I'd like that. It was just my mom, grandma, and me most Thanksgivings. But yes, let's do that. I'm grateful for this land providing us with food." Haley turns to Calvin.

"Me next?" Calvin says.

"Yes."

"Right, I'm . . . grateful for all of you. I wouldn't have made it this far without the rest of you . . ." He takes a step back and shakes his head, his eyes on the float in the water.

Sam's next. "That the current brought me here. But I guess that's not something on the island." He blinks. "That Penny and Pepper get along. Well, I guess for Pepper too. I've never really had a cat. She's a nice one."

Zane's standing next to Sam. "That the bloody rainy season has ended."

"Amen," Dante says. "I'll go next. I'm grateful for the stove in the derelict, but also the treehouse. The rainy season would have been a lot worse without it. Zane, you were an ass while you were making it, but I'm damn glad we have it now. And the fish weir that Calvin made. Without it, we would have been a lot hungrier."

"What you got, Rockwell?" Zane asks.

I'm the only one left. My brain whirls because they've said everything. Dante cleared the rest out.

And then it snaps in me. It's wrong, but I'm going to say it, anyway.

"I'm grateful we wrecked. I'm grateful for the island being here. That my whole life was turned upside down. I'm sorry that I had to drag all of you with me. But this is the best damn thing that's ever happened to me. Better than winning the gold or being born into a rich family. This circumstance, this place—it's made me better. It's given me a rich and unique family, one that I never want to give up. It's made me realize who I am and what I want. And what needs are and aren't." I'm staring at the float. It has me in a trance. It's spinning in the middle of the pool, deciding if it wants to take a ride on the current down the stream. And then it shoots off, flowing away.

"Should we go after it? I don't want it to start a fire." Haley takes a step behind the rock toward the entrance path.

"There's not much fuel on it. It will burn out soon," Calvin says, reaching for her.

"But . . . only *you* can prevent a jungle fire." Dante laughs. "I'll get it, Sassy. Be right back."

Chapter 25

R & R

Calvin

Haley's crying, and it's because of what Rockwell said.

He's grateful for us being here? It's both sweet and a horrible thing to say. It makes me want to punch him. Because he's not wrong. I'm glad I'm here. I wouldn't have chosen it, but . . . I push out the thought of it. You can't choose what you get served. Life isn't a restaurant. You can't pick from a menu. You eat what you're served or you go fucking hungry.

The rest of them are circling around Haley. And I'm standing back, watching, listening to the fucking jungle. Waiting. For what, I don't know. Enough time has passed that if the pirates were going to come after us, they would have already. I shut down my inner alarms and focus on the light around Haley's hair.

The flashlights are wedged into the sides of the rocks. It's where we normally put them. It gives enough light to see when we're swimming. But now it gives a ghostly effect as it shines on the underside of everyone's chins.

Easton wipes the tears from her cheek and kisses up the trail of tears.

"Do you really mean it?" Haley places her hand in the middle of Easton's chest.

"Absolutely I do. There is no place I would rather be than here." Easton's eyes are locked on her.

"I agree." Sam's voice is on edge.

"I third that. But running water would be nice," Zane says. "And maybe some take away?" He moves around to her other side.

"What's wrong with the food?" Dante laughs. He places the bedraggled float on the ledge next to us.

"Fuck, am I the only one who hasn't gone completely nuts?" The five of them turn and stare at me. "What? I'm not saying that I don't appreciate all the things we just said, and I meant every word I said."

Haley turns from Easton to me. "I . . ." She puts both her hands on my chest like she just had them on Easton. But then she pushes, hard enough for my feet to fly out from under me, and my ass hits the water with such a big splash that I hear the cries and laughter from the rest of them as I douse them with water before I sink down.

Only for a moment. My feet hit the bottom of the pool and I jet upward. In time to see Easton swipe Haley's feet out from under her. He tosses her in the water five feet from me. I'm on her as she comes up, shaking her hair out from in front of her face.

"Chiefie," I growl out a warning. "That wasn't very nice, now, was it?"

It's dark, but I can see the panic in her eyes about what I'm going to do back to her. I internally laugh, because the evilest thing I could do to her now is nothing. Make her think something's coming.

"No, I suppose it wasn't."

There's a splash behind me. But unlike Haley and me, the rest of the guys have surely taken their clothes off.

"So, how are you going to punish me?" She splashes water in my face and swims backwards, away from me. It's hard to laugh and swim at the same time, but she's managing it.

Fuck, the way the moonlight picks up her smile . . . I'm pulling off my shirt and tossing it to the rock as I swim. My shorts are next. I'm to her before she makes it to the weak side of the waterfall. The side that's a little drizzle.

There's a thin ledge that lets you wiggle past the rougher rocks to where the years of rushing water has smoothed the rocks. It's refreshing and a damn good hiding place. If my ass wasn't so damn large, I'd love to push her to the wall and take her. Two good strokes and I'm able to get my thumb and forefinger around her ankle with a quick pull and I have her at my side.

"You got your shirt wet there, Bunny."

Her arms loop around my neck. "Yeah, you're right. What are you going to do about it?"

I pull her back from the waterfall, back to the ledge. Because as much as I'd like to rip her shirt off her, I do care about what happens to it. I do care. She's going to need what she has for as long as I can protect her.

I keep the backward strokes going until Easton and Dante are beside us.

"I've got you, Sassy. Hands off the Viking. Let's get this thing off your pretty titties, and then we'll work on getting that kitty of yours unwrapped."

"Titties and kitties?" Haley laughs but does as the chef commands.

I put my knee up, giving her a place to sit while they yank at the shirt. Dante tosses it to the big rock with a swack. Then I lean back and hold her around her waist, leaning her on my chest, one hand on her stomach and the other on her breast. My hand covers the entire thing. It's the perfect size. Never thought I would say there's the perfect size, but there it is under my fingers.

I pinch her nipple between my index finger and ring finger. I'm lost in her. In this part of the pool, I can just barely stand. I'm the only one who can. I lick along the shell of her ear.

"Calvin." It's husky and breathy, and it makes me want more. So much more. More than I can ever tell her.

"Haley."

"What, no Bunny?" Sam growls and leans over her, kissing her.

I laugh. "Ready, Bunny?" I'm a bastard because I don't want to share, not yet.

She pushes Sam away, knowing what's about to happen. I pull her under with me. My flat feet hit the pebbled bottom of the swimming hole and I shoot up, launching her into the air. Her laugh fills the night breeze before she splashes down into the water. Easton and Sam are there, instantly buoying her up. The loss of her solo attention on me rakes against the inside of my ribs. I'm hollow without her in my arms. No matter—this is what I signed up for. It's who we are now. I can't change it, and I'm not sure I'd want to.

My right arm's asleep. And there's a head on my chest. Haley's tight body is pressed against me to my left. I crack open my eyes and pull my arm out from underneath Zane's chest. The guy sleeps like the dead. He rolls over, grumbling.

But then I smell it. Bacon. Well, not bacon—we haven't had the time to cure the beast yet. Dante's got a whole plan.

I roll toward Haley, pulling her into my side. After swimming for ten minutes, Haley crawled onto the big rock and fell asleep. But she's rubbing her naked self over me now. I smooth her hair back and skim my fingers down the sides of her arm. She moans. It's light, and my dick twitches in reply.

"Hey!" Dante yells from below. "No starting Thanks-o-weenie without me." He laughs.

"The guy has sex-dar," Zane says sleepily.

"Indeed," I agree.

Haley rolls over. "Five more minutes, just five minutes."

I kiss her on the back of her neck. "Take all the time you want, Bunny." I cover her up with the sheet and make my way out of the sleeping loft.

"What's that?" I stare at the brown liquid in the cup Dante's offering me. It definitely doesn't taste like the tea that Haley and Dante have been perfecting. Honestly, the tea isn't that bad, or maybe I've just lost my addiction to caffeine.

"It's coffee. We've got enough for a few more pots. And I figure for as tired as everyone was after the Island Olympics, the boar, and then swimming at the waterfall?

Yeah, we're going to need a little bit to have the best Thanks-o-weenie day."

"You're . . . Whatever, we're not going to break her. Okay?"

"You wound me, Viking. I would never dream of hurting Sassy. I just don't want anyone falling asleep."

I take the cup out of his hand, and fuck . . . "This is the best cup of coffee I've ever had."

Dante brings his up to his lips and has a sip. "Not me. Mine was in a cafe in a little village in Southern France. Made by this woman who had to have been over a hundred. I speak halfway decent French, but she wasn't telling me her secret. She had the best smile, though." He shrugs, looking over my shoulder like he can still see her.

He's less than ten years older than me, but it's like he's lived twice as long. Chefs do that, though—they come and go. One season or two at the most. A guy like Dante? I'm sure he's a leave-them-wanting-more kind of guy.

It gets me thinking. "What's your endgame?"

"You talking about when we get off this lovely island? Damn, Green. You really are changing."

I shrug. Because no, I don't think we're getting off here alive. "That's not what I asked."

He sits down on the end of the new table, testing its legs before fully committing his weight to it. "You asking me if my intentions are honorable?"

"I suppose."

"You don't live through something like this and then walk away. At least, I couldn't. I've always been a nomad. But Sassy? Sure. I could figure out how to stay in one place if that's what she wants."

I nod.

"Did I pass your test?"

"Sure." There's no test to pass. I'm not his keeper. I'm not anyone's keeper.

"What about you?"

I take a small sip of my coffee, savoring it. "I've never been big on change."

"Not sure what that means, Viking, but okay. You want some breakfast? I have pig with a side of pig."

"I'll take the pig."

"Good choice." He slides off the table and makes me a bowl. There's more than pig in it. It's good.

"Thanks." I pull up a stump. With enough work, I can make some chairs to go around the table. But first, I want to get the WaveRunner working. It will make going to the other side of the island easier and use less fuel.

I'm taking the tub of dishes from last night out to the beach to wash them when Haley tiptoes down the ladder.

"Morning." I put the box down and pull her into a hug.

"Morning. Where's everyone else?"

"Sam and Easton are off on another secret project," Dante says. "They should be back soon. No one wants to miss—"

"Thanks-o-weenie," Haley and I say together. Her laugh vibrates through my chest.

Soon turns out to be not soon at all. I've got the dishes washed. I peer at the WaveRunner. I guess I've got some time. I flip open the toolbox and sift through the few tools I have.

The carburetor was a gummy wreck—the whole machine was. It reeked of stale fuel. I drained it as soon as I had it back here on the beach. But I need to finish removing the carburetor.

I steady my hands, and with my smallest wrench, I loosen the bolts and lift the carburetor free. The fuel bowl has a murky liquid in it—definitely water contamination. I was hoping it hadn't gotten this bad. It's slow, meticulous work, but it has to be done right. It's going to take a lot to get the gunk out of everything. You'd think I'd have all the time in the world to work on it. But somehow I don't.

Someone's running down the path from camp. Zane pops out onto the beach. "Let's go. We're ready."

"Ready?"

"The thing, the day—you know." Zane pivots and zips away.

I tuck everything back under one of the few tarps we have. Easton might have come up with this holiday, but I'm sure it's Dante who's made the agenda. And that scares me just a little.

Chapter 26

On the Rocks

Sam

"You smell good." Haley nuzzles her nose into my neck. "What is it? I can't quite put my finger on it."

"My new cologne. Do you like it?" I laugh.

"I do." Her lips purse.

Easton shakes his head, and he pulls out a small cloth bag. "All right, everyone grab a rock. Don't show it." He starts with Dante, then Zane. Calvin takes the bag out of his hand, shakes it and pulls one. He passes it to me. I swish my hand around in the stiff fabric bag. My chin flicks to Easton. There are only two rocks left. But Haley, Easton, and I still need to pick a rock.

"I'll take that from you, Sam," says Easton.

"I want a rock." Haley grabs at the bag.

Easton frowns. "No, trust me, Haley, you don't."

"I'll share my rock with you, Sassy."

"There's no rock sharing," Easton says.

"What sort of game have you gotten us into?" Zane laughs.

"Relax, I'll explain after we reveal rocks."

"Last time I heard something like that, I lost twenty quid. But okay, let's do it." Zane thrusts his hand out in front of his chest, and the rest of us do the same. Haley's got her arms crossed over her chest, her lips in a slight pout; it has me thinking about making her do other things with them.

"Firefly, if you would do the honors." Easton wiggles his eyebrows, and Haley drops her arms.

"Reveal," she giggles. "I don't know why I get such a kick out of saying that. Makes me feel like a game show host."

We all turn our palms over, and they have four white rocks, but in the middle of my hand is a dark rock.

"Sam, you've got the dark rock."

"Indeed. Now are you going to explain my fate?"

"It's simple: to honor the day, you're Haley's servant."

"Oh, bloody hell. Trade you, Sam." Zane holds out his rock.

"Not a chance." I slide the smooth stone into my shorts pocket. "How can I serve you, my queen?"

Haley clasps her hand over her face. She's shaking her head. "Oh, I . . ."

"We could all have done that." Dante grimaces. "Heck, I do that every—"

"Shut it," Calvin says.

When I see how red Haley's turning, Easton's point is evident. If he'd plopped a crown on the top of her head and declared her island queen, she'd freeze up. She might even with just me. She's used to being the one to solve the problems, even after we've all shown her how much she means to us. Yeah.

"In fact, leave them alone. I need your help." Calvin walks toward the stream.

"Who are you talking to?" Easton asks.

"Everyone but Sam and Haley. Move." He gestures.

"Hold up here. We're not *your* servants," Dante protests, but he walks down the path with Easton and Zane after Calvin.

"Now, how can I be of service, my lady?" I ask.

"I want to weave a new mat for the living platform—"

I cut her off. "No work. Just relaxing."

"But what if I want to?" she asks.

"Then think of how much fun you'll have tomorrow. Why don't I make you a glass of wine? And set you up with a chair on the beach, and you can read."

"I've read that book four times."

"You can pretend to read while you nap. Then I can wash your hair for you."

"Oh, that part sounds nice. Do you think you could cut it?"

"Cut it?" I'm being such a guy—I see how much work it is. "Sure, I will promise to do my best."

"That's not very reassuring."

I shrug. "A straight line, I can do."

"That's all I want. Just a few inches." She laughs. "You should have seen the look on your face. What did you think I wanted you to give me—a pixie cut?"

"If that's what you want."

"Never. I have the weirdest-shaped head. In all my baby pictures, I have a hat on. It's really like a cone or a bullet. Horrible." Her eyes flick to the sky and back to me. "Just a trim."

"What were you thinking there?"

"It's nothing. My ex. I'm trying to reprogram myself from all the things he said to me over the years."

"Yes, he was not only an ass but a fool. Your head is a lovely shape."

"Right." She crosses her arms over her chest.

"Now sit. I'll open a bottle of wine."

"Are you sure? Maybe we should wait."

"You heard Easton. You get what you want. Do you want a glass of wine?"

"Yes, please."

She's patient as I open the bottle of wine. I don't mangle the cork, but I'm not a sommelier or a chief stew.

I pick up a bowl of fruit that Dante has out. I can't help but wonder if Easton let him in on the plan, because under a cloth there's what certainly looks like a picnic to me.

"I'll just run up and get the scissors and my shampoo."

"No, Sugar. You're going to come with me and sit while I get everything else."

"Okay."

I take one of the two beach chairs, the food, wine, and a glass. "Right this way, Ms. Brewster. I believe we have a beach picnic for you."

"Let me carry something, Sam."

"The primary never carries anything."

Her eyes go wide. "Unless they want to." She holds out her hand and wiggles her fingers. I hand her the bottle of wine. She raises her eyebrows but holds the bottle to her chest and leads us to the shady spot on the beach. It's a nice spot away from the fish weir. "I had a primary a few years ago—they weren't owners, but they'd rented the yacht for two months. She was nice—too nice. It was a battle to get her to not make her own drinks." Haley sets the bottle of wine down on a large stone, anointing our spot.

"So you see what I'm dealing with here?" I rake the sand away from her chair, like the deck crew would have done for a yacht guest. Only I use my fingers until I find a stick with two little branches. I'm sure I look crazy grooming the sand with a twig, but Haley's laughing, so I don't care.

"That wasn't the point of my story, but I can see how you twisted it to help your agenda." She giggles and takes my twig away from me, twirling it between her fingers. Then she waits patiently for me to set up the chair. When she's sitting, I hand her the glass. I retrieve the bottle and pour a taste of the wine. I've seen stews do this, but I've never actually done it myself. My pour is a little large, but she doesn't mention it. She swirls the wine and sniffs it before taking a dainty sip. "Damn, Rocky has good taste in wine."

"It's to your liking?" I've got a cocky smirk on.

"I'm not sending it back, if that's what you mean. Unless?" She shifts left and right, gazing out at the horizon. No boat in sight. She holds the glass up, and I pour more. "I think you should have some too."

"You think?" This is a lot for her, but if she's going to get everything she wants out of life, I need to push her. I'm going to have her ordering me around by the time the day is over. "I think I could arrange that. Stay put. I'll be right back." I run along the zigzag path to the treehouse.

Penny is curious as to what I'm doing, but then she puts her head down on her paws and huffs. She just wants Pepper to play, but she's not having it. Pepper gazes down at Penny from the living room platform.

Up on the sleeping platform, I grab the bedraggled

paperback, one of the small mats we sometimes take down to the beach, a few towels, things to wash her hair with, some clean clothes, and anything else I think we might need. I nestle my pile into one of Haley's baskets. This one looks more like a basket than her previous ones.

I snatch another one of the glasses I brought on that very first trip here from the kitchen area too, and I'm back on the beach.

My girl has her eyes closed, her hands folded over her lap. She's not asleep. I see her twitch as I approach.

"Hey, Sugar."

She breaks out into a wide smile. "I love it when you call me that," she says, her eyes still closed. She brings her glass to her lips and takes a sip. "This really is good wine." She licks her lips.

I pour some for myself and plop down on the mat next to her chair.

It's oaky with a little chocolate undertone, and the flavors zing across my tastebuds. I haven't really had wine since that day back on the boat, on Haley's birthday. I take her hand from where it rests on the arm of the chair and bring it to my mouth, pressing a light kiss to her knuckles. "It's good. So you like being called 'Sugar?'"

Her blue eyes sparkle in the afternoon sunlight. "I do. I like all my nicknames."

I cock my head at her. "Really? There are quite a few."

"There are." She smiles, her eyes closing again. She sucks her lips into her mouth, wetting them.

I take a few things out of the basket. "I have your book."

Haley takes it, bringing it to her lap. "It's a good book. But if I'd known it was going to be the only book I had to read for the rest of my life . . ."

"I don't know," I say. "I like the part where he sneaks into her bedroom."

"You do?" She laughs. "You've read it?"

"Haley, Sugar, Sweetie, we've all read it multiple times. Even Easton. I had to stop Dante from reading it out loud. I still can't believe the heroine forgave him for what he did."

Haley nods, her eyes closed. "You'll do funny things for love."

"Yeah, that's not real love. He was selfish and there were red flags everywhere."

"I suppose he did kill her stalker."

"And then made her an accomplice," I groan.

"It's a dark romance, Sam. There's supposed to be red flags." She leans forward and kisses me. The wine on her lips is sweeter than the liquid in my glass, that's for sure. I place my glass on the rock next to hers, and she loops her hands around my neck, then slides off the chair into my lap.

When our lips part, my cock is hard and her eyes are dazed. "What can I get you now, my queen? A lot of guests order beach massages."

"But however will you find a masseuse on such short notice?"

"I happen to know a guy." I take both of her hands and help her stand up. She waits while I de-sand the mat and a towel which I roll up for a pillow. I reach for the bottom of her T-shirt, but she's ahead of me and pulls her shirt off.

Now she's smirking at me. "I love you, my queen."

"I love you, Sam."

My smile's so big it covers my face. "What, no king? Ah, true, you're not a queen—you're the empress with five kings." I wiggle the fingers on my right hand at her.

She laughs, her fingers tugging on the hem of my shirt. It lands in the sand at our feet. Her hand lands flat on my chest. We stare into each other's eyes. "I love fun, playful Sam. I mean, I love serious, badass Sam too. My king."

"Massage or hair first?" I raise my eyebrows at her. I take her hand and look at the supplies for her hair.

She brings her ponytail to her nose and sniffs. "No one should have to smell this rat's nest."

"Let's take care of that. But then we have some playing to do," I say, squeezing her hand three times.

Chapter 27

Royal Fleet

Haley

The way he growled *"We have some playing to do"* makes me want to wash my hair myself and get to the good stuff, but Sam sets me on the big rock. The tide is high enough that the water's close by. "I can—"

"Lie down. Tilt your head over the edge of the rock." He points.

I pull my hair out from under me, and Sam takes a small plastic container and carefully pours water over my hair. With one knee popped up in the air, it's actually comfortable. And it's surreal watching the clouds go by.

"You good?" Sam's serious face pops into view.

"Uh-huh." He's gentle but firm as he rubs the soap through my hair. "I'm seeing the appeal of being petted. If I had a tail, I'd be wagging it."

He rinses my hair and wraps it in a towel before helping me off the rock. He sweeps my feet from the sand and carries me back to the mat. He points. "Lie down, Haley."

I don't go all the way down onto the mat. Nope, I stop

on my knees. Am I testing him? Yes. This holiday isn't at all what I thought it was going to be. I worked myself up for being the one doing a lot of the work. But now? Now I'm the one getting all the attention when I thought it was going to be me giving them the attention.

But now I want badass Sam to come out. I smirk up at him, my hand skating down the front of his pants.

"No. All the way down, Haley."

I blink and reach. I want to please him. I want to make him fall apart on my tongue.

"No, this is about you."

My body acts on impulse, and I follow through without another word. Face up, I stare at him, the sun behind his head, his long muscular legs and that delicious V that starts at the top of his shorts. He shakes his head at me.

"This is about us," I say.

A guttural sound bursts from him. It's quick. His eyes twinkle at me. "Take your swim shorts off and roll over. I get pleasure from making you fall apart. Now roll."

I bite my lip and wiggle out of my shorts, but I don't roll over. I can't stop staring at him.

His eyes crinkle, and in a flash, he grabs me by my ankles and flips me over. "You need to follow directions, Haley." There's gravel in his voice. He pulls the tie on my bikini, and the straps fall away.

I'm panting. I should know by now that I like it when they do things like that. Maybe I like a little red flag. "Yes, Captain." I move the towel under my neck. I place my hands over my head. I'm half expecting him to tap my butt and tell me, "Ass in the air." But that doesn't happen.

There's a warm drizzle of the coconut oil that Dante's been making on my shoulders. Then Sam lightly straddles my hips, his large hands skimming lightly over the back of my shoulder blades. He works the oil into my skin, applying more and more pressure as I melt into the mat.

"Oh, that's good. Right there."

"You have big knots in your shoulders." He moves from them to my neck. "And your neck is tight too."

It's from weaving. I hunch over the fronds. The darn things cut up my fingers too. But I like it, and it's useful. I open my mouth to say all of that, but only a soft moan comes out.

"Right there?"

I moan again.

"I'll take that as a yes." He works his fingers perfectly on the pressure points of my back.

I've had more than a few massages in my life. I had one owner who insisted I get a massage before she did to make sure the masseuse was good enough. And she wanted a massage in every port. That was a good season. But Sam . . . he's amazing. Those fingers know how to do lots of things.

"Oh, you're really good at this."

"Thank you. I . . ."

My eyes roll back in my head. There's drool running out of my mouth. "I'm turning into a limp poodle. So good."

He laughs.

"Noodle . . . I mean noodle." I'm not letting my brain go off wondering how he's this good at it. Nope. That isn't happening. Focus.

Sam's touch changes. He shifts positions, scooting down my body. His focus moves to my lower back. His touch is lighter. "Hey, Sugar. Don't tense up on me."

"I'm . . ." I let out a cleansing breath, a yoga breath.

"That's right, just like that." He moves down to my butt cheeks, and honestly, I've never been a fan of someone massaging my ass. But then I've never had Sam working his magic until now.

I've lost the ability to tell time. "Am I purring?"

"No, that's Pepper." Sam laughs. She's helping. That's when I feel her little paws on my back. "She's kneading biscuits."

I cock my head to the side and wiggle my fingers. Pepper rubs up against my hand for a few minutes before trotting away.

"Where'd she go?"

"Over to the supervisors."

I turn my head the other way. The rest of the guys are sitting on the big rock, watching. Their hair is wet like they've been for a swim. I let out another breath and cock my head up at Sam.

"Time to flip." He taps my hip and lifts himself off me.

I roll and blink up at him again.

"Water or wine?" he asks.

"Both." I push up on my elbows. I half expected the other guys to come running over when I flipped, but they're staying by the big rock and I'm not sure how I feel about it.

"Water first." He hands me my bottle.

When I've had my fill, I exchange it for my wine and we clink glasses. It tastes even better now. He feeds me a piece of coveted mango. And I hold one out for him to take. He sucks my fingers into his mouth. And I close my eyes—I'm vibrating with need.

Sam straddles me again. His large chest hovers over mine, his lips a whisper away from my ear. "What does my queen wish for now? Do you want the court jesters to come play with you too?"

"Aren't they my kings?" I giggle and run my hand over his beard.

Sam's eyes twinkle. "Not in front of them. I wouldn't want to inflate their egos any more."

I take his lips in mine. He planks over me, caging me in. My legs wrap around his hips. When did he take his pants off? I run my fingernails down his back, and he hisses. His cock rubs down my core, and I wrench myself up against him.

"Fuck," Dante says, the restraint in his voice strong. Sam's body hides the others from my view down the beach.

Sam deepens our kiss, and when my head falls back to the mat, the blue in his eyes matches the cloudless sky above his head. He winks at me. And damn if his charm doesn't send a bolt of electricity around my body.

He rests his forehead against mine. "I think this party of two is about to get much larger."

"Oh." I drop my legs to the mat.

"Here or the loft?" It's a simple question.

"No sand. Loft."

"Good choice," he whispers. "Get on my back." He thrusts up to standing, like he's doing a workout. And I follow suit, jumping onto his back. Then he's off running down the path to the camp. He's up the ladder before I can even try to get off. A quick dusting off of our feet and I'm hauling him down on top of me.

My fingers skim the tips of his shoulders as the other guys arrive on the platform. Our bodies press together, and I squeeze my hand between us, reaching for his cock. But Sam's hand lands in the middle of my chest and he eases down my body. His warm mouth settles on my core, and I'm lost. My neck bends, and the top of my head pushes the pillow away. My vision blackens as I break apart. Catching my breath, I slowly come back. My eyes snap open, and

Sam's there. His blues glowing at me as he crawls up my body. There's a rustle to my side. Dante.

"Look at him, not me," Dante commands.

Sam gives a robust chuckle and takes my chin in hand. His kiss centers me. Even in the glow of an orgasm, my need for him builds. I lock my feet around his back and rock my hips, and he enters me with a swift thrust that has me slurping down air. "Sam." I buck against him. But he doesn't move, not yet. I shouldn't either. I need to let things stretch out.

I love feeling him inside me. Holding on to his biceps, I close my eyes and tilt my head back.

They're here, but I need to finish what I started with Sam. He grabs my hips and tilts them upward, driving himself deeper into me. His pace pushes me into the mattress. He surrounds me, a wall of muscle. A fortress. In his arms, I'm safe. I'm free to be the queen.

Until the island, orgasms were generally something I had alone. But my second orgasm races at me, drowning all of my senses. Sam's fingers are in my hair, and he tugs on my wet, uncut locks. I'm over the edge again, dragging him with me.

"Fuck, Haley." He's clamped on to my shoulders with one hand, the other holding him up until it doesn't and his whole body crashes into mine.

My eyes fly open. I love it. I love how he's locked me in. If I could, I'd stay here forever. Flattened under one of my kings.

Chapter 28

Code Breaker

Haley

"Haley? Haley?" Zane calls to me.

"Shut it, Morris. She needs her rest," Easton says louder than Zane.

I roll over. I'm disoriented. The rest of last night was a blur. Wine, so much wine. And more of everything. I'm drooling. I reach out my arm and find an empty mattress.

"Well, she's got to be awake now. How are you feeling, Sassy?" Dante asks.

"Are you okay?" I lean over the side of the railing.

"I'm better than okay. I think I figured it out. Well, I think I figured a little section of it out. Translating this is going to take bloody forever." Zane waves a piece of paper at me.

"Rocky's agenda?" I ask.

"Yes, it's bloody amazing. Come here. I mean . . ." He clears his throat. "Or I've been staring at it long enough to make me think I've figured it out. And honestly, I don't have it all yet, just . . . Well, come here and see." His smile covers his entire face.

"No way." Easton shakes his head. He's leaning over Zane's shoulder. I'm the only one who's been encouraging Zane to continue figuring out the agenda. All the other guys think it's a lost cause. Admittedly, lately I've thought it might be impossible too.

"Give me a second. I'll be right down."

"Take your time," Zane says, like a man who wants me to hurry.

I laugh. "Just a minute." I run my fingers through my hair. I don't need a mirror to know that it might be clean now, but going to bed with it wet—or rather, having sex with it wet—and then falling asleep without brushing it? Yeah, I'm going to have to take a dunk in the ocean to get it to even go into a ponytail.

I'm down the ladder, and Dante hands me a cup of coffee as my toes hit the sand. "Enjoy it, Sassy. We have enough for two more pots. I'm thinking about Christmas morning and New Year's Day."

"Good idea. Thank you." I take a small sip and slide onto a seat at the table next to Zane. "Show me."

Easton's sitting next to Zane, and Dante's across the table.

I take another sip of coffee. "Where are Calvin and Sam?"

"Around," Dante says. Which has been the answer a lot lately. Well, not Calvin and Sam. Mostly Sam and someone else.

"Oh." I raise my eyebrows and stare at Dante over my mug.

He shrugs. "Okay, Zane, give us the goods."

"Well, I don't have all the goods yet." Zane laughs.

Dante moans.

And I shoot him a look. "Don't mind the naysayers. They never spot genius." I rest my hand on Zane's shoulder. He's not paying any attention to Dante.

"Right, well. I don't have all of it yet. But the numbers go from 1 to 50, which is confusing because the alphabet has 26 letters. But then I thought, what if he's used the other numbers as words he's memorized? Like important names or frequent words. Which is why it's harder to solve. Because normally you can look for three numbers that are repeated more frequently and boom, you have the word "the." But not here. But there are an awful lot of 5s. What if 5 is the key? And then I thought, what if he's got the alphabet numbered back from 50? But there are a lot of 50s but not many 25s. So that bloke did it backwards, but there aren't enough 25s either. I've tried it both ways. On this passageway. But there's a heck of a lot of 46s and that's the most common letter in English. So I've been using this passage. Over and over. Thinking maybe he added a few numbers that equaled important words to him. Easton said Rocky's been doing this for ages. Before he merged with Harding, before Candy."

"And they could be 50 and 49. But how many whole word numbers would he have added?"

"That's what I've been trying to figure out. And moving from the back seems the most logical. Again with so many 46s. I don't know why that didn't stand out to me months ago? I'd been jumping all over. So now I'm using this passage as a test." He points to a part in the book.

4 49 / 34 46 46 47 / 8 / 38 37 29 46 / 9 25 9 26 / 46 33 37 38.

"These two? 4 and 49 seem to be together a lot. Then there's that 8, so forget about that. Here—the last three phrases are the ones I'm working on. And I just got it, using the alphabet backwards. Making 48 the letter B—"

"Not A?"

"A's one of those high-frequency words. I believe it's 9."

"Right." I think I understand it. Maybe.

"Get to it already." Dante's leaning over the table.

He flips to a different page. "Right. The last three words here would be 'moved away from.'"

"What if 4 is Rocky and 49 is Harding?" Easton's a lot more invested now.

"Could be." Zane writes it under the corresponding numbers.

"Rockwell Harding. What's the next bit then?"

Zane looks at his key, which is a mess of things crossed out and underlined. "Need?"

"Then 8 could be the word too. That's a common word, right?"

"Sure is, Little Bird." He pumps his hand in the air. "I think we've got enough to really figure out what's in here."

I plant a kiss on his cheek. "Do you want any help with it?"

His head is bowed, and he's deep in thought. "What? Oh, I don't think so. But thank you."

Christmas. It's weird to think about. How can we have been here for that long? But here we are. I used to love Christmas.

"Are you okay?" Easton's hand lands on my shoulder.

I'm staring out at the ocean. "It's fine. It makes me think about my mom. Last year I was still with Steven. But it didn't feel like Christmas. It wasn't fun." I huff. "There were so many signs. You know? I should have known that Steven wasn't the answer. Things had spun into the realm of not fun for a while."

Easton wraps his arms around me, his chin resting lightly on the top of my head. "Let the scumbag float out to sea. Tell me about your mom. What did you do for the holidays?"

"Maryland gets cold but not Maine-cold. Sometimes we would get snow. But not usually for Christmas. A couple of days before Christmas, we'd put on our snow hats. Mine was a Capitals' hockey one with a blue pom-pom. Mom's was an Orioles' skullcap hat with a black pom-pom. We'd make cocoa and watch *A White Christmas*. It was our version of a rain dance. If we did it just the right way, savored the peppermint candy cane stir sticks long enough, we'd get snow on Christmas. Not a lot. Not like I bet you got in Maine when you were little. An inch or two. It would shut the city down, and Mom wouldn't have to go to work. She was a receptionist for a dentist. They worked right up to Christmas. But if we got snow a few days before her vacation started, we had a longer vacation. That was the best. Then we'd lie around the house watching movies. As many marathons as we could get in—well, of ones that we both loved. The really old black and white ones and all the stop-motion ones."

"Oh, there's more material for Zane. I think it's possible that he might actually finish the entire Marvel universe in his bedtime stories."

"What about you?"

"Before my mom died? Or after?" He hugs me tighter into his chest, pulling my shoulders back so we're flush.

"What were your good Christmases?"

His breath whispers in my ear. "That's hard to say. I don't suppose I've talked about my mom much."

"You've talked about Maine. And how Susan moved you to Miami, and that's how you got into swimming. But not about your mom, no." I want to turn around and look at him. But at the same time, the ocean has me mesmerized, and something tells me this is going to be a lot easier for Easton if I don't.

"I was little, you know. Nine. A lot of my swimming friends . . . A lot of them have told me they don't remember much before their eleventh birthday. For me, I've got the before Mom time and the after. Moments from when I was really little. She wanted Emily and me to live a normal life. She'd come from a normal middle-class family in California. She met Dad in college. The photos of their wedding are like a fairytale."

"I'm guessing her dress didn't have a horse on it?"

His warm laugh shakes me. "No, it did not. Like a real Grimm fairytale, things weren't all roses in their marriage. I remember waking up to them fighting. I don't know what about. They were just voices in the dark. The next morning, there would be a large flower basket on the front hall table. Mom would pretend like nothing happened. When Dad traveled, though, I could hear my mother crying at night."

I run my fingers over his hands. "That's hard. I never heard my parents argue. Not when they were married and not after the divorce, either."

"You're lucky."

His rapid heart pounds against my shoulder blades.

"We don't have to talk about this. I didn't mean to bring you down."

"No, it's good to let it out. Then one day she was gone. Pills. No goodbye, no nothing. At least, that's what I heard the new housekeeper say a month later. Things changed. Which, of course, they would have had to. Dad worked a lot. Emily and I were little. Suddenly, it wasn't just the four of us in the house. There was a housekeeper and a cook. Then eventually a driver. All Susan's ideas."

That has me tilting my head to look up at his blue eyes. "Susan? How soon after your mother died was she in the picture?"

"She was my dad's executive secretary, as they called them back then."

"Oh."

"Yeah, oh."

"Do you think something was going on before your mom died?"

"No clue. But she didn't waste any time moving in on him, that's for sure."

"Gross."

"Yeah, but she wasn't all bad."

"Swimming." I hold his hands tightly around my waist.

"Yeah, swimming. And you know, she loves Christmas. Every inch of the house was filled with decorations the year after my mom died. I don't think you could add another bow to the place if you tried. And then when we moved to Miami, she hired a company to do the lights. Our house was its own nighttime spectacular. But I still liked my mom's homemade decorations better. Emily insisted we put them up. She was little and capable of throwing an amazing tantrum when she tried. By the time we were in high school,

Susan had a tree placed in Emily's room for all the 'crafty decorations,' as she called them."

"We should make some." I roll in his arms, my forehead inches from his lips until I stand on my tiptoes.

Easton smiles. "We should."

"I'd like to make some gifts. I'm working on some ideas. There's one I need some help with, though. Could I borrow you?"

"You can't borrow what you already own."

My stomach warms. I know it's corny, but I don't care. I take his lips in mine. He deepens the kiss and I'm moaning into his mouth. My core's on fire.

He pulls back. The sun pokes out from behind the jungle above his head, making me squint into the sun. I haven't seen my sunglasses in a few days. "Now, Firefly, what do you need? I'm at your service."

Shoot, I didn't think about the state of his arm before I asked him. I suck on my lips and run my hands down the sides of his arms. "No, it's okay. I'll ask—"

"Whatever it is, I can do it." His tone has dropped.

I'm not sure he can with his arm, but then it's not fair of me to ask and then rescind. It's not hard to pick out that he's having problems with his arm, but more so it hurts his ego that he can't do what he's used to doing. "Down by the waterfall, I saw—"

"All you have to say is waterfall and I'm there." He laughs.

I playfully slap at his firm abs. "Not waterfall time." Although it doesn't sound like a bad idea right now. "No, I saw a flat rock that looks like something chalk might work on. I thought I could make Zane a chalkboard to work out the code on."

"That's perfect. What are you going to do for chalk?"

"I . . . I hadn't gotten that far? Burnt charcoal?"

"Crushed shells might work."

When we get to the waterfall and I'm staring down at the rock that I saw a few weeks ago, I realize it's a lot bigger than I thought it was. It's sticking half in the water and half out. And the memory of the chest in the cave floods into my head. I never mentioned it to any of the guys.

The excitement clogs my throat. "Cave—there's a box in the cave!"

Chapter 29

Lost Cargo

Haley

"What?" Easton's staring at the rock.

I take a deep breath and slow down. "In the cave where we tied the WaveRunner up, there's a box covered in seaweed and barnacles. I completely forgot about it. I was too worked up about the knots in the vests and you and Calvin being missing."

Easton sinks to the big flat rock, his feet dangling over into the water. His neck twists up at me, then back to the spot where we buried the Phoenix diamond. "Like buried treasure?"

"Maybe. I didn't exactly get a good look at it."

"That sounds like a fun mission. But we'll need to group it with a trip over to the pomelo beach." He pats the rock. "This is the one?" He pats the smaller rock, which isn't small at all.

"Yeah, never mind, it's too big."

"It's too big to move like this, for sure. But if I find another rock to use as an awl, we can split it."

We're back in camp in no time. It's weird how far away I used to think the waterfall was.

Easton leans over me and whispers, "You distract Zane, and I'll grab the hammer."

Zane and Dante are sitting close together when we come back into camp. Dante throws a lid over the top of his pot with an extra dramatic flair.

I sit down in Zane's lap, and he rotates, turning me away from Dante. "How are you doing, Little Bird? What's Easton up to?"

I fling my arms around his neck and kiss him on his collarbone. I have lava spots on my body, but so does my Birmingham Boy.

He tilts his head, giving me better access. "I no longer care what he's bloody doing. Fuck, Haley."

"Hmm." I go higher and nibble his ear.

"Where are you going with that?" Zane's head cocks to the side.

"With what?" I slide off Zane's lap and wiggle my eyebrows at him, then take off down the path to the waterfall with Easton.

"How about this one?" I hold up another solid rock. I took geology in college, but I don't remember much.

"I'll give it a go." Easton takes the triangular-shaped rock and holds it against the edge of the one we want to use. He smacks it, and the wedge shatters into pieces. We try three more wedges before the rock cracks. I can see the split happening.

"You did it!"

"We did it." Easton looks up from the split rock.

"We did," I say, staring at him.

"We're a good team."

I sit down on the edge of a nearby boulder, and Easton

places the newly manageable-sized rock next to me. I brush my hand over it, taking a corner of a rag and wiping it down.

"This is really going to work. He'll be able to decipher the rest of the notebook and have room to write his answers in the rest of the agenda," I add, glancing at Easton.

Easton smiles, his eyes glistening as he nods. "Yeah, he's really gonna love it. You did good."

"Come on, you did all the work," I reply.

"Sure, I'm just the muscle, but you had the idea. That's the most important part." He flexes his biceps at me and laughs. Then he glances away, over the top of the waterfall, and back to me. "I just want you to know I really still believe that we're going to get off this island, and when that happens . . . Haley Brewster, I need you in my life. I don't want you to vanish. Please tell me you won't vanish."

I grab his hands and laugh. "I have the same fear about you. I don't want you to vanish out of my life either."

"Good, good," he says thoughtfully, nodding with his lips closed. "Then it's settled—no vanishing."

"No vanishing," I agree.

I don't know which of us moves first, but our lips entwine, and he pulls me over the new slate to sit in his lap. We kiss until I'm dizzy.

"Do you want to take a dip?" I ask.

Easton squeezes his eyes shut tight. "Oh, I wish I hadn't promised Sam—"

"You promised Sam what? What's going on?"

"I also promised not to tell, so . . . I don't know what you're talking about," Easton says, trying to sound casual.

"I don't know what you're talking about," I mimic back at him, my jaw locking tightly, arms crossing over my chest. "Okay, I suppose this is the season of surprises."

"It is the season of surprises," Easton replies, interlocking his fingers with mine, the slate tucked underneath his arm.

I glance back to where we did the work. "Oh, wait, I should clean up the evidence."

I push the shards around so they're hidden and nothing sharp can hurt us when we come back at night. Then I join him on the path, our fingers locking together again.

I hide the slate in my ever-growing pile in my cubby.

Luckily, the camp kitchen is empty. Everyone else must have scurried away to do secret things in this time of secrecy. Easton gives me another kiss.

"Okay, now, turn around. I'll see you later," Easton says.

"It's fine. I'm going to the beach anyway," I say, taking my notebook and heading for the sea. I plop down in the shade, my back resting against a rock.

One gift down, four to go. Now I just have to come up with four more good ideas. I'm . . . vibrating inside. I'm honestly happy. Maybe this Christmas won't be so bad.

"Hey there, Chiefie!" Calvin's working on the Wave-Runner again.

I jump off the rock and tuck my notebook under my arm. "How's it going? Did you get the carburetor back in?" I ask.

Calvin nods. "Yup. I think it might actually be time to see if it's working."

"You're kidding. Really?"

"Nope. Let's do it. You want to do the honors?" He closes the panel on the backside. "Well, no. Maybe you should stand over there. I don't want you to get all mucky if it spurts things."

I watch the tick in Calvin's neck. I don't think he really means "mucky"—I think he means if it explodes. But I nod and step to the side.

He turns the key once, and nothing happens. He tries again, and it sputters, starts, and then stops again. Calvin wrinkles his nose. He grabs a tool from the box, opens the panel, and fiddles with something. Then he steps back, turns the key, and this time the engine turns over. He lets it run for a minute, then turns it off.

"I think we're good to go. Want to take a spin with me and see how it works?"

I glance at the ocean, then back at Calvin.

"We haven't taken the tender out in a long time . . . or at least, I haven't been on it in a while," I say, unsure if I want to go or not. "Shouldn't we tell the others first?"

Calvin glances at the jungle. "I suppose we should. Let me see if I can find somebody. I'll be right back."

He runs off to the camp, and I sit down again, pondering while staring at my notebook, pen in hand, my lips twitching left and right. I'm coming up blank, and I don't like it. I tap my pen on my pad, but no good ideas come to mind for the other guys.

By the time Calvin returns with life vests in hand, Zane is with him.

"Zane's going to help," Calvin says.

"Okay," I reply. I tuck my notebook underneath the toolbox, then second-guess myself. "I'll be right back." I run it all the way to my cubby, and Dante's there in the kitchen.

"What's going on?" he asks.

I'm out of breath. This is exciting. I didn't doubt that Calvin would get the WaveRunner fixed. The other guys? Yeah, not so much. Easton's been calling it Calvin's salvaged sculpture. "Calvin got the WaveRunner fixed. We're gonna take it for a spin," I say to Dante.

"Oh, I want to see!" Dante quickly covers up his lunch in progress and follows me out.

Calvin and Zane are hauling the WaveRunner to the water on a bamboo sled. Dante joins in to help while I hold the life jackets.

After a few minutes of fiddling, Calvin gets on it and starts it right up. He's cautious and takes it only twenty feet out into the shallows. But it's not spouting flames or even smoke anymore. He widens his loop from the shallows, taking it farther out before he carefully brings it back in, avoiding the rocks on the beach.

"Are you ready for that ride I promised, Haley?" Calvin asks.

I nod, handing him a life jacket. He begrudgingly puts it on, and I do as well.

"We'll be right back," he tells the others.

I scream with laughter as he spins off the beach. As chief stew, I didn't get much opportunity to actually play in the water—I was too busy working. I think I can count the number of times I've been on a WaveRunner before the Rock Candy died on one hand.

Calvin turns to me. "Anything you want to do while we have it out?"

I hesitate, then lean forward. "When I was searching for you in the cave, I noticed there's a large box underneath where we used to tie the WaveRunner up. Did you see it when you were in the cave?"

"No, I didn't." Calvin turns the WaveRunner toward the Rock Candy alcove. "But I want to now."

"Shouldn't we be getting back? We said we were only going out for a short spin."

"This won't take long," Calvin says. "Besides, the tide's low, and if we're going to look at it at some point, we might as well do it now. I want to run all the gas I put in here through it, just to make sure it's completely clean."

At least, I think that's what he says—he's screaming into the wind.

I nod and glance back at the beach. Easton and Sam are there now too. I wonder if Easton will tell them what we're doing. Since I mentioned the box earlier today, I'm hoping that's what happens.

I hold on to Calvin's waist and press my head into his large back. It's amazing the difference his wide shoulders make as a windbreak.

The ride over to the cave feels twice as long as it does when we take the tender. But the weather is perfect today, the skies clear, the ocean like glass. Of course, that doesn't mean a thing during the rainy season. But now, we're good. It won't rain today.

No matter how many times I see this place without the Rock Candy, my stomach is going to drop. It's like cursed water now. The place where our hope washed out to sea. I turn my head the other way and watch the waves coming in. My heart thuds in my chest. The last time I was here, I thought Calvin and Easton might be dead. I cling tightly to him.

He pulls into the cave, slowly putting the machine into neutral. "I'm going to tie up the WaveRunner, but I don't want to turn it off. Just in case." Calvin tugs on my ponytail. "Where's the box?"

I lean to the side and find the shadow. "There." I point it out.

"Hold on to the handlebars. It shouldn't move, but . . ." Calvin slides out of his life vest and dives. I'm holding on to the handles so hard my knuckles are turning white. I'm doing my best to keep the machine steady while watching what he's doing.

He pops up a minute later, shaking the water from his

head.

"Damn, Chiefie, I think you found sunken treasure."

Chapter 30

The Bubble

Calvin

I climb back onto the WaveRunner. "It's crazy. I have no idea how we're going to open that box, let alone move it. It's made of thick wooden planks, and it's wrapped tightly with rope. Maybe we could cut the rope." Haley hands me my vest, and I put it on.

"You'll figure it out. I know it!" she says into my ear and wraps her arms around my waist.

Thank fuck the WaveRunner slides right into gear. The light outside the cave has changed drastically as I head back out. I'm shocked at how much darker it's become. Clouds hang low overhead. It's only a matter of minutes, if not seconds, before a storm lands on top of us, overtakes us. There's thunder in the distance—this has come out of nowhere.

Haley tucks her head into my back, her fingers locked around my sides. When the rain starts, it doesn't do that gentle one-or-two-drops thing; no, it comes down in sheets, like someone's throwing us into the waves. The ocean has gone from pure glass to nothing but 100% chop. The Wave-Runner rides up the sides of the strong waves and crashes down. We're trying to slide against the current, and it's putting the machine to the test. My stomach is somewhere underneath my ears.

Holy fuck, I've never gotten seasick on a WaveRunner before, but I guess there's a first time for everything. "Hold on!" I yell back at Haley. "This is gonna get worse."

"Just go," she says. "Go, go." There's a light panic in her voice, but she's holding on. The ride that took us eight minutes to get to the cave takes at least twenty-five minutes back. We're still not past the bluffs. I'm starting to worry we might run out of fuel. I give the fuel gauge a tap. When we round the corner to our beach, the big rock welcomes us back.

Thank fuck. I know where all the rocks are, but if the waves want to throw us into them, there's nothing I'm going to be able to do to stop it. I avoid one, then two, then a third rock. When I see a fourth one coming, I yell to Haley, "Bail!"

We're close enough to shore that the waves are going to push her in and not out, I hope. She jumps, and the momentum of her jumping off is just enough to get me to the opposite side of the rock that was coming straight at us.

I run the WaveRunner right onto the sand, hitting the off button as I bail, taking large steps, going back to find her. Zane and Easton are running down to the shore. Haley's stumbling out of the water. Zane wraps her in his arms and heads for camp.

I go back to the WaveRunner. Easton's there. We move it to the sled and haul it to the tree line.

"You good?" Easton yells into the wind.

I wipe my hand through my hair. "Yeah. Let's get off the

beach." Storms this time of year haven't been lasting long. But hell if I know what's going to happen.

Easton's ten steps in front of me as I head up to camp. Haley's discarded life jacket is on the living room platform. I put mine with hers and climb up the ladder. The shutters are drawn tight, and the door is pulled shut. Sam opens it for me as I approach and seals it tightly behind him. Everyone's on the sleeping platform.

"Are you okay?" Haley hands me a towel, even as Dante's trying to dry her off.

"Thanks," I say, running the towel through my hair, peeling my wet clothes from my body. When I have dry shorts and a T-shirt on, I turn and face the four other guys, all glaring at me.

Sam opens his mouth, but it's Dante who steps forward. "What the hell do you think you were doing?" he demands.

"It's not his fault." Haley raises her hand to put it on Dante's chest.

"Like hell it's not," Dante replies. "He knows better. What if the WaveRunner had stopped and you were next to the bluff?"

"It didn't stop," Calvin says.

"But it could have." Sam's voice is deep. He's not happy.

Haley holds her hands up to Sam this time. "There's no way we could have known the weather was going to change that abruptly."

"And I know what's going to be said next," I mutter.

Sam and Zane say together, "Prepare for the worst." It's Sam's motto, and one that Zane has taken as his own.

"We're fine," Haley says. "We're fine, we're fine, we're fine."

"I'm glad you're fine, Sassy, but numb-nuts over here could have really gotten you both hurt."

"He didn't, and we're fine," Haley repeats.

"Where did the damn dog go?" Sam ducks his head outside. "Come home," he yells out into the jungle. "Penny, home." He cups his hands and yells it again, "Home!"

"Besides, we discovered something really exciting," she says.

"Oh yeah, what was that, Little Bird?" Zane asks, smiling at her.

"Calvin, you tell him. You're the one who dove and saw it."

"Right. It's thick oak wood, something really water-tolerant, wrapped in heavy, old-style boat rope. There's no way we're gonna get it up. I tried budging it. The thing is really heavy, but we could cut the rope if we wanted to see what's in there."

Zane nods. "You think the planks are the same sort of wood as this?" He knocks on the floor. "Because there's no oak trees around here."

"Yeah, I do," Calvin replies.

I study the floor and think back to what I saw underwater. "I do. I think they're the same."

"That's interesting." Zane rubs his chin. "Maybe it was something the derelict had in its hull. Maybe they were hiding it before they got thrown back onto the shoals."

"Could be," I nod, making one last pass with the towel over my head. I slump down into the pile of pillows in the corner, the pile that Penny and Pepper like to sleep in, just as a wet dog comes racing in from the storm.

"What in the hell?" Dante says.

"Only useful thing Jenifer ever did. It's Penny's strongest command. She'll run wherever she thinks of as home."

"Impressive," Dante says to Sam, and then he turns to me and gives me a look that says the dog is smarter than me.

I could have really hurt Haley. They're not wrong. And what the fuck am I doing? Sometimes it's like I get a burst of energy from the wild, younger me and I stop thinking. They're right. Of course it could have ended differently.

I close my eyes and listen to the rain on the roof. When I open them, Sam is still glaring while the others have moved along. Zane and Haley have their heads close together, probably talking about Rocky's agenda or maybe theorizing what could be in the box. But I've got bigger worries.

Sam sits down next to me. He doesn't say anything at first. Fuck, I hate disappointing this man. For a long time, I thought of him as, well, my hero, someone I wanted to be like. It's a little different now, now that we're in this . . . whatever we are in.

"I don't expect you to live life in a bubble, but I sure as hell think you need to change your perspective. You've been living like we're already dead, taking chances that don't need to be taken. It's one thing when you do it with your-self; it's another when you do it with Haley. I won't have it." He raises his eyebrows at me.

I give him one good nod because he's right. I haven't really cared about things in a while, certainly not since the pirates. It's only a matter of time.

I close my eyes, the rain on the metal roof thankfully drowning out the rest of the group. Sam moves to the other side of the platform, not waiting for my response.

The warm ball of fuzz—Pepper—is pulled away.

"Hey," Haley says.

I crack open my eyes. Haley's holding Pepper on her lap, her body parallel with mine.

"You doing okay?" She wraps her arm around mine, intertwining us, and rests her head on my shoulder. "You looked awfully deep in thought."

I nod. In reality, I was almost asleep. It's easier just to switch off than to think about things.

"I'm sorry they came down so hard on you," she says.

"No, they're right. I shouldn't have taken you out like that. We should have come back in and waited for the tender to be ready, just in case something happened to the WaveRunner."

"It's not your fault. I could have stopped you."

I cock my head at her. "Nice try."

She playfully slaps my arm. "I could have," she insists.

"That's cute," I think, because I'm awfully stubborn and when I get an idea in my head, be it good or bad, it's just there.

"The guys had some good points, though." She looks up at me, her clear blue eyes darker now in the low light of the storm. "But we're fine, we're good, and we'll just move on from here. You don't need to ruminate on it for days on end." She covers her mouth. She does that a lot when she's regretful of what she said, like she can stop the words from coming out or pull them back in.

"No, they're right and you're right," I say. "But really, what does it matter? We're gonna die here. It's just a matter of time."

Haley snuggles her head down onto my chest. With my free hand, I pet Pepper. She stands up and rubs her face along Haley's chin.

"Calvin, you need to have hope," Haley says after a long time. The rain has slowed; there are just fat drops echoing on the metal now. "Really—you need to have more hope. We're gonna figure this out, right?"

"Right," I say, too loudly. Pepper scurries away.

"Oh, come on. Now we've lost our lap warmer." Haley repositions herself, kneeling between my legs. She holds my forearms in her hands, her chin tilted upwards to look at me. "I guess it's no use. I can't make you feel something that you don't feel, so I'll just have to have enough hope for both of us." She rises up and kisses me. It's a light kiss. Then she stands and crosses the room.

I miss her immediately. Why do I have to be this way? Being a realist sucks.

Chapter 31

Hall-Mark

Dante

"Morning, Sassy." I lean over my former morning girl and give her a kiss. "You told me you wanted me to wake you up early."

She rolls over, her eyes shut. Sam and Calvin both crack their eyes open at me. Sam immediately moves to sitting. Zane is already gone—well, I don't know what he's doing. He's off making something for someone, I'm sure.

Sam stands like a zombie, pulls on a shirt, and disappears down the ladder, Penny chasing after him. I bend over and give Haley another kiss on the cheek. "Let's go, Sassy. Sun is shining. It's going to be a great Christmas Eve."

Her eyes flutter open. "Did it snow?" she asks in her best little girl voice.

"Only in Calvin's heart," I say, and I turn in time to catch the pillow he throws at me.

"Ha ha." He's up and pulling on his pants over his thick thighs. "Come on, let's go. We've got things to do. You know, the primary—she's an ornery one," he says, putting a smile on.

Sassy slips out of bed, awake. "I'll be down in a minute," she says.

"I'll be waiting for you," I say.

Haley and I have planned this thoroughly. There's a lot of things that we don't have much left of—flour, sugar, cocoa —and we're going to make all of them count. In the last few weeks, Calvin, Zane, and I have figured out how to make some mud bricks, and I've recreated the oven that I saw on the pomelo beach. Well, ours is a little less crumbly. I've been able to cook a few things in it over the last week, and I've almost gotten the hang of it. I'm hoping that we can mix together some cookies, or at least attempt a cookie and some biscuits . . . but we'll see.

The fire is going already, and actually there's a slight chill to the air, which is refreshing. I wouldn't say it's cold by any means, but it's less like a sauna and more like a comfortable 82 in the shade.

The thing is, for me . . . I know that this Christmas will be a letdown for, I guess, everyone else here, but it's kind of normal for me. I'm used to not having anything. I'm used to a barren tree with one or no presents underneath it. But today will be different. We might not have the pierogi that my mom used to make or an array of Christmas cookies, but I also won't have the drawn-out family fights that used to happen when I was younger. Oh, it's different now, of course. It's vastly different now. My mom and sister and my niece and nephew—they have a nice place, and there are plenty of presents under the tree for the kids. Or at least . . . fuck, I hope there is. I always send them something, lots of things.

I don't like thinking about it. I don't like thinking about

how they must think I'm dead, because how could they not? It's been so long. There's no other logical explanation. But we're not dead, unlike what Calvin thinks. Fuck, I'm sick and tired of him. What is life if there's no hope? Sure, it doesn't look good, but you don't know until you're out, and even then, you don't know at all. Because then you're gone.

No, today is going to be amazing.

I glance up at the sleeping platform, seeing those long tan legs coming down. "Hey there, Sassy. Are you ready?"

"I think so." She glances over at the tub where she's been collecting supplies. "I know it's weird—we could have done this a long time ago—but my mom and I always decorated the tree on Christmas Eve. Sure, we had lots of other things up beforehand, but the tree went up on Christmas Eve. And I guess, well, I know it's not a tree, but . . . I bet it's still an evergreen tree. It's still what it represents—family, love, celebration."

"That's the spirit, Sassy," I say. I'd begun to think that she was down about Christmas. I kiss the top of her head. "I know this is tough on you."

She smiles up at me, her eyes glazed over, tears not quite dripping from her lashes. "It is. It's so hard. I miss my mom so much. She was really good, you know? She was a really good human, and it's not fair. It's not fair what happened to her." She looks up at me, tears dripping down her cheeks.

"I know, Sassy. Sometimes life's not fair. But she wouldn't want you to be sad."

Haley nods. "You're right. She really wouldn't want me to be sad, not today. I'm not going to be sad today. Today is about family and love and happiness."

"Did someone say happiness?" Zane comes around the corner. He has something behind his back.

"Oh, wow, is that what I think it is?" Sassy leans left and

then right. "It's a Christmas tree!" she says, her eyes going wide.

"This is part of your Christmas present. Well, I guess it's a present to everybody, but I made it for you." He puts it down on the table.

"It's beautiful," she says.

Zane's made a four-and-a-half-foot-tall Christmas tree out of driftwood attached to a main trunk. The little pieces of driftwood hang low at an angle, giving it the shape of a pine tree.

"Oh my gosh," she says. She wraps her arms around his neck and peppers kisses all over his face. "It's so beautiful. Thank you so much."

"Well, when you told us that everyone should make an ornament or two for our tree, I thought, 'What tree?' So ta-da," Zane says, waving his arms around it like a game show host. Then he pulls a straw star out of his back pocket and holds it out in front of his chest. "You said you wanted us to make some ornaments, so I did. My neighbors were Swedish, and they always had little straw ornaments hanging all over their tree—little horses and hearts and things—so I made this." He places it on top of the tree.

Her voice goes up two octaves. "It's pretty cool. It's perfect."

"I'm glad you like it," he says, pulling her in for another hug. Before heading over to his cubby, he grabs another box and hands it to her. "I don't know . . . I was having fun, and well, I made a few more . . . just in case other people didn't make any for you."

I roll my eyes. "I made mine, Sassy, and it's not just a shell on a string. But I'm going to give it to you later." I drop a kiss on her forehead as well.

She cracks open the box. "Oh my gosh, Zane, these are

so incredible!" She pulls out one after another—little straw horses, hearts, and even a little elf made out of straw with a red hat. "How did you do this?" she asks.

"Oh, I dyed it with some"—Zane pauses—"something I found on the beach. Came out pretty good, didn't it? Father Christmas would be right proud."

"I don't know about Father Christmas," I say, "but Santa would like it." I cock my head at Zane.

He groans and throws his hands up. "Well, I gotta go. I've got somewhere to . . . I'll see you later, Little Bird. Love you." He looks guilty as hell. Like he's dipping out on her. Not going to help Sam finish his Christmas present.

"Love you too," she sings, blowing a kiss in his direction. She laughs. "It really is the season of secrets, isn't it?"

"Indeed, Sassy, it is. You're not a fan, are you? Of presents."

She shakes her head at me. "I mean, of course people can do what they want to do, but . . . and of course, I love presents. I mean, who doesn't? Someone buys you something or makes you something because they want you to feel special . . . but sometimes . . ."

"Sometimes," I say, "you have a hard time accepting that?"

She nods. "Yeah, exactly. Sometimes it just makes me uncomfortable. That's weird, right?" She grimaces.

"No, Sassy. It's not weird. You're allowed to feel however you feel. Do you want me to tell all the guys to stop the secrecy? No more surprises?"

She closes her eyes and her mouth. "No, no. That's . . . that's no. I mean, I do like it. I will like it. I like it. It's fine. It's good, it's good, it's really . . . it's good."

"I think you doth complain too much. At least, I think that's what Shakespeare says." I laugh and turn back to my batter. "All right, well, no surprises from me." From under the counter, I grab a banana-leaf-wrapped package. "Here, open it."

"Oh, I can wait," she says.

I incline my head at the tree. "Oh, it's an ornament."

"Okay, yeah, I'll open it now. That's great," she says excitedly. "Dante!" Her eyes go wide. "It's perfect." She holds it up.

"I'm not as good of an artist as Zane is, but you know, it's fun," I say.

"Look at Pepper and Penny together." She holds the threaded cord. "I love it." She places it on the box with Zane's ornaments.

"You're not going to put it on the tree now?" I ask.

"No, can we do that later, together, all at once?"

"Ah, I do like a good tradition. Let's keep it."

"I really love it, Dante. Pepper and Penny on our beach looking at a sunrise."

I smile at her. "I should have asked Zane about how he made those colors."

"Oh, no, it's perfect as is. I love it in black and white."

"Thanks," I say. "Now, are you decorating the table, or are you doing something else?"

"Right," she says, coming out of a daze.

"Whoa, this place looks absolutely beautiful, Firefly." Easton wraps his arms around Haley's waist.

"Thank you! It does look festive, doesn't it?"

"Zane, your tree turned out great. Oh, wait." Easton hands Haley a small package wrapped in a piece of plastic.

"Thank you." She carefully unwraps it and holds it up. It's a round ball. Well, more ball-shaped. With shiny pebbles around it. "Wow. How did you get them to stick?"

"It's a hollow core, from a scrap of plastic. I used some of the clay we found while making the oven. When a few of the larger ones fell out, I tried to use resin from tree sap to make them stick. But Zane took pity on me and I used a few drops of the caulk that he'd brought from the yacht."

"It's really pretty. Like a natural disco ball." She gives it a delicate slow twirl, and we all ignore the tink as two stones fall to the table.

"I had fun making it, Haley, but I've never been good at arts and crafts."

She hooks it on one of the branches.

"Here Haley, open mine next." Sam hands her a parcel wrapped in one of Penny's red bandanas.

She peels the fabric back and holds up a cluster of little shells, attached with a cord.

"Oh, that's so sweet." She hangs it on the tree.

"Sweet?" I say.

"Yes, sweet. There are five white shells and one pink shell." She holds it up.

"And?" Easton adds.

"Yeah, and?" There's something I'm clearly not getting.

"Six shells. Five of you, one of—"

"Oh, that is kind of nice," Calvin rumbles. "I didn't wrap mine. Close your eyes."

Haley does and puts out her hands.

"You can open them," he says.

Haley glances at her empty hands and then looks at what Calvin's holding. A strand of stars carved from shells.

"I thought you would need a garland."

"It's lovely!" She moves to hug Calvin but stops to keep from crushing the garland, which is over five feet long.

"Seriously dude, you need to sleep more," Easton says.

"You need to sleep less." Calvin holds the garland up. "Do you want to put it on now? It tangles easily."

"Wait one minute." Haley adds my ornament, and the three thousand that Zane made. "Ready."

When he's done, we stand back and gaze at it. "It looks good, but it's missing one more thing." Sam scurries off and digs through the tubs under the treehouse. "I found these a month ago but thought we should keep them until the others died." He holds up a set of solar-powered lights. He and Haley weave the lights around the tree, minding the ornaments. "They'll come on tomorrow."

Haley hooks her arm around Sam's bicep, a huge grin on her face. "Just in time for Christmas morning."

Chapter 32

Holiday Leave Denied

Haley

"Happy Christmas, Haley." Zane runs his fingers down my arm. "Everyone's awake and waiting for you, Little Bird."

I sit upright with a start. "Merry Christmas, Zane." I yawn. "Oh . . . oh. I never sleep in." I never sleep in on Christmas morning. I was always the one to run downstairs first. Last year I was the first one up, but then I was on charter and I was up before the chef. I never sleep in.

Zane is smirking at me. Because yeah, that's not true anymore.

"I'll be right down. Give me a minute to get ready."

"Take your time. We thought you'd like a biscuit, while they're warm."

I glance around the empty space. I really did sleep in. "That's what that smell on the wind is." Dante made one yesterday as a test to see if it would work out. That one bite had me dreaming all last night.

I find the one red tank top I own and my not so white

shorts, then head down to the kitchen. The tree's so lovely I almost burst into tears.

There's only one present under the tree. Which seems odd considering all the secrecy. I turn away, and there's a snicker from behind me.

"Merry Christmas," I say and give Easton a kiss.

"Now it is. You look Christmassy this morning, Firefly."

"Thank you." I pull out my tank top, ignoring the spot on the bottom that I can't get off. "Merry Christmas, Calvin." I give him a kiss, too. I vanish into his bear hug.

"Merry Christmas, Chiefie. Did you dream of sugar plums?" Calvin asks.

"Something better," I say.

"Really, now?" Calvin wiggles his eyebrows. I did have good dreams. And they were Christmas ones. We weren't here. I'm not sure where we were. But I still gave the guys the gifts I made, and they loved them. But then we had electricity and running water.

"Merry Christmas," Sam says from the other side of the table, though he's not smiling when he says it. His eyes flick to the tree for a second, and it confuses me even more.

I'm about to head over to my cubby when Dante grabs me around the waist, dips me, and claims my lips. "Good morning, Sassy. I hope you're ready for a fucking fantastic day?"

"I am," I say as I catch my balance. Dante hands me a cup of coffee and a bowl with a biscuit in it that's topped with mango puree. "Oh, this looks like heaven."

Dante laughs. He passes out bowls to the guys, each with only half a biscuit. Guilt rises up my throat.

"Don't even start, Sassy. They all wanted a taste, so they've had half of theirs already."

"Oh." I savor the next few bites. We all do, in silence. I'm not the only one who licks the bowl.

"Present time!" Zane yells. The guys rearrange the two deck chairs and a bunch of the wooden stumps we use as stools in a semicircle around the tree. "Sit here, Little Bird." Zane positions me in a deck chair. "Sam, get it rolling."

"Let me get mine." I step over to my cubby.

But Easton spins me around and ushers me to sit. "In a second, Firefly. Open Sam's present first."

Sam bends and slowly walks over to me. "I hope you like it."

Zane elbows Sam and shakes his head. I'm a little nervous to open it. It's heavy-ish, ten inches long and almost square. It's wrapped in banana leaves and tied shut with a bit of string. I hold it in my lap for a second and gaze up at Sam. Whatever he's made, I'm absolutely sure I'm going to love it. And I'm trying not to worry about how nervous he seems. I hold it up to my ear and give a careful little shake. Not after Easton's ornament dropped stones on the table yesterday. "It doesn't rattle. Guess it's not Legos."

"Not Legos, but that would be brilliant, Little Bird. Think of how much fun we would have putting together one of those huge adult sets."

"Legos have erotic building kits?" Dante smirks.

"No, you turd," Zane says.

Dante laughs and slaps Zane's back.

"Hush, don't ruin this," Calvin growls.

"Should I open it?" I ask Sam, who's taken the seat next to me.

"Please. But carefully."

I untie the string and slowly open the leaves. In front of me is an orange and red square of the raft plastic. "It's a book."

"It's a notebook," Sam says. "Some of the pages are still a little bumpy. It's taken me a while to figure out how to get the paper smooth. But those are the best ones."

I open the cover slowly, like I should have on white conservatory gloves. The plastic cover must have something thick in the middle. The first page has a dried orchid pressed into it. Beside it, Sam has written: *To Haley, Merry Christmas. I love you, Sam.*

It's weird—I've heard them all say it, but this is the first time I've seen it written down and it makes a difference. It really does. There's no way I'm letting my fat tears land on the pages. I wipe them away with the back of my hand. I should pop up and tell him how much it means to me, but I'm speechless as I turn the thick pages. He made paper! He said they're bumpy, but they're perfect. I turn the pages carefully.

That shakes me out of it. "It's beyond perfect. How . . . I . . . It's . . ." I hold it to my chest and bounce to standing. "I love it, and you. And thank you so much. This must have taken forever." I place the notebook on my chair and give Sam a kiss that I hope makes him understand how much I appreciate all the time this must have taken.

"Damn, Sassy, wish I'd made you a notebook. But I did help."

Sam ends the kissing. When he does, I'm dizzy. "Everyone helped. There was a lot of experimenting. Which brings us to . . ." From behind them and under the table, the guys fill up the space underneath the tree. There're all kinds of wrapped presents. Wrapped in what must be some of Sam's first attempts. The paper is bumpy and has holes. But the guys have colored it with patterns.

"Holy . . . Night." It's the prettiest thing I've ever seen. "Wait, I want to—"

Zane hands me his phone. It's already powered up. "Figured you might want to."

"Thanks!" I take a bunch of shots of the tree and the pile of gifts and my notebook. Then Calvin, with his long arms, takes a shot of us all with the tree and Penny. Because she, of course, appears out of nowhere.

"All right, Sassy. Sam might have the—"

"I want to go next. Well, partially next," Calvin says.

"Okay?" I shrug.

He jogs down the trail, Penny at his heels. He's back in a few minutes with two chairs. They're made of driftwood and what looks like part of the derelict. Zane rolls two stumps away, and Calvin sets them in place. "I've only made two so far. I kind of want feedback."

"Damn, Viking. When did you make these?"

"I don't sleep," Calvin says.

"Right but . . . Never mind. May I?" Dante asks.

"Sure. As long as Chiefie tries this one out. I made it more to her size."

I sit tenderly at first. I don't know why. Calvin would never make something that's not quality. "It's really comfortable."

"It is. And unlike Haley, I have no problems hurting the Viking's feelings," Dante says.

"Dante!"

"What? It's true, Sassy. Well done, Calvin."

"Thanks," Calvin says standing in front of me.

I place my notebook on my chair and give Calvin a long kiss. When I pull back, he's smiling from ear to ear, and that in itself is a Christmas miracle.

"Okay, my turn." Dante gathers a plastic box from the kitchen. "I have two things for you. One was too bulky to wrap, and then this one. Not Legos, but don't shake it. Open it first."

It's a small bottle of oil. With caution, I open the lid, and I can smell it already.

"We only have so much shampoo left, but I think I've come up with a good recipe."

"It smells lovely," I say.

"And I made you this. It's a flower press. I thought you might like to press specimens of the plants you've been collecting, and write about them in your new notebook," Dante says.

I'm oohing and aahing, and there's another round of kisses.

"This one's from the two of us." Easton hands me a small, wrapped package and nods his head at Calvin.

Inside is a bracelet of pearls. And hanging from the strand are six little wooden circle charms carved with the first initial of each of the guys and me.

"It's so pretty. Easton when did you find the time to do so much diving without me seeing?"

"I'm stealthy."

"Will you put it on for me?"

"I'm still working on a clasp."

"Tie it on. I'm never taking it off," I say. I kiss Easton, then Calvin again.

Zane's standing in front of me, his cheeks rouged. "Okay, now, mine isn't as dramatic as the rest. It's also two parts."

The other guys groan.

"You're like the kid with the A+ project who tells the teacher that they could have done better," Dante says.

"Right, okay, here, Little Bird." He hands me a piece of paper from Rocky's planner.

I don't quite know what I'm looking at. Then it hits me. It's the treehouse, only there's another platform.

"I'm building you a water closet platform. Well, without water. Or mostly without water. I've got a good portion of the pieces cut. But it was hard to install and have it be a surprise."

I place the sketch inside my new book and kiss him. I'm excited about the washroom space, but even more so that he didn't turn into a beast while working on it in secret. Last time, he was so stressed he drove everyone crazy.

"Oh, and here's the second half of my gift." He hands me a beautiful picture of a house. "It's what I will build you when we're rescued. Well, maybe not with the sea view. That's kind of a here thing." Zane smiles.

Notebook on my lap, I sit and stare at his sketch. It's just the sort of house I would want. Where there's an inside without sand or bugs, but there are tons of windows so that you feel like you're outside. Mid-century modern meets craftsman with a zippy energy to it. It's a hundred-percent Zane. "I love it. I can't wait to see it."

He scrubs his hand over his chin and turns away.

"What? Did I say something wrong?" I'm at his shoulder.

"No, Little Bird. You said something right. The fact that you love it and have enough faith that we're not only going to get off the island but that you'll see my creation . . . That means the world to me." He squeezes me tightly in his arms.

When he lets go, I sink into my new chair. I'm overwhelmed, and then I remember. "I haven't given you your gifts yet!"

Chapter 33

A Full Hull

Sam

"Yes, you have, Sugar. Letting us watch you be showered with love—that's the best gift yet." It's true. I've always loved watching people open gifts that I've gotten them, rather than opening ones given to me.

She's smiling at me as she heads to her cubby; two trips later, she's put hers under the tree. "That's really sweet of you to say, Sam. I guess I don't need to pass these out, then?"

"You're like the opposite of Father Christmas." Zane lightly punches my arm.

"Hey, don't be the Grinch, Sam. I want my present," Dante says.

"Grinch. Exactly," says Zane.

"I'm not the Grinch." I sit down.

"No way Sam's the Grinch. That would be me," Calvin says.

"You're not the Grinch either." Haley hands him a small, leaf-wrapped package. "Merry Christmas."

"Thank you, Haley." He pulls her into his lap and opens it.

"It's a salve for your knees," she says.

"My knees. Thank you."

"You think we don't all know your knees hurt you like fuck?" Dante leans forward in the camp chair.

"I thought I covered it pretty well," Calvin says. "Guess not." He opens the jar and sniffs it. "Nice." Taking a dab, he reaches between Haley's legs and rubs some on his knee. "It tingles."

"It's a mixture of aloe I found, ginger, turmeric, and an oil from a tree. I've found a lot of plants in the last month."

Zane points at Dante. "Ginger—that was what you added to the coconut grits last week."

"Indeed. Sassy didn't want me to spill her secret."

"Man, that feels good." Calvin's mouth is hanging open. Although, that might be because Haley is rubbing the salve over his other knee.

Zane laughs. "Careful, Little Bird. I think his eyes are going to roll into the back of his head."

"No careful. No stop," Calvin grunts, his head hitting the back of the camp chair.

"More later." Haley kisses the top of his nose. "I'm glad you like it."

"Like isn't anywhere near enough to describe it," Calvin moans.

Haley hops off his lap and takes another package out. This one's larger. "Dante." She hands it to him, beaming.

"Sassy, whatever could this be?"

"Hush, I told you to stay off the beach. You weren't supposed to know."

He carefully unwraps a beautiful basket. It's honestly the best she's made.

"It's perfect, thank you." He places it in the middle of the table and pulls her in for a deep kiss.

"Easton." She hands him a small package. Everyone else seems to know what's going to be in it. But then, I've been on the derelict beach for weeks. There's a lot I've missed.

"Thank you." Inside his package is a piece of sea glass encased in a twine cage hanging from a leather strap. "This is beautiful. The bubble inside looks like a heart."

Haley's ponytail bobs. "That's what I thought too."

"I love it." He puts it on and gives her a long kiss as well.

"Zane." Whatever is wrapped in the leaves looks heavy.

"Whoa, Little Bird, what's in here?"

"You don't know? I thought I had given away all my surprises." She claps.

"I haven't the faintest."

"Wait, open this one first." Haley hands him a smaller package. "I've been doing some experimenting, too. I think this should work, but I want to keep trying to get it perfect."

Zane peels away the leaves and holds up a white drop of I'm not sure what.

"Okay, now the other one."

Zane's eyebrows shoot up, and his smile consumes his face. "No way. A slate and chalk to help me figure out the rest of the code without using up the last of the agenda paper. Brilliant."

"I didn't know about Sam's—"

"It's bloody brilliant. I won't waste anything this way. Agenda or Sam's paper."

"I'm glad you like it. Easton helped a lot with it."

"Thank you, mate." Zane draws a smiley face on the

slate and a soccer ball. "This is my favorite gift ever." He puts his supplies on the table and dips Haley in a kiss.

"Whoa is right." She laughs. "Now I'm dizzy." She stands and then comes to me.

I hold my arms open for her, and she sits on my lap.

"Now he looks like Father Christmas, with all that salt in his beard."

I shoot Zane the finger behind Haley's back, and he laughs so hard he falls off the stool. "Have you been a good girl?" I ask Haley.

"No, but I've already gotten my gifts, so." She laughs. "Here, Sam. I hope you like it."

I'm painfully slow opening the leaves, one after the other.

"Open it already," Dante yells.

"Patience, Jones. Anticipation is part of the gift." The last leaf falls away and there's a bracelet with different types of knots in it. "You learned how to do all these yourself?"

"I had some help—lots of help—from the guys. But I can do them by myself now."

"They're really good." I slip the bracelet over my wrist. "I love it. Thank you." Damn, I could kiss this girl for the rest of the day. For the rest of the year. Hell, for the rest of my life.

Her eyes are sparkling blue when her lips leave mine.

"Catch, Sam." Calvin throws a small paper-wrapped package at me.

"Thank you." I hold it up and take my time opening this one as well. More because they're all groaning. "Wow." He's carved a mini-Penny. She's sitting with her head cocked to one side.

Calvin runs his fingers behind Penny's ears. "She was a really good model."

She barks and wags her tail. In her don't-stop-petting-me way.

"I love it."

Then packages are tossed around the circle left and right. Easton's made Dante a rack to hang above the potbelly stove to hold his spoons. Calvin's carved Zane a Union Jack. Dante's made Calvin some lube. Actually, Dante's made everyone some lube. *"Thoughtful and useful,"* to quote him.

But my favorite part of the chaos of the guys' gift exchange is watching Haley. Her eyes are beaming. She talks about a family, and she's right. That's what we are now. A family that nothing can pull apart.

Zane gathers the wrappings, both leaves and paper. While Dante's making a fish course, Easton and Calvin are playing a game of checkers with the board Zane made Calvin. Haley's rocking in the hammock Easton made for Dante. This new chair that Calvin made cradles my back in a way that's the most comfortable I've been in months. And I can't stop smiling. Pepper's on my lap. Penny's head is on my foot.

I've always thought of myself as someone who likes the quiet. A cup of coffee on an empty deck. The sun beating down on me. But then I'd never really been completely alone before. Penny scooches closer to my foot. Oh, I wasn't completely alone all that time. I had Penny, but her conversation wasn't the best. I thought I was a quiet kind of guy. But this? This is the best.

The only thing missing is my brother and my sister with her husband and kids. This isn't bad. Nothing about it. Which is bonkers. We're stuck in the middle of the ocean, yet I've had the best Christmas morning of my life. There's a little pile of presents beside me: My Penny carving, which

I'm definitely going to make sure Penny doesn't treat as a chew toy. I run my thumb over the bracelet. She did a good job on the bowline and the other knots in the bracelet. It means so much more than something bought. The Mancala board from Zane, a shell-decorated dog bowl from Easton, and the oil from Dante.

"You can't do that," Easton says. And I'm not sure if he's being serious or not, the way he says it.

"Fuck, you suck at this, Swimmer Boy." Dante laughs, watching over the game of checkers.

"I can. You lined your pieces up for me to jump them. I thought you were doing it on purpose. I mean, seriously. Look at this, Zane." Calvin replays the triple-jump of Easton's pieces in a slow-motion reenactment.

"It's fair play. Why did you . . . ? Oh, never mind," Easton says.

"Oh no, I've lost. Zane, you said you wanted to play the winner? I'll help you, Haley." Easton pushes up from the table.

"You lost on purpose?" Zane growls.

"I know, right? Weird." He pulls Haley into a kiss. When he comes up for air, he laughs. "Want to take a swim?"

"I'm up for a swim too." I put Pepper on the chair, and she curls up into a ball.

"Yeah, yeah, I do," Haley says. "We should all go. Do you have time for a swim, Dante?"

"I have time for anything that has to do with you, Sassy. But yeah, this just has to simmer, and I'm letting the fire go out—for today, anyway. By the time it's done, we'll be able to eat our afternoon meal. Let's swim." Dante picks Haley up and races three steps. "Ugh, I love you, Sassy, but my dick isn't going to let me run and carry you."

She slides down his chest, laughing. "I'll walk." She pivots and announces to the rest of us: "I'll walk—no, I'll beat you all there!" She takes off running, and Calvin's not wrong calling her a bunny. She's got a good amount of hop in her step as she takes off for the ocean. Sand flies up from her feet.

I'm off after her, but so is Penny. Penny's going vertical beside her?

"You ready, Penny?" Haley high-steps into the surf, knowing full well there's no way on the planet that my dog is going to go into the water willingly. Seaweed? Hell yeah. Mud, deer scat, anything that smells like shit? Yes, please. But water? Nope.

But then she runs straight into the waves.

Haley skids to a stop. "Penny?"

Penny's only in up to her shoulders, but that old saying that all dogs know how to instinctively swim? Not true. So not true.

I reach Penny at the same time that Haley does. Does the damn dog think she's got her life vest on? My heart rises up my throat as her head sinks below the water like she's trying to walk to the mainland. Haley has Penny's head, and I have her haunches as we pull her out of the waves. Penny gives a good sneeze all over Haley's chest.

Haley ignores it. "Are you okay?" Haley pulls Penny into a hug as the dog shakes herself over both of us.

"Penny," I say. "What were you thinking, girl?"

The other guys have caught up to us.

"She was thinking that she'd follow Little Bird anywhere. Just like the rest of us."

"Don't be a lemming. That's not smart!" Haley holds Penny's head up and stares into her eyes. "You're a smart girl. Use that brain of yours." She kisses Penny on the nose and hugs her again. Then Penny gets up and trots away, racing after a dead palm frond blowing down the beach, like *I don't know what your problem is.*

"Are you okay?" Haley holds on to my biceps.

"I'm fine. I'm not the one who almost drowned. Thank you for getting to her."

"You were there too," Haley says.

"I know, but you didn't hesitate to chase after her. She's not a small dog."

"She's family. I'll do anything for my family."

"Anything, Sassy?" Dante wiggles his eyebrows.

"I've already proven that, haven't I?" She laughs and slips away from me, heading straight into the surf. "But first, a Christmas Day swim." When she gets in up to her waist, she dives under a shallow wave and swims out beyond the breakers.

I'm not the only one frozen by her beauty. Watching.

Easton breaks first, taking off. And we all follow. There are no games today. Just floating. Haley moves around the five of us. Light touches. A kiss here and there.

I don't remember the last time we all swam together, staying out so long. But it's another layer of the perfect day. Another tick of time building the life that I didn't know I wanted. A life of less, not more. Of slower. Of people, not things. Of providing for my body, not indulgence.

Haley floats next to me. Her skin has turned pink enough in the sun that we need to get her into the jungle shade. "Today is perfect," she says.

"Yes, yes, it is, Sugar. Merry Christmas."

Chapter 34

New Contract

Calvin

As a kid, I lived for this week. The week between Christmas and New Year is like days that don't matter. They don't exist. They're not even ticks on the calendar.

Don't get me wrong, Dad still ran the farm, so it wasn't like we didn't have things to do. There's always something to do. I've never once told my parents I was bored. And no fucking way would I have ever said that to my grandfather—he would have come up with a chore so heinous that I'd still be able to smell it now.

But this month, I've made mounds of gifts, and they're all adamant that the chairs are good. They need to sit in them longer and give me feedback before I go and make any more. The WaveRunner is tuned up, and the motor on the tender is purring better than the day it came off the factory line.

I could run over to the other side of the island and dig

another hole. That's the only thing that needs doing on this side of the island.

I push that thought away. Everyone else seems to be in full holiday mode. Even Sam has stopped going up to the lookout as much as he normally does. It's true there's no real reason to keep going up there. No reason at all. If we haven't seen a non-pirate ship in seven months, we're not going to see one now.

Zane and Haley are playing checkers. Sam and Easton are playing fetch with Penny at the beach, and Dante's taking his turn with the book, his feet sticking out of the top of the hammock.

"I'm going to go check on the boar traps," I say.

"Didn't you do that an hour ago?" Dante's head pokes out of the hammock.

"No."

"Yes, you did," Zane says.

"I'm just taking a walk," I shoot back.

"On this side of the island." Haley holds up two of Zane's checkers.

"Yes, on this side of the island."

She's worried that I'm going to wander off to Pomelo Beach. Which I haven't done for a while, but soon we're going to need some more fruit. And then . . . I can finish up.

I move the chicken tractor a few feet down the strip of land we've cleared between some trees. They race around, clucking excitedly at the fresh dirt to dig in. The little ones are getting big enough that I should make them a bigger pen. Soon. But not today. I'd have a battle on my hands if I interrupted a do-nothing week.

I really used to like this. But now this do-nothing thing makes me anxious. Walking helps to clear my head, but doing—doing helps turn things off. I've never been one to relax without doing. Sitting on a beach and not moving? Not for me.

We've only made two traps. And they're not that deep and don't have any of the spikes that we first thought about putting in them. Not with Penny around. No, these would only catch the boars. It's one of the reasons why I check them all the time.

The first one's covered in its layer of palm fronds. But farther down the path, the second one's open. The covering of fronds is partially gone.

"Holy shit, it worked," I yell. Down in the pit is a boar. The thing landed right, so we didn't need any spikes to finish it off after all.

"I can tend the fire," I say to Dante.

"I'm good." He looks up from a scrap of Sam's wrapping paper.

"What are you doing?"

"Tomorrow's New Year's Day."

"And I asked what are you doing?"

"It's New Year's."

"And you're writing your New Year's resolutions?"

"Resolutions? That implies I have something I need to change. You fucking know I'm perfect, so no. But I always take the last day of the year to reflect on what I want to happen in the next." Dante glares at me.

"So resolutions," I say.

"No. I put it out into the universe what I want. And then I get it."

"Well, fucker, why didn't you tell the universe you

wanted the yacht to be fixed when we still had it? Or a nice cargo captain to spot our fire? Or hell, I don't know, plumbing? That would be fucking fantastic."

"Because maybe I don't want any of those things. Maybe I'm happy being perfect just the way I am. You, on the other hand, need to change your surroundings to be happy."

"You're telling me that you don't want to eat in a Michelin-starred restaurant again? Or own a Michelin-starred restaurant?"

"Fuck no. That shit is toxic. I'm the best. I don't need another owner of a tire company telling me I'm good enough."

Like some sort of fucking Beetlejuice, Rockwell strolls out onto the beach. "What about a tire company?"

"Calvin thinks I need a Michelin star to have a good sense of self-worth."

"Not what I said, but whatever."

"It is what you said. That I would wish for validation from a company that makes tires."

"It's a crock. Still, my grandfather would have sold his kidney to have come up with the idea." Easton sits on a stump next to Dante. "But yeah, fuck 'em. I've eaten in Michelin-starred restaurants that don't come anywhere near to what you make, on a beach with almost nothing." Easton nods in a I've-said-my-piece way.

"I just don't need validation like that in my life. When I was a kid, I just wanted my blockhead uncle to throw me some damn scraps. 'Good job, Dante. You're nothing like your dad. You work hard. Your mom's proud of you. I'm proud of you,' or whatever shit it was I wished for. I came home from whatever fucking job he had me working one day. I was like thirteen. I was crying and my mom found me. She told me, 'You don't need him or me to tell you you're amazing, Dante. I mean, I need to say it more. Because you're better than all of us. But the only way you're going to know it for sure is if you believe it. I believe it. Do you?' And that was fucking it. I don't need anyone to tell me I'm great. Because I already know I'm a fucking special snowflake. And a Michelin-starred chef? No fucking way. They work themselves into drug overdoses and ulcers. They have to keep doing the same shit for years because they become the weird sausage guy or the queen of exotic cheese. Fucking hate cheese. So no. No, no to all of that."

"What do you say yes to?" Haley asks. I hadn't even heard her coming up behind me. She puts one hand on Easton's shoulder and the other on Dante's.

"I say yes to you, Sassy."

She laughs. "That's not what I mean, and you know it."

"Right. In the new year, I say yes to creativity. I say yes to spontaneity. I say yes to fucking—"

"Cheese," Easton interrupts.

Haley laughs.

"I was just going to say fucking." Dante pulls Haley onto his lap.

"Fucking is nice. But then so is cheese."

"And how are we going to get cheese, Sassy?"

Haley's eyes flick to the mountain.

"Goats?" Easton asks.

"No," I say.

"Well, I say yes. Because I say yes to Sassy."

"Keeping goats isn't the same as moving the chicken tractor a couple of times a day," I say. "We'd need a fence. Good fence. Those are wild goats."

"I'm going to side with Green on this one," Easton agrees. "The one close encounter I had with a goat on the mountain didn't leave me wanting more."

"We need pasture," Haley says, like it's easy enough to snap her fingers.

I inwardly groan. "You don't need pasture. Goats make pastures. Goats could clear the Amazon rainforest with enough fencing and time." Am I kicking myself inside? Yes, yes, I am.

"I'll wash the dishes," Haley says.

"No, I'll do it." I stand, grabbing the tub from under the counter and placing my bowl in it first. "Good dinner, Dante. I'd say Michelin-star-worthy."

He shoots me the middle finger, and I smile as I take his plate.

"What's up with Green, jumping up to do the dishes?" Zane asks as he places his bowl in the tub. It's not that I don't do the dishes a lot. It's that I tend to find something else that needs to be done. But tonight . . . tonight, I'm trying to stay away from the hype. I've always hated New Year's Eve. The hats, the party where everyone pretends to be happy. Or get so drunk they can't stand. Then I end up driving them home. Worse, the stupid countdown. Ten, nine, searching for someone to kiss, eight, seven. It's all a crock of bull, six, it's just another night, another day . . .

"I can help," Haley says, jumping up.

"I . . . I've got it." I nod and head to the beach.

"What's going on?" Haley's trailing me, taking three

steps to my one. "Hey, slow down." She waves the dish towel at me.

"I've got it, Haley. You've got plans for tonight. Go and do them."

"My plans include you." She crosses her arms over her chest. And fuck. "I made hats."

"I'm sure you did." I keep walking to the rock where we wash the dishes.

"You don't have to wear one. You don't even have to say what you want out of the new year."

I grunt and wash the first bowl.

"If we don't celebrate the passage of time, are we even really living?"

I cock my head at her and raise my eyebrows. My hands are deep in scrubbing the fish stew off.

She wrinkles her nose. "That sounds like a barrel of bull. I know, I know. But it's not. It's the little moments that make a life. At least, I think it is." Her shoulders slump.

"It's hard for me."

"Yeah, I know. I'm not sure why."

"The little moments to me are the ones with my brother. Playing in the barn. Making cardboard mazes for kittens to run through. Having fights with hay when we were supposed to bring in the cows."

"She hurt you."

"No, I don't give a fuck about her. He hurt me. The one person who my grandmother said would always have my back. My brother. She and her sister were inseparable. I'm just . . . It's horrible, but I'm glad she died before . . ."

"That's not horrible. Being upset with what your brother did is horrible."

"I'm not upset. I'm changed. I'm a realist. That's all.

That mindset shit Dante was talking about? I'm not woo-woo. I can't change my stripes."

"What color were your stripes before your brother—Please," she says, taking a clean dish from my hands. She dries it, sets it on the dry spot on the rock, and waits for the next dish. "You don't have to say a thing. Just be with us. I promise I won't hurt you."

"Okay." I can't. Please? This girl fucking kills me. But there's no fucking way I'm getting out of this without being hurt. Life—my life at least—doesn't work that way.

"Can I put it on your head?" Haley's holding a hat made out of three elephant leaves.

I glance around the circle. The rest of them are already wearing theirs. "Sure." I'm an ass because I don't bend down.

She smirks at me. Damn, she's fucking cute in the twinkle lights of the driftwood Christmas tree. On her tiptoes, she reaches and manages to get it on my head. She takes my hand and then Sam's on the other side of her. "Come on, join hands."

I stare at Dante, who's next to me, but take his hand.

When we're all linked up, she nods. "On this last day of this year, let's all take a moment to think about all the good we've had. All that we've overcome. Let's close our eyes."

It's almost silent. The jungle chirps over the crashing waves on the beach behind us.

A whisper of Haley's breath slips into my ear. "It's going to be a good year." She squeezes my hand three times, then she gently lets it go. But she's wrong.

"Five, four, three, two, one," they're chanting.

A cork pops, and I open my eyes. Dante's holding a bottle of champagne. The smokey vapor twists out from the top on the wind, slipping away from us into the jungle sky like Haley's wish.

Chapter 35

Closure

Easton

"What exactly is that?" I point at the very small raft that Calvin's constructing on the beach. "You're not thinking we're going to float away on that, are you?"

"Fuck no, Rockwell." He doesn't look up. "It's a platform for when we go back to the cave."

"The cave?" I ask. "Like, on the mountain? I thought we decided we're not going over there unless we have to for food."

"Nah, man," he says, "the water cave. You know, the one she found when she was looking for us—with the box wrapped in a thick rope."

"Oh, right. But why? Just leave it alone."

"You're not in the least bit curious?"

"No, man, not at all," I say. I might be a little curious, though.

"Okay, well, I am, so I'm making a raft to tether on the

back of the WaveRunner. I mean, we can use it for other things too, right?"

"I suppose so. Just . . . you're not going to get me all Tom Hanks, holding on to a volleyball, riding the currents. We haven't seen anything out there but unfriendlies."

"No, just relax. This isn't for anything other than pulling behind the WaveRunner so we can use it to help float up the box."

"Got it," I say. "You want some help?"

An hour later, we have a two-sided bamboo raft with a layer of the emergency raft sandwiched between it.

"So when are we going to do this?"

He cranes his neck up at the sky. "Not today."

"Yeah, you're right. It looks like it's gonna rain again. I thought the rainy season was supposed to be back in the fall, not in February."

He shrugs. "I'm not the damn weatherman."

I nod. With each passing week, he seems to be getting crankier. It's becoming a bit of a thorn in everyone's side. If he wants to take the WaveRunner for a little spin and see what's under the water, why the hell not?

"Let's do it," I say.

"By the look of the sky, it should only rain for a little bit."

"Now you're the weatherman?" he says.

"It's not hard. Rain comes from east of the island and moves west, to the other side. All you have to do is look." I motion my hand across the horizon like a presenter.

"So we go this afternoon."

"With Haley," I add.

"Obviously," Calvin grunts.

And the rain starts. We take cover, running for the camp. In the last few weeks, Zane's been working on his

Christmas gift to Haley. There's a side platform coming off our sleeping platform, just big enough for washing up and some storage. But we've also now got a cover over the table and most of the kitchen area—it's part tarp, part roof, and mostly waterproof.

Sam and Dante are sitting at the table with their lunch.

Dante cups his hands at the sleep platform. "You coming down?"

A few seconds later, Zane pokes his head out. "In a minute or two."

"There might not be any left in a minute or two—Calvin just showed up," Dante announces.

"Hardy har," Calvin says.

I look between Haley and Sam. "So, after lunch, it looks like it's going to clear up."

Sam puts his spoon down and holds my gaze. "There's definitely more to that statement," he says.

"Right, yeah. So after lunch, I'm thinking that Haley, Calvin, and I'll take the WaveRunner and Calvin's new raft and go see what's in that crate."

"No," Sam says. "That's a waste of gas. If you're going to do it, go tomorrow. Take the whole day. Take supplies, do what needs to be done. Get some fruit, then drop the raft off."

"Or we could take the tender and all go," Dante says.

Calvin's head jerks to the right. I'm not the only one who picks up on it—Haley does too. "What, you don't think I can help you bury the villagers?"

"You're right. This needs to be done. We've gone this long without doing it, and it's time," Sam says.

Calvin nods. "Okay, then we go tomorrow. But not all of us. Sam's right. We shouldn't be using all of our gas at once. We'll get up early, drop the raft off, take the WaveRunner around the side of the island, and do what we need to do. And then, as time allows, we can investigate the cave some more and what's under it."

The sun rose on a clear blue sky half an hour ago. There's a tinge of pink left on the horizon. Sam was right—yesterday would have been a rush. Today's tides are perfect. We'll drop the raft off at the cave, go around the other side of the island, and make it home before dark.

The new raft smacks into the low surf, splashing up a wave that hits me in the face.

"You're sure about this?" Haley crosses her arms over her chest. "Of course you are."

"We'll know if the thing is going to hold together before we get to the bluff. I can swim back. And yes, before you ask, I'm going to wear a life jacket." Even though the thing gets in the way of my stroking, especially with my right shoulder. But if the raft flips and knocks me unconscious? Yeah, it's a good idea.

"Or the three of us can ride on the seat?"

"This will be a workout on the way over. I'll do that on the way back." The plan was to fill our largest bag with coconuts and more durable fruit and trail it behind us.

"More mangos," Dante yells as the WaveRunner pulls us out through the surf. "And make sure Sassy comes back in one piece."

I'm sure that has Sam scowling. But I'm not looking back. I'm holding on to the ropes hanging from the corners of the raft. Haley sits between Calvin's legs. But he's the one driving. There's no room for her to hold on behind him because he's wearing a huge pack. A pack that will turn into a small floating fruit storage on the way back.

Calvin takes it easy getting out past the breakers. But I'm regretting my decision. We should have crowded together on the seat. I'm being tossed about. But on the other side of the breakers, the sideways crashing of the waves against the raft is more invigorating than terrifying. I whoop as we pass the bluffs.

Calvin slows near the cave. It being low tide, he pulls right in. It's an easy turn around. Haley slides into the water and helps me untie the raft.

"I know we're doing the crate later, but I'm going down for a quick look," I say.

Calvin's silent.

"I'll come with you." Haley takes off her thin backpack and life jacket, hands them to Calvin, and dives in. She's a few strokes ahead of me when we get to the box.

They're right, it's old. And it's been down here a while. Not that I'm an expert—Calvin's the archeologist—but it's been at least ten years, maybe longer. There are long strands of seaweed tangled in the rope, and there are a ton of things growing on it. I run my fingers over it, and it doesn't feel like rope, more like crystals and mineral deposits. Holding on to the box, I make my way around it.

Haley brushes my shoulder with her fingers and signals she's going up. I've got enough air left to make my way around the whole box. I pull on the rope, but it doesn't budge. The lid's not going to come off without the rope gone. I head up to the surface and come up on the side of the raft. I want to look at the box again.

"We've got a plan," Calvin says. "Stick to the plan for the day."

"Fine. Your raft is going to work well whenever we figure out what's in the box," Haley says.

"That's yet to be seen," I say, treading water next to the WaveRunner while Haley situates herself behind Calvin.

"Ready?" Haley reaches down and gives me a hand up behind her. I shake off the water and take the smaller pack from her, slinging it on my back.

I have one hand around her, and the other clutches the seat.

Calvin turns us around. With the raft tied up at the cave, Calvin's pack—converted into a fruit float for the return trip—bobs in the water behind us. The fruit float has been so useful to bring back a decent amount of food. We've been making runs with the WaveRunner every few weeks, for the last two months, to get fruit. But usually only two people go.

"Chicken Beach," Haley shouts into the wind.

"Yes," Calvin says as we race by.

But Haley hasn't been out here, not yet. I lean in and whisper in her ear. "Hold on. When we round the peninsula, the current changes and the waves really kick up."

She flattens herself against Calvin.

Maybe it's because it's low tide, but the waves aren't much of anything today. We call the side of the beach between Chicken Beach and the stream Pomelo Beach now, and the rest of it the Village.

Haley's head turns to watch Pomelo Beach vanish. Calvin takes us onto the Village beach. There are remnants of a pier that I didn't notice the last time I was here.

I'm pretty sure Zane and Calvin have been coming this far whenever they come, though they don't talk about it.

There's a piling near the shore solid enough to tie the WaveRunner to.

Calvin lifts Haley off and carries her to the beach, even though she's still wet from her dive in the cave. But then he just likes carrying her around.

"Full disclosure, Chiefie: Whenever I make fruit runs, I've been working on digging."

"I know," Haley says. "We all knew."

"You're not mad?"

"No. It's not you to go hiking or running over the top of the mountain by yourself or doing the journey for no reason. I'm sorry. I thought you knew I knew."

He nods. "Makes sense."

"Calvin." Haley reaches for his arm. But he's got the supply bag and is heading for a path up to where the huts were—are. "I thought he knew. I . . ."

"It's not you, Haley. Calvin made a choice to keep this place secret from you, from all of us. He's stubborn. He wanted it to go down one way, and it didn't. In a way, he's trying to carry the pain for us, them, it's fucking noble. But it's also—"

"Stupid," she says.

"Yeah, it is."

"But I still love him."

"Didn't say you shouldn't. But it's never going to be easy."

"I didn't sign up for easy."

"No, no, you didn't." I follow her up the path.

Chapter 36

Crosshairs

Calvin

Sweat comes out of every pore in my body. Easton's too. Even Haley has taken a turn. But the digging's done. A month ago, Zane and I decided to make a spot that overlooks the beach. One cemetery. Someday I'll move the others that I buried last fall. But not today. I really didn't think Haley would want to be here.

I flick my eyes over to Haley. "Why don't the two of you go collect the fruit while I—"

"Do all the hard, painful stuff by yourself? No." She's got a hand on her hip. The early afternoon sun shines from around her back, castling a halo above her head.

"Thank you," I say.

"Wow, he might be changing," Easton grunts.

"No, that's not happening," I say.

"What next?" Haley asks.

There are five mounds; all the details are written in my notebook in my pocket. In college one summer, I worked for an archeological firm that moved a small family cemetery. There's a new highway that goes through their old family plot now. We haven't done things exactly to the same standard.

Haley's on one side of me, her head close to my shoulder, Easton on my other side. "Do we say something now?"

I glance at her. Because I don't . . . That doesn't matter to me . . . but then, that's another layer of the respect I wanted to give to them. The respect they weren't given when they left this earth. The respect I'm expecting to not have when we leave it too.

"Wait, I did bring something." Haley scurries down the side of the hill to the beach.

"You doing okay, Green?" Rockwell doesn't turn when he talks to me. He's watching Haley reappear into view on the beach, grabbing her backpack. She's trying to entice a mostly feral cat to take some fish jerky from her hand.

"Yeah, I'm fine. Why?"

"You haven't seemed fine in a long time."

Now I'm giving him the look. I know it well—it's a family look. Furrows between the eyes, a cocked smile, one that says you're wrong and you're nuts.

"I'm right as rain," I say.

"What the fuck does that mean?"

"I have no damn idea. It's something my grandfather used to say. I'm good. Don't worry about me. I'm worried about what this is going to do to her. She holds it together during the day. But . . ."

"Yeah, she has nightmares," he says.

"She thinks we don't notice."

Easton turns sideways. We've both taken our shirts off in the heat. There's a set of bruises along his back that he points to. "From when she woke up a few nights ago."

"Damn."

"Damn, what?" Haley says. She's already crested the hill.

"Damn, you're fast," Easton replies.

She scoffs, not believing him, but doesn't press further. "I brought flowers." From her pack, she pulls a few birds of paradise. "I don't like picking them. But this is different." She places the first couple, pausing to pluck a spent flower off and toss it to the side before putting the rest down. "Do you mind if I say a few words?"

"That would be nice," Easton answers for both of us.

"I've thought about all of you for a while. Actually, I think I kind of knew you were here before." Her eyes flick to mine. "That's kind of woo-woo, but this place has almost always felt safe. What would it have been like if you were all alive when we arrived? Would we have been friends? Would you have gotten us help? I'd like to think the answer is yes. But we'll never know. But in my imagination, you're all happy. You're happy that we're here and that we're trying to be as respectful of your home as possible. Our home. I'm sorry we didn't do this sooner. I hope you can forgive me for being cautious." She squeezes my hand. I'm not sure if she's talking to them or me now.

Easton glances at me and then starts singing. I have no idea what he's singing, but Haley knows it and she sings along while I stare at the flowers in the dirt. I don't know what I thought I would feel when we finally finished, but this isn't it.

I lie on the edge of the platform, floating outside the cave. I've lost track of how many times Easton and I have come here. We've cut through two ropes. That's it. We're no closer to opening the lid. When the ropes are gone, we'll have to figure out how to pry the top off. Whatever's in there is heavy. Not even Easton, Sam, and I together could budge it.

Easton's still down there. I'll give it to him—he really can hold his breath a hell of a lot longer than the rest of us. Everyone's been out here at least once. But we only stop by after we've made a fruit run. About once every two weeks.

I'm staring at the stalagmites on the ceiling of the cave, catching my breath, thinking about everything and nothing, when I realize that next week is my birthday. I'm fucking hoping that Haley's forgotten. But I know she won't have.

Easton bursts to the surface and tosses a two-foot length of rope onto the raft. "Three pieces down. A million more to go. I'm ready to go back. You?"

"Yeah, let's call it."

We're halfway past the bluff when I see a flicker of a glint on the horizon.

"Watch where you're going," Easton calls out into the wind.

The glint distracts me, and I turn the machine into the current. The waves crash hard against the sides of our legs.

"Out there." I incline my head. "Is that something?" I yell into the wind.

Rockwell's body shifts. "Yeah, it's something. With the waves, I can't get a handle on it, though." I'm already turning into our camp beach when he answers.

I race the WaveRunner up onto its sled. Easton jumps off as I lash it down, and then we yank it up to its blind. "Fuck." I scan the beach. It screams we're here. But there's nothing I can do about it now. "Get things secure," I say to Dante and Zane as I head straight up the ladder.

"What's going on?" Zane asks, following me.

"Easton will fill you in." The binoculars are on the peg on the living room platform. I grab them and scamper up the ladder. The tree shakes with someone else coming up as I'm still tuning the lenses for my eyes.

"What is it?" Sam asks.

"Not sure . . . incoming. Fuck. It's the same pirate boat that took the Rock Candy." My stomach lurches. But then, I knew this would happen.

"You're sure?"

"Same half-inflated red fenders hanging over the side. Yeah. I'm sure. We've got maybe ten minutes from their speed. And they'll have to launch their tender."

"Fuck. Can you make out anyone on deck?"

"A couple of guys on the bow. One with a gun strapped to his back." I take the binoculars away from my face.

Sam scrubs his hand over his scruff, but then he's making his way down the ladder. Descending like a captain of a submarine. I'm right on his heels.

"Haley?" Sam yells.

"She's using the head," Dante replies.

"Pirates are coming in hot," Sam tells him. "We've got maybe a ten-minute head start."

Dante, Zane and Easton are there. Easton's already

moving around the campsite, collecting things into a backpack.

"We don't have much time," says Sam. "Calvin, take Haley and Penny and head for the cave near where you first found me. Take the gun. Like we planned."

"Gun's already in there." Easton hands me the pack. "Water, clothes, and some of Dante's jerky."

"Good." Sam says. "Now make one for yourself. You need to head the other way and go toward the derelict into the thicket. Dante, Zane, we're going to greet our guests. With Zane's bag of tricks." Sam's got Penny's vest and her leash. "Go with Calvin." He clasps the lead onto her collar, and for once she doesn't twist away.

"Bloody right. Get going," Zane says.

"What's going on?" Haley turns the corner. "Sam, you were calling for me?"

"Yeah, Sugar. Pirates are on their way in." He gives her a quick kiss and a hug.

"We've talked about this. It was a hell of a long time ago. But what do they want? Rockwell, most likely, and you. So as much as I hate to do it, we split up," Sam says. We've talked about only part of the plan with Haley. But not all of it.

"That always works so well in horror movies." Dante mumbles. I shoot him a look.

"There are supplies in there from last fall. I checked them not long ago."

"No. You need the gun here," Haley says.

"If they catch up to you in the cave, you'll need it more than us. Go."

I've got a rope around Penny's collar. She's on alert. Sam grabs Haley and gives her a quick kiss. Dante, Easton, and Zane do the same.

"I don't like it, but okay? I don't want to leave you all." Haley's sitting in the chair I made, pulling on her tennis shoes.

"Go—we can take care of ourselves," Zane says.

"Let's go." I stand next to her, wanting to pull her away, but she's still putting on her shoes. "Easton, you're the other thing they want. They're going to follow all of our trails. Get going."

Easton gives a nod and runs down the path to the derelict. He'll cross the stream and head into the jungle afterwards.

"Now we can crush some stormtrooper ass." Zane wiggles his eyebrows.

"Get going," Dante says and pushes us out down the path.

"All right, Bunny, show us what you can do. I want to get as much distance between us and the beach as possible." We head down the trail.

"Give me the leash; you've got the pack." Haley cocks her head to the side and holds her hand out as she's lightly jogging.

"I can do it," I say.

"You go first. You know she loves you as much as Sam. She'll run faster if she's running after you."

"No, you first."

"Calvin?"

"No, Haley. I'm a bigger target."

"I'll go first, but give me Penny."

I hand her Penny because arguing is just slowing us down. Haley kicks up, and Penny stays glued to her side. When it counts, this dog seems to know what the hell is going on.

The jungle's loud and the ocean beyond it is even

louder, but I can't help straining to hear anything that might be happening behind us.

Above the normal din, there's a bang. Haley falters for a second but then continues her charge forward. "What was that?"

"Don't know. Keep going." The damn waterfall and the mountain beyond it have never felt this far away before.

And of course it starts raining.

Chapter 37

Rodger

Sam

I can just barely see Zane from where I'm hiding. The rain's a slow drizzle; from experience, I know it's going to shift to a downpour soon.

The tripwires are in place. They're something we added after they took the Rock Candy. Every week, we've been testing them to make sure they're not buried too deep. And to think I almost suggested Zane should use them for securing the new bathroom platform.

I give the end of the wire a test, raising the bit in the jungle just an inch. It's going to work—as long as they come up the path and not straight through the underbrush.

Dante's up on the platform. He's watching to make sure they don't launch a second tender.

I'm not thinking about how my gut stirred watching Haley and Penny run for the cave. No good can come from that.

Focus, Sam.

Under cover it's swelteringly hot, and sweat runs down the side of my face. There's a trio of flies buzzing around too. I ignore all of it. If ever there was a time I needed to focus, it's now. I need to keep her and my whole crew safe. This clusterfuck is my fault, after all. I should never have left the shipyard. The Rock Candy had already been mucked with, and I should have seen it. No, we're coming out of this, and I'm going to fucking take down the people who left us here.

I glance back at the ocean. Their damn boat is slower than anything. They must have another ship to come alongside cargo ships. When they get to the bay, they launch a tender. I think I see four men on board, which might give us a chance. Even without the gun.

I'm fucking hoping this gives Calvin and Haley a chance. It's something that the five of us talked about a while ago. We went round and round about whether to tell Haley or not. We took a vote about whether we should tell her. Three to two against. Zane and Easton wanted to tell her. There's no way she would have gone with Calvin, if we had told her. No way. We're planning on giving up our lives if it means saving her.

Fuck, I hope I get to see how pissed she is when she finds out we left her out of the plans. That means she's alive and I am too.

I almost swung the other way with Zane sitting on my shoulder like the good angel saying, "She'd want to take care of Penny." Calvin and Dante, they wanted her to start living in the cave that very day.

But it all comes down to what we believe the pirates know about us. And our theory was that they don't know Haley's here and they most likely didn't get a good look at

Calvin, not in the twilight. So if the pirates attacked, it would be Easton they'd want. As Rocky's son, and an Olympian, his picture has to have gone around the world. If they find Easton straight out, they'd most likely kill us all. If they didn't, they might take us all prisoner. Which is better than dead.

I'm hoping they're all as horrible a shot as the guy back on Chicken Beach. Not that Easton's arm getting hit wasn't bad. Again, not dead. That's what I want for all of us.

But they only put four of them on the tender. We have a fucking chance. They're betting on us just welcoming them like saviors. Or being so weak from hunger that we'll be no trouble to defeat. We're fucking neither of those things.

Calvin's been attacked by pirates before, back when he was on a cargo ship. But I've never come face-to-face with them. The closest I've ever gotten was the ship that motored by my six when the Rocky Candy was adrift. Then there was nothing I could do. But now, this is our home. Our turf.

At first, it felt like it was hopeless. Like back on the Rock Candy when I watched and waited to see if they would notice me. This is our island, and we're going to protect the damn thing and the woman we love.

In my peripheral, I see Dante scramble down the tree-house ladder and take position. He holds up one finger and then four, confirming what I saw. One tender with four men on it. Dante moves into position on the other side of camp.

"Attention castaways. We are here to save you. Surrender." A bull horn squeaks off. The speaker's English is stilted with a French accent. It's one I think I remember hearing on the radio. "Come out of the jungle. No harm." They're not on the beach yet. Their old outboard motor is loud enough to hear over the crashing waves.

I can't see Zane's eyes roll, but I know they do. If it wasn't the same pirate ship that took the Rock Candy and shot a bullet through Easton's arm . . . maybe we might have believed them.

Then the motor's off. Do they tie it off? Or run right up the beach? I risk the slightest movement, peeking out from my green palm frond cover. The best fucking idea. They're out of the tender. I signal as much to Zane and give him a nod. I'm clenching my jaw tight enough it ticks all the way in my chest. My palms are sweating around the bamboo handle.

They pull the tender onto the beach. It's at such an angle that I can't see exactly what they're doing. But the waft of gas fumes tickles my nose. I've always loved the smell of gasoline, but that changes now.

These are only the first two obstacles we've laid out. Zane's controlling the first one. I've got the second one.

Their boots are closer. Zane pulls, and it hits the first guy's boot. He drops onto his chest. A sand cloud puffs up around him, obscuring whether we got either of the others, but at least one has tumbled into the first. He's swearing in a language I don't know.

Zane holds his position. The other two are sweeping side to side while the first one tries to get up. The one in the back is coughing while the other is yelling into his radio. The pirate in the sand pushes up, and sand pours from his shirt and gun. I'm holding the bamboo and the wire, waiting, holding, holding . . . waiting for the other two to step forward.

At last, one of them lifts his left foot, then his right foot comes down, and I pull it. I yank as hard as I can. It cuts right through his boot, and he drops. His radio flies out of his hand. And now Zane and I both dart away in opposite directions—because that was the plan, that we'd both create motion after the second wire was triggered.

They're swearing and muttering, and general chaos erupts. My throat is raw and dry, but I can't afford to let fear take control. I can't afford to fail. Haley's life depends on it. She's the reason why we were all living this last year. The bond that keeps us waking up every morning. My reason for living. I've never known what this kind of love is before. But I will willingly give my life if it means she lives. The thought of them hurting her? Of even touching her? No, I won't let it happen.

My heart beats in my ears with each strong step I take away from camp. The plan will succeed. I'll protect her with everything I have.

I round the map tree, around the backside to where I meet up with the path. Zane should be heading the other way into the thicket.

I can hear them now. There are two behind me. The others must have taken off after Zane. Two . . . I can do this. I can do this. Hopefully they've been slowed down by whatever damage the wires did to their legs.

I thunder down the trail toward the derelict, away from Easton, away from Haley and Calvin, away from my Penny. I'd rather stay and fight. But bringing a knife to a gun fight? Never a good idea. I need them to chase me. And then end up finding Haley instead? No, they're on my tail. They'll take the bait.

It's always loud here—birds, the water, buzzing insects—but now all I can hear is the sound of my feet hitting the sand of the trail. When I turn off the path, each dried palm frond crunch echoes in the base of my skull.

I need to get them to the derelict. It's one of the two locations that made the most sense. If they don't fall for my ruse, I can fall back and use the heavy side planks of the one wall that's left as cover before swimming around the edge of the rocky bay. That's the plan, but there's no way I'm letting that happen.

My steps are elongated, and no matter how hard I try to run without making a sound, I'm thundering. I've never run this hard—not even the time in high school when I thought I could be a track star at tryouts. Not even the time when I thought my sister was going to run into traffic.

My thighs are cramping. I'm darting in and out on the trail. Off the trail, I make my way to a stream, crossing it. I jump past where the stream ends, emptying into the ocean. I'm close but not quite to the derelict. I'm heading down to an area where I can hopefully fight them off, protect myself from any bullets that might fly.

Loud voices scream and yell, "Americano! Americano, come back here. We won't hurt you. We won't hurt you." He screams in a French-Asian combo way. *Like shit you won't hurt me. Why is that AK-47 strapped to your chest if you didn't plan to hurt me?*

I pass the trail where I know Easton will have gone and continue into the jungle. Part of me wishes I had done this weeks ago, months ago, back when I was still making fire every day at the derelict, working on my surprise to make Haley paper. Back when I had my tools here, tools I could use as weapons. Now, my hope is they follow me into the other pit. I need them to be close but not too close.

I jump to the left and hide behind one of the large banyan trees. I need to wait. The pit's up ahead. They need to be closer, close enough that they fall for it. I hear them coming, and I take steps. I go. I run next to the pit, careful not to trigger it myself. Nimble steps to the side of it.

The two of them come up behind me.

"Stop right there!" one yells.

But I don't. I keep going. I hear the palm fronds and bamboo break, the hole opening up, swallowing them. One of them screams, but the other one hasn't been caught. I hear the gun cock.

"Stop!" he yells and fires next to me.

Chapter 38

Battle Plans

Dante

I've scurried my way up the tree to the platform that Zane made. I'm not sure this is going to fucking work, but from the screaming and yelling on the beach path, the wires at least did something. I wipe drops of rain from my eyes. My heart is beating in my throat as I wait for whatever is going to come. I've got my knife in hand, braced against the rope.

There's no way this is going to work. This sort of thing only works in cartoons and Star Wars movies. But it's at least something. And Zane said he's done the math: it should come down in the right spot. I'm watching the shining rock in the path. He's told me that if I cut through the rope as soon as the first person steps over the rock, it should trigger the net to fall. Then I have to cut the next one before I jump and run like hell.

I'm flattened behind my blind when the sand-covered pirate stumbles into the middle of camp. He swipes everything off the counter with the front of his gun—dishes go scattering. I want to fucking kill him just for that.

He's mumbling in some language I can barely understand, and I'm only picking up a little bit of it. Fuck, I wish I'd spent more time learning whatever language a pirate who lives off the coast of the Philippines would speak, but I never thought I'd need to know more than the names of a few vegetables and "hello," "goodbye," and "where's the closest bar?"

Still, I'm getting a few of the expletives he's throwing down. He sits in one of the chairs that Calvin made. He kicks another chair sideways, and it skids across camp. He's rubbing his ankle. His neck cranes as he looks up at the observation platform. He holds his gun up, and I brace myself, expecting him to fire a round, but he's just looking through the scope. He drops it, grunts, and starts my way.

He stops at another of Calvin's chairs and takes the crew sweatshirt from it. He glares at the Rock Candy logo and brings it to his nose and huffs it in. The guy is seriously out of his mind. We wash our clothes but not often, not by the standards back home. We've been saving soap, and while Haley's mixture of flowers and herbs helps to freshen us all up, other than Haley, none of us are sniff-worthy. Especially not Easton's second-hand deck jacket.

The pirate throws it on the ground. His eyes scan but not fucking high enough to see me. Thank fuck I'm good at sitting still. It's not a skill a lot would think I'm good at, not with my wild mouth. I'm kinetic energy, that's what my nan used to say. But then they didn't have my uncle. I can be still, small, invisible when I want to be. It's just that I never want to be.

Calvin taking the gun was the right decision, but if I had it? Damn, I could drop this stinky-jacket-huffer to the ground. The winds are strong but not strong enough that his big nose is going to pick up my scent on the breeze.

My fingers are loose around the bamboo connected to the line that will drop the load of rocks and coconuts on this fucker. While he was making these Ewok-Home Alone traps, Zane was happier than . . . actually, that fucker's always happy.

But I say a little prayer to Saint Jude. Sister Maria Elizabeth would be damn proud of me. At graduation, she said she would keep praying for me. I'm hoping that works in my favor in the next few minutes.

The huffer is walking like he's got all day. I guess he has; we haven't gotten off the island in almost a year, and he's holding the damn gun. But what was supposed to happen was half of them were to take off after Sam, the others off after Zane. I'm sure Zane's just as busy with the one after him as I am frustrated about huffer taking an afternoon stroll.

Come on, man . . . I've got things to do. My fingers twitch, but I hold the knife to the rope. He's really taking his time, which is going to work out a hell of a lot better for the debris smashing into his huffy little skull.

Two more steps and he'll be on the spot for me to release the net. He's over the rock, his head bent, looking at it. I wait. He takes two steps forward as he cranes his neck up. I pull the bamboo handle and the net crashes down, opening up. He screams as gravel and coconuts rain down. I cut the second rope, and the rocks pummel down.

His moaning stops. His feet stick out from under the net like the witch from the *Wizard of Oz*. Damn, I'm turning into Zane. But they don't move—well, a twitch when a coconut rolls into his foot. Huffer is either out cold or dead. Either is fine with me.

I scramble down the makeshift ladder and examine the pile. Somewhere under there is the huffer's gun. I lift the edge of the net. No. First, I grab a rock the size of a roast to serve twenty and swing it down.

Sam

There's screaming coming out of the pit. There's nowhere to duck out of the way of a bullet. I didn't make it to the derelict as I hoped. The fucking rain has slowed me down.

"Stop or I shoot again."

I freeze, my hands in the air. They vibrate back and forth, even though I'm trying to hold them steady. He's behind me. I assume he's got a gun.

"Turn," he says sharply. "Now. Go." His words are crisp and demanding. I turn slowly.

He's wearing khaki green, his jacket buttoned up to his neck. He can't be more than mid-twenties. His English is tinted with a French accent. In the hole in front of me, his accomplice is scrambling, pulling at the palm fronds, trying to climb out, but using them for stability isn't working.

The one in the pit hollers up to the other, the one holding the gun on me. He's spitting and swearing in a language that I don't recognize. Every once in a while, though, he yells out "motherfucker," but it doesn't have the same venom that the other words have, as if he doesn't really understand the meaning behind it.

My jaw is clenched, and the tick in my neck is back.

He points the gun at the ground. "Down," he says, and

I'm not sure what he wants me to do. Does he want me in the hole? "Down," he repeats, motioning with the barrel of the gun.

He strings together a sentence of French and whatever his native tongue is, but I don't get any of it. His eyes glare at me, his forehead furrowed.

"Down lie," he says, his English coming out backward.

I crouch next to the pit and reach my hand down for the pirate. He's scrambling at the walls, clawing at them. "Here," I say, holding my hand out. He looks at it like I have daggers for fingernails. "Take it," I say softly, trying to assure him that I'm not going to bash him with my forehead—which, under other circumstances, sounds like a good idea, but the gun pointed at my head says maybe it's not such a good idea.

He grabs my wrist, and I grab his. Then we do the same with our other hands. I lean back, and he walk-climbs up the side. He lands on the ground next to me. I'm ready for it, so I roll away. He comes after me.

They're shouting back and forth between the pit guy and the one pointing the gun at me. There's a brief second that I think I might be able to dodge away . . . but then the younger one pulls himself together. He leans over, getting in my face, and spits on my cheek.

The other one narrows his eyes, ignoring the spit on my face. I do the same. He wants a reaction. He's not getting one from me. I don't reach to wipe it or even acknowledge it. I keep my eyes on the hands of the guy with the gun. Oh, I'm watching the other one with my peripheral vision. You don't become captain of a boat without being able to do five things at once. My sister told me it was great practice for being a dad at some point.

Fuck. I want to see my niece and nephew again. I want

to see Haley pregnant, my ring on her hand. Yeah, I'm going to do everything I can to keep her safe. To get all of us out of here alive.

The gun-less young one limps over to the other one and reaches for the gun. There's more shouting and a momentary split second where the gun isn't on me but in the middle of the chest of the one from the pit. It's not long, not enough for me to make a run for it. The other one throws his hands up in the air and shouts.

After a minute, the gunman motions for me to walk back to camp. Fuck, it feels like I've been here for a long time, but it's not even fifteen minutes. Much less, even.

"Go." The one with the gun motions and pushes me in the back as I walk past. "Faster." I'm walking as slow as I can to be considered fast. The longer I give Haley and Calvin and Easton to get away, the better.

We pass the cut-off path where Easton would have gone. I walk quickly past it, keeping my steps even. But the one with the gun pauses. He says something to the other one, and I think he's going to run the other way, but the young one shouts back.

They both come with me back to camp. I'm hoping that Dante's net worked.

The gunman grabs my arm and presses the barrel of the gun into the middle of my back. Then I see why. Dante's holding a gun. A gun he has aimed at the young guy from the pit.

Dante yells at him in French. I understand, "You and . . ." well, that's it. My French is horrible. But I'm watching Dante, waiting for him to give me a signal or anything that might mean duck, dodge, or fight back. Until then, I'm letting the two with the guns be in charge.

The man behind me yells back in rapid-fire French.

"*Non*," Dante says.

"*Oui*," the man behind me says, followed by a long stretch that I catch none of.

Dante looks at me and shakes his head.

There's shouting from the jungle from the direction Zane ran. And in a heartbeat, the kid who spat in my face darts off with a limp, but damn, he's still fast.

Dante kicks over the table with a thud and ducks behind it.

The gun pushes harder into my back. And fuck. The pirate lets out a string of words.

Dante says something. And the gunman grabs my hair with his free hand, ratcheting my head back. "*Oui*."

Dante pushes the gun out and comes around the table with his hands up.

Fuck.

Chapter 39

Tactics

Zane

I fucking overshot the pit. I thought I had him, but he ran right by it. The thicket's kept me hidden, though he's sniffing around me. He'll be around again, and the next time he does, I'm doing a cut-back. It's my favorite football play. Sure, it doesn't always work, but what else do I have to try? He's going to find me here eventually. Though the sun is dropping in the sky.

I freeze, contemplating my next move. There's a chance I might be able to dart off, round back to where the thicket on the other side of the island is. I'd have to cross the stream behind the pool, but I could still do it. Meet up with Easton.

But no, we need to keep him safe too. Haley first, Easton next. Sam's right. They want Easton—he's the money item. I've been bouncing back and forth between two ways of thinking: either they want him alive for ransom, or they want him dead because he was supposed to be killed the first time around.

But I don't think these guys were involved with the

saboteur. They're not that suave. They don't seem to have an overall game plan. It's more of a money grab. So now I think they're after the ransom or reward, whatever you want to call it. But they still don't want to give the ship up, so they can't exactly just hand us over.

Something doesn't fit. There's part of this puzzle I'm missing and have been for months now. I feel like I can almost reach it, but it's out of my grasp.

My pursuer circles back around again. I think this might be the time that I need to do it. I crouch under the large clump of ferns that I've been tucked beneath and ready myself for takeoff. I hold myself in a sprint position until he's close enough to see me but too far to take a good shot. Unlike the one who chased after Sam, this one isn't sporting an AK-47—he's got a handgun. And so far, he's fired no shots, something else I need to be cognizant of.

He takes a few more steps. The wind is blowing in through the jungle from the ocean. It's that time of late afternoon that if we're going to get more rain, it's going to happen now. Instead of that little burst we had right as they landed, it could turn into a full-blown storm, or it could blow over. That's the nature of this place.

I hold, waiting, just like when we were pulling the wire. The wire worked. It didn't quite work how I thought it was going to—I was hoping it would really slice into them, cause them more damage, instead of just slowing them down. But it's allowed us to at least try and work the plan this far. I hold, and I hold, sweat pouring from my brow, the muscles in my legs twitching, wanting to go.

I see him from the corner of my eye, 50 feet behind, and I take off, sprinting through the ferns, jumping over the logs that I know are there, and scrambling through the under-growth. But what I didn't account for is him screaming. He's screaming bloody murder. He's been silent up until this point, and I don't know why he's screaming, but I'm not stopping. I'm not going to let him affect me. *Keep going.* Steady steps pound the leaf litter of the jungle floor.

Just when I think he's behind me, I can see the pit up ahead. Someone else bursts through the jungle too—one of the guys who had been following Sam, I guess. Now I've got two of them, one coming at me, the other coming behind me. The pit's in the middle, and I'm not sure what to do. I don't hesitate, though. I run straight for it.

This is the one that I built with Calvin, and I know it well enough. I know that in the corner there are some heavier bamboo poles that are holding up the rest of the palm fronds. I nimbly step as close to it as I can, just as the two of them are coming up on me.

The one ahead of me doesn't appear to have a gun. He's just running, running straight at us. He's yelling now, something in French or an Asian language, I don't know which one it is. I don't understand it. Mom told me to stay in French class, but I didn't want to.

I hit the corner of the pit just as the two of them are almost on top of me, and I burst forward back to the beach. I hear it collapse behind me. They're shouting and screaming, and then there's utter silence. Nothing.

It couldn't have been that easy, could it? I keep taking steps, running away from it, but there's no noise. I dart behind a large banyan tree and wait. I peek out from around it, and the jungle is empty behind me. I can see a bit of the pit covering left behind, so I zigzag back from tree to tree, using the cover of the largest trees possible, until I get to the pit.

And there, down in it, are two mangled bodies. Unlike the pit on the other side, we used sharpened skewers in this one. Spikes that worked really well. It's caught two boars over the last few months. We've trained Penny to stay away from them.

I crouch, looking for where the gun might have got too, avoiding the vacant eyes of the one that landed face up. It's there somewhere. I'm walking around the side of the pit when I hear a twig break from the direction of camp. But I'm not fast enough. Sam's walking toward me with his hands in the air.

"Easton," Sam calls. "Easton."

I stand, and only then do I see the guy with the gun pressed to his back.

"Where's—"

"Back at camp."

I nod. I have no idea why Sam's calling me Easton. Anyone with access to the internet can look up what Easton Rockwell looks like, and it sure as hell isn't me.

"Right," I say. First law of improv: never contradict another speaker. One of my sister's rules.

"Move," the pirate says. Then he sees the pit and he jostles Sam to the edge and looks in. "Motherfucker."

For a second I think he's going to push Sam in too. Though the corpses below might keep him from being too injured.

"Go." He cocks his head at me, and I step back and away from the pit, heading in the direction of camp. "Hands up. I die him, no funny."

"Right, got it, mate." I put my hands up and walk beside Sam. Four came off the tender. Where's the other one? I'm searching ahead of me. If Dante's back at camp, is the other one there too?

The guy holding the gun behind me must be a heartless bloody bastard; he didn't even flinch seeing his two dead crewmen in the pit. Didn't even lean far enough over to see if they were really dead. Though I'll give him some credit—they looked really dead. Like beyond dead dead.

We march into camp, our captor busy chatting it up on his radio. There's a lot of short bursts of angry words before he pockets the thing again. Dante's tied to a tree on the far side of camp, near where my net worked. I shouldn't smile. This isn't the time for smiling. I swallow it down and cock my head away from the gunman to hide my glee at the two feet sticking out from under the bundle of rocks.

The radio goes off in his pocket again.

Dante's eyebrows rise, and when the gunman steps away from Sam to look through the jungle to the beach, Dante smirks and winks at me. I have no bloody clue what the hell the wink means. But it seems hopeful, or the chef's finally gone all the way off his rocker.

The gunman moves all of us to the beach facing the boat. We're waiting and waiting while the sun sinks lower. At last, two crewmen jump from the ship into the water and start swimming for the beach. When they crawl out of the waves, neither of them are happy. One has large zip ties, the kind the cops use. The other guy pats us down. *Mate, if I'd had a gun, I would have already used it on you.* But then I did what Calvin told me to do with my pocketknife back in camp: I slid it into my underwear behind my cock.

Ziptie grunts at Sam, and he puts his hands out. The wet pirate yanks them so tight on Sam I'm worried for his circulation. Dante's next and then me. I do the trick my sister taught me when she was going to the rallies for the Just Stop Oil demonstrations. She was never arrested, but she studied it up in case she was. I tuck my thumbs into my palms, making my hands as wide as possible before the zipties are tightened, then relax them after, creating just enough slack for me to wriggle free later. The guy is wet and mad and doesn't notice what I've done.

"In," he says, pointing to the tender.

Ziptie guy sits down and stays on the beach, while wet guy number two and our gunman usher us into their tender. I'm not sure how long wet guy number two has been working on boats, but he hasn't been driving a tender long. He revs the engine before Ziptie pops up and has untied the line, and we lurch toward the big rock. There's more swearing, and I'm pretty sure I know "fuckturd" in Tagalog now, for as much as the gunman is yelling it at him. But then we're off, and he doesn't do such a bad job lining up at the aft of the pirate's ship.

Dante leans over to Sam to whisper something to him, but the gunman grunts and pokes him in the back with the barrel of the gun.

Climbing onto deck when your hands are zip-tied in front of you, though? Yeah, it's not easy. Sam goes first, followed by Dante, then me. There are two more guys with guns pointed at us on deck, and one unarmed. The gunman from the beach doesn't come aboard the ship. No, another guy jumps into the tender. And then we're led along the starboard side of the ship and down another ladder. I've seen ships like this before; this is where they would keep the fish if they were earning an honest living. The door slams with a thud.

"What the hell were they saying?" I turn to Dante, I think. It's so dark I can't make anything out, but there's a crack of light coming around where the aft hull meets the deck. They have a light leak. Where there's a light leak, there's a water leak. I wiggle my hands free and push the looped cuff into my pocket, retrieving my knife. "Give me your hands, Sam."

He turns, and his cuffed hands slap into my side. "Sorry," he says.

"No worries, Cap."

"Your hands are free?"

"Better than that, I've got my knife. Now hold still so I don't cut you." I snip the bit off and catch it before it falls. "Keep a hold of this so we can pretend to be cuffed."

Dante's already got his hands where I can reach them. "What the hell were you winking about, Dante?" I hand him his cuff back.

"Half the crew speaks Indonesian and the other Tagalog. Half of their radio communications are them saying What and huh in broken French. But what I did get is the guy in charge wants us alive. Something about they won't get paid unless they have the four guys."

"Four?" Sam says.

"Yeah, four."

"Whoever's paying them doesn't know about you," I say to Sam.

"And that's going to be to our advantage," Sam replies.

Chapter 40

Double knotted

Haley

"We could go over the top of the mountain, down to the village instead of the cave."

"That's a long way. I don't want to get stuck out in the open." I don't want to get stuck anywhere. "Penny and I can stay in the cave, and you can go back and help them."

"No, I'm staying with you," Calvin grunts.

"But the others need help," I say.

"Going over to the village would be better. They'd never suspect that we could go that far."

"Exactly, because we can't. Not in a day. Adrenaline was the only thing that got me over and back when we were searching for you." I'm scrambling up the rocks, pulling myself. Calvin puts Penny next to me and gives my dangling foot a boost.

"You've got adrenaline now. And there was a while that I was going over every day and back before anyone noticed I was missing. You can do this, Chiefie. You're fast."

Arguing with Calvin on a good day doesn't go well. "Leave me in the cave and go back for them. Please." It's a dirty thing to do. I know how he feels about me saying please. All the guys—it's their Achilles' heel.

"We have to get up to the caves first."

My heart races. I look back over my shoulder. Penny copies me.

"Stop, Haley. Just focus. Climb up. Let me hand Penny to you."

I pull myself up onto a large boulder and turn around. Penny has her front paws on the edge near my toes. Calvin boosts her up. This section of the mountain is the steepest, but then Calvin just steps up like it's a normal staircase. I suppose it wasn't that hard for him to go back and forth, but back then we didn't even have a shovel.

It goes on like that for a good twenty minutes before Calvin says, "Let's take a break. There's a larger ledge over there, so we can press ourselves into the mountain and maybe they won't be able to see us."

"Yes," I respond.

He pulls a water bottle out of the pack, opens it, and hands it to me.

"You first," I say.

He shakes his head, and we both stare at the bottle hovering between us.

"Fine. Thank you." I take a quick sip and hand it back to him. He takes a sip and then pours a little into his hand and offers it to the dog.

She laps it up, licking his skin and looking up at him with devoted eyes.

I know the feeling. Despite everything that's happened, I trust him. So why am I questioning what he thinks is for the best? I'm not sure. Just something about it feels wrong.

It feels like we should be closer—that if he could go down and help the guys, things might turn out differently.

"Let's get going. We're almost to the caves." I yank myself up and gingerly scramble and slide through the rubble of the mountain over to the caves. From here, you can see down into the ocean, and shit—there's the pirate boat. It's right there.

I can see it. If I can see it, it can see me. I look at Calvin, speechless for a moment, but then it rushes to me. "They can see us. We have to move. We can't stay here."

"What?" Calvin says. He's busy holding on to Penny. For such a fierce friend, she can be rather timid, especially on trails like this. That's why Sam usually carries her up the mountain.

"Look, there, in our bay," I say, pointing over the edge of the far bluff. The pirate ship is just hanging there.

"Fuck," Calvin's deep voice echoes, startling a bird from the side of the mountain. Penny barks twice.

"Penny," I say, shushing her. "Quiet, girl." I know the ship can't hear us, but that doesn't mean any pirates who've come ashore can't. "I think . . . you might be right. Maybe we should go over the mountain," I suggest.

Calvin shakes his head. "No, no, we need to keep going."

"Wait, see that glint on the far edge? That's gotta be somebody looking at us. If they have binoculars like the good ones we have, they're counting the hairs on the top of Penny's head right now." I flatten myself against the mountain, but there's not really anywhere to hide. "They're going to see us going into the cave."

"Yeah, I think it is. I mean, it's a little hard to see with the naked eye, but . . ." Calvin trails off, his eyes narrowing as he scans the area.

"We need to switch this around," I say, urgency in my voice. "They're going to know we're on the mountain. They're going to come this way. The cave isn't safe. The other side of the mountain isn't safe either."

"You're right. There are more places to hide on this side and it's bigger. We pivot," Calvin says, his voice firm. "The safest place would be over in the thicket where Easton is hunkered down. We can get there by going around the backside of the waterfall. I've done it once before. It's not comfortable, it's really overgrown, but we're here—we might as well try."

I nod in agreement.

We're moving with more efficiency now, but going down takes just as long as it did getting up with Penny. I sort of slide from one boulder to the next on my belly. Easton's sister's high school T-shirt is taking the brunt of my sliding. The thin fabric now sports a hole on the side. I'm not going to die wearing Emily's T-shirt. That would be too much for Easton.

Damn that's a weird thought. I push it out. My brain is always there for me, coming up with the worst of the worst-case scenarios.

My foot skids on loose pebbles.

Calvin grabs my forearm, stopping me from sliding any farther. "You good?" His blue eyes stare at me, his hand gripping the top part of my forearm, holding me steady.

"Yeah, yeah, I got it, thanks."

Even Penny's looking at me like I might fall.

I cock my head at her. "You're the one who has to be carried." I scratch her between her ears. "Let's go."

Up took a while. Down doesn't take as long. There was urgency before, but it's doubled now. Those on the boat know where we are, which means if they have radios—

which most boats do—those on the island know where we are too.

"This way," Calvin says.

"I thought we were going to the thicket."

"Another change of plans."

"Change of plans? Where to, then?"

"I don't know about you, but if I were a pirate, I wouldn't be looking behind a waterfall."

"What do we do with Penny?"

"Oh, good point," Calvin grunts. Our four-legged friend hates water, tolerates it on a good day, but most days, she'll do anything to not get anywhere near it. "All right, back to the original plan. Let's go to the thicket, but we'll take the route above it."

"Great." I stare at the waterfall on the side of the mountain. A few months back, Easton jumped from the top of the waterfall into the pool. I asked him to never do it again. It scared the living daylights out of me. He said it was fine, but when even the littlest of injuries, as we've learned, can be life-threatening here, it isn't worth it.

He took me up there a few days later to see the top. While the stream widens out before it goes over the waterfall, there is a section where you can almost step over it.

"Okay, let's do it."

We make our way laterally across the mountain. Penny really is insightful. She's not complaining at all. It's like she understands something is amiss.

When we get to the top, Calvin takes my hand. "This way—we'll be able to cross up here. It's not far." The stream narrows here, and Calvin examines it. "It's pretty deep, but I think we can get Penny to jump it, and then I'll reach out and help you over."

"I can do it myself," I say.

"No time for heroism, Haley. Just let me help you."

Calvin takes a big leap. The rock on the other side wobbles a little, but then steadies.

"Toss me the pack," he says.

I do, and he catches it, putting it on dry ground.

"Okay, now toss me the leash."

I toss it to him, and he catches it with his fingertips. Penny looks back at me like, "Are you sure you know what you're doing?"

"There's no way she can make this jump, Calvin—it's too far." The last thing I want is for her to tumble over the top of the waterfall.

"Right, okay," he says. Then he calls her. "Penny, come."

Somehow, she jumps in the air—straight, vertical—and it's almost like she levitates over the water. Her front paws catch the rock and her back paws dip into the water, but Calvin's able to grab her and yank her to land. She takes a few steps and goes into the jungle, shaking herself off.

"Holy shit," Calvin says. "That was close. Okay, your turn." He holds his hands out for me.

I hesitate. There are definitely times when I wish I was more physical, but the last year on the island has changed my body quite a bit. My legs are more toned, and while I've always liked running, I've gotten a lot better. I can do this. I take a few steps back to get a running start. I launch myself into the air, my right leg forward, my left back.

Calvin snatches my shoulders and pulls me into him. We stumble back a few steps but stay upright.

"I did it," I say, slightly breathless. "Good. Let's keep going." I head into the dense undergrowth.

I've never been to this side of the island. The farthest

I've ever gone is the Birds of Paradise cluster. Beyond that, it's a thicket of jungle from here to there.

"Do you know where we're going?" I ask Calvin.

He nods. "This way. There's no real path. I don't think the boars are over here as much as the other side, but we're going to have to fight our way through. It's not going to be easy without a machete. But then, it won't be easy for the pirates either."

"We'll manage. We have to." I've got the pack on.

We head down around the backside of the waterfall. I can still hear the water running inside the island and the ocean from the southern side, but Calvin's right—it's hard going. The ferns are densely grouped, and the jungle thickens and thins along the way.

We have to squeeze between trees, and we've given up on Penny's leash altogether. It's pointless. You would think a year living in the jungle would teach her how to not get twisted around a tree. But no. And at this point, we just need to keep moving.

It's amazing how fast we're going and how silent we're actually being. Penny trails between the two of us.

"Keep to the right," Calvin says quietly. "There's a bluff toward the water."

As he says it, I step on my right shoelace and pull it out. I motion for him to keep going and crouch to tie my shoe.

He nods that he's going to check out what's around the large banyan tree up ahead. Penny trots after him.

With my shoe double-knotted, I stand to round the large banyan tree.

"Go home, Penny," Calvin yells loud enough for the mainland to hear.

Chapter 41

Special Forces

Calvin

"Penny, go home," I yell.

She looks at me with mournful eyes. Eyes that seem to say *let me bite him*. But then she turns and takes off. I just hope she doesn't run into any other pirates. I'm hoping to hell that Haley gets my signal. The asswipe doesn't, so I don't move.

He screams, "Go."

I watch as Penny runs through the jungle away from me. Thank fuck she doesn't turn back around and look at Haley behind the tree. I'm holding my breath, hoping that Haley understands I would never yell. But the one command that damn dog knows certainly is helpful right now. I can only see the fluff of her tail.

The pirate follows my eyes; he has the gun pointed directly at my chest. I see him flick his eyes to the dog. It's a momentary decision he makes. He fires into the jungle.

I scream "No!" as loud as I can, not necessarily because I think he's going to hit the dog—there are too many things in the way—but because I'm afraid that Haley is going to scream as well behind the tree, or worse yet, show her face. I need Haley to know that I'm not hit.

But neither thing happens. She's a fucking brilliant woman. We're lucky to have her in our lives.

Now I'm just hoping she doesn't try anything stupid, like taking the gun out of the pack and coming after us. Not looking back where I know she's hiding is killing me.

"Go," the pirate says again.

I'm grateful for his command. I'm more than willing to get out of here, to put some distance between me and Haley. I have no idea how many of them are on the island; I can only hope they don't find her.

He's got the barrel pushed into the middle of my back, and he seems to know where he's going. I do too. He's leading me right back to camp. It's not the easiest way—there's a stream to cross—and I'm hoping that at some point he gets distracted and I can overpower him.

He's not much of a man—scratch that. He's a good foot shorter than I am, but he's got some muscle to him, so I have a feeling it would be a fair fight, but he won't go down without trying. What I really need to do is get far enough away from Haley that he doesn't realize she was with me. Because right now, I don't think he does. I'm just a castaway lost in the woods with his dog.

He cuts a sharp right, heading north. The stream's pretty wide right here, but he pushes me in. "Go," he barks.

This is the spot. This is where I'm going to overpower him. I walk through the water, hands still in the air. He's got the gun on my back. The rock under my foot wobbles but steadies under the weight of my second foot. The balance changes as the pirate steps onto it. I step off it with my left foot, and with my right heel I push it downstream. It knocks him off-balance, and with the force of the rushing water, he stumbles. His gun disappears into the stream, his eyes flare, and I smile. It's not nice to smile.

He comes straight at my core. I don't know what he thinks he's doing. He pushes me back, but I'm braced for him, like he's a linebacker blitzing at me in a game. I wrap him up, throw him over, and drop him under the water.

I hold him there, my frustration at this whole island playing out in front of me. I hold him down for Haley. I hold him down for Emily and the crew on the other raft. I fucking hold him down for the murdered villagers on the other side of the island.

I'm going to hell for sure. Because his squirming and gasping open mouth are bringing me a rush of fucking joy. He pulls at my arms as bubbles leak out his mouth . . . until they don't anymore. I hold him there for another second until I'm sure he's not going to be able to come back from this. I'm definitely not coming back from this, but one thing is clear as day: he won't shoot at another dog.

I should have just let him go, because then I hear it—the cock of a gun behind me.

"Hands in the air," another pirate says.

I clench my eyes shut and turn around, one hand still on the drowned man, the other in the air. But it's not just one man, one pirate—it's three. The one who gave the command waves with his gun.

I come out on the other bank. These fuckers must really want us alive. He watched me finish off one of his men and didn't shoot. I crawl up onto the bank. One of them kicks me in the ass, and I go sputtering to the ground, ferns in my face, but I jump up as quickly as I went down.

There's no running, not with three of them.

"Move."

One of them picks up his radio. They're talking, but I don't understand anything. It's fast, but it almost feels like he doesn't understand what the other guy is saying either—there's confusion on his face.

One of the others jumps into the stream, pulls the guy out of the water, but not a second later, the one who seems to be in command has all four of us marching away from the water, away from Penny, away from Haley and the body on the bank. And I'm hoping they don't have anybody else. But there's nothing I can do. I'm outmanned, outgunned.

Easton

I'm sitting in the thicket. I have been for a while, my arms sore and stiff from not moving. I fucking hate this. I fucking hate hiding—hiding because of my family, hiding because of who I am. We're here because some crazy person needed to off my family, wanted us all dead, and here I am again, hiding. It's fucking wrong. I don't know why I ever let them talk me into it, but I'm not gonna go bursting out of here now.

We had a plan. I'm supposed to stick to it. I'm supposed to wait until either I don't hear anything else or it's dark, or until they push the compressed air blast telling me to come in. Still fucking hate it.

There's a gunshot. It's the first thing I've heard over the water in an hour—maybe ninety minutes. I have no idea how long I've been here. I can't get a good read on the time of day through the tightly packed vegetation. I strain, listening for anything else, but there's nothing. I reposition myself. Maybe I should move to another spot, but no, I stay put. I stretch out my muscles.

Five minutes pass, ten, and then I hear something. Is it a boar? There's rustling. It's not loud enough to be a person.

Then I see it—a flash of white, low to the ground, behind a clump of ferns to the north of my thicket. A brown nose pokes in at me.

"What are you doing here, girl?" I ask.

She pushes at me. If ever there was a dog that wanted me to go, it's this one right now.

"You want me to follow, Penny?"

She sneezes.

"I'll take that as a yes. Okay, okay, yeah, take me. Where do I need to go? Let's go."

Somehow, the dog is walking silently through the woods, and I practice all the things that Green taught me— around the thicket, around the side, near the rocks of the bluff on the southern side. Why the hell didn't I study this part of the island better? I should have explored more. Damn, I hope the dog knows where she's going, but her nose is to the ground.

We're moving and moving. I'm going as fast as she can, staying with her, stepping carefully. My eyes scan the horizon as best I can.

This area of the jungle is so dense, but I can still hear the ocean to my right. We're heading toward Pomelo Beach, toward the waterfall. We go and go and go. Penny darts forward, around a tree.

"Oh my, Penny, I could have shot you." It's Haley.

"Haley, it's me," I say, coming around the edge of the tree.

Haley's holding a gun. "Easton." She puts the gun down on the pack next to her and throws her arms around my neck. "It's horrible. They took Calvin, but I knew I should stay here because they didn't know I was here."

"They took Calvin?"

"Yes, there was a pirate, and he had a gun. I didn't want to look too much because the pirate hadn't seen me, but I think with the two of us, we should go after him."

I take the gun from the pack and swing the pack over my shoulder. "Good girl, Penny," I say. "Yeah, let's go after them. But silently. I think I know just the way."

We walk back through my thicket, past the Bird of Paradise field, close to where the other pit was. The bamboo is all broken—someone has fallen into the pit. We look down. There's no one.

Twenty minutes later, we're close to camp.

"Stay here," I say.

"I'm not staying here."

"Okay, all right. Together. We'll do it together. No more splitting up."

"Exactly," Haley nods and whispers to me. "That's what I said all along."

"Stay here, Penny," I say. Penny cocks her head, then lies down.

"Good girl," Haley praises her quietly.

I can't help but wink at Haley when she says it, and her eyes widen. This isn't the time for flirting, but with Haley, I can't stop myself.

The best way to see what's going on in camp is to go around the back, underneath the treehouse, near the ramp that Zane and Calvin installed for Penny. Haley and I move with stealth. I have the gun raised, and Haley's behind me— at least she's letting me go first.

It's quiet, though—quieter than it's ever been here. I can hear the ocean, but the jungle is silent. There are no birds, and the wind has stopped with the rain and storm passing. I peek around the banyan map tree. There's no one in camp, but the net we had hanging over the trail to the waterfall has definitely been deployed. The rope hangs silent, still, from the tree.

I cock my head at Haley and motion for her to stay put, to run if something happens. She nods. I move into the kitchen, crouching low, keeping myself out of view. The table has been knocked over, and when I round it, that's when I see there's a body underneath the rubble of rocks. But there's no one else here.

I go back and get Haley. "I think . . . I think they're gone," I say with uncertainty.

Haley nods. "I think you might be right. Only one way to tell," she says.

Together, we sneak out onto the beach. Our tender is there under the pile of palm fronds, but the one we saw coming ashore is definitely gone. The pirate ship, however, is still out in the harbor. The sun's almost set.

"Do you think they have them?" Haley asks.

"I don't know, but we should go check out where Zane was hiding," I say.

Haley agrees.

"Whoa," I say. "Don't come over here." I put my hand up. "You don't need to see this." Two more dead pirates.

"I think they're gone, but maybe they're coming back to get their dead," she says.

"I don't think so . . ."

"Well, we can't let them take the guys."

"I agree, but we can't do anything about it right now. When it gets dark, we'll take the WaveRunner out, climb up one of their own ladders. We run the risk of them hearing us, but . . ."

Haley's holding on to me tightly. We've got about an hour before the moon rises. I wonder aloud about swimming all the way out, but Haley makes a good point—it would be hard to keep the gun dry.

We use the binoculars, and while they have guards on their ship, they're not very observant. They're mostly dangling their feet over the edge of the deck, smoking.

"If we're lucky—and I sure as hell hope we are—we'll be able to get close enough that we can grab a rope, turn the WaveRunner off, and hope that we can get back to it before it floats away."

Either way, we have the gun wrapped in plastic, shoved in a bag. It's not like we're going to be able to use it, firing from a WaveRunner anyway. I'm not 007. And three lessons from another Olympian with a gun don't make you an expert.

Chapter 42

Boarding

Haley

We're crouched on the edge of the jungle, waiting. From what we've seen, they've been changing the guard every two hours. There's only two of them. And one is definitely not getting a Christmas bonus. He's sitting on the edge of the deck, smoking. The other one has almost been doing his job.

I want to get going. Do this. I'm scared the boat is going to take off. But we're waiting for the other one to come back on shift.

"We could just swim? Are you worried they're going to leave?"

"I was. I'm not sure why they haven't left yet. But I'm not worried anymore." Easton hands me the binoculars.

We're nestled behind a clump of short palms and dense scrub away from camp and the treehouse. I've got on the darkest clothing available to me: a pair of dark pants, my dark trainers, and another one of Emily's shirts, this one a dark green, long-sleeve shirt with the name of her high school in yellow on it, so I'm wearing it inside out. The name still shows, but not as prominently. It's well-worn and loved and I almost didn't put it on, but Easton handed it to me.

He's wearing a black crew T-shirt, a dark warmup jacket, and dark swim shorts. They were the most similar outfits we could find to the three dead guys. I'm wearing two sports bras to make me look as much like a man as possible. And I don't care about what we had to do to my hair. It's hair; it will grow back.

I adjust the binoculars to see. There's something going on in the aft. "They're launching the tender."

"I think so. We can take off running now or—"

"I'm done hiding."

"Same," Easton growls.

"We take their tender," I blurt out. "They won't know it's us coming in. They'll be looking for their crew.

"Fuck, Haley. That's—"

"No more dangerous than trying to grab a rope ladder from a WaveRunner. What's the alternative? Leave the guys on board the pirate ship? No. Not happening. Stay here and wait? Wait to be slaughtered?"

"No. But I could go without—"

"I said I'm done hiding, Easton, and I mean it."

"True, same. But I don't like bringing you on board their ship."

My fingers ache. I want to snap off. I want to go now. I'm like one of those poor racehorses shaking their heads behind the gates. Holding while they get into their tender makes me want to charge into the water. I glance at Easton. "How can you be so calm?"

"How were you calm when you had the primary who drank all the champagne in the first two nights and then made one of your stews quit? And you had a captain who didn't back you up. But you stood up to her and got her to be almost a decent human being. You did that by keeping your cool. This is no different than a billionaire diva or a world-class swimming meet."

"Other than it's our lives."

"We risk our lives every day by getting out of bed. But today we risk our lives for our family."

"You're amazing," I say.

"No, you are amazing. I'm just better with you." He cocks his head to the boat.

The tender's away. He hands me the binoculars again. I lift the binoculars; the lazy crew member is back on duty. There's three men in the tender. I'm just hoping they don't leave anyone there to guard it.

"You pilot the boat," he says. "I'll hold the gun."

"Right." I can do it. Zane's been teaching me how to drive our tender. And theirs, from the look of it, is a hell of a lot smaller. I don't want to hold the gun. Though Calvin's shown me how to do that in the last few months too.

I glance back at camp. We took Penny out behind the map tree, off to the side, and gave her a dose of her anti-anxiety tablets in a large fish, then tucked her out of the way behind the treehouse. I hate that we had to drug her, but having her bark when we leave isn't going to help her or us.

The tender bounces onto the shore. They take it way too far. I can only imagine what Charlie would have done last season if one of his guys had driven the tender all the way onto the sand. They jump out, and one of them tosses the rope around the big rock, like he's been here before. Another one lights a cigarette. The first guy smacks it out of his hand and points to the blind up to camp.

The other one is already on his way. He scans up and

down the beach but doesn't glance as far as us. Instead, he turns to the fish weir. He picks up a fish and tosses it back into the ocean. Then he kicks down three of the posts, the same way Calvin does when we have too large a stockpile of fish.

My heart pounds with each step the guy takes toward the camp. He vanishes behind the blind.

We wait a good ten minutes until we're sure they're far enough into the jungle to not hear us on the beach. "Ready?" I whisper.

We're silently flying down the beach. It's so different from the run we did on our island festival day. Or the times when we're goofing around challenging each other.

I jump in and go to the outboard. Zane's voice echoes in my head. I'm looking for the kill switch lanyard. But of course, there isn't one. *Don't fall out, then, Haley.* I go to turn the fuel valve to the "on" position, but it's already on, and since they just shut it off, there's no need to prime it.

Easton tosses the rope in and gives us a good shove. He points the boat in the right direction before rolling into the tender. "Go." He's already getting the gun out of the pack.

The gear shift is in neutral, and I start the engine, one hand in place on the motor to steady it. I pull the cord sharply, and the engine sputters and coughs but turns over, roaring to life. A quick switch to the run position and we're off. I'm sitting as low as I can. No need for my head to be a target.

It's just another day, and it's a good one to live. I'm going to get my guys.

A handheld radio in the bottom of the raft squawks.

Easton and I both stare at it. It's rapid-fire French.

"It's the ship, I think. They're asking if the tender is returning. My French isn't as good as Dante's," Easton says.

It goes off again. Easton picks it up with one hand, the gun in his other hand. We're getting closer to the ship, but there's no one on deck.

"The jungle is thick. I always had problems with my radio too far into town. The away team might not be able to hear it," I say into the wind.

"*Oui,*" Easton says into the radio.

Another long string of French comes through, but we're almost to the aft of their ship where they launched it from.

Easton throws me a look when I don't pull alongside the rope ladder like we talked about for the WaveRunner. Instead, I take the tender around the back where they launched from. I'm doing my best to not lose my nerve. Doing this is crazy. But also, not doing this will cause them to know it's not their guys. This way, they'll be one guy at most. Hopefully the lazy one, who will not have his gun strapped to his chest.

I slow the throttle and do the best I can to get close to the ship. I keep my head down. Easton turns the radio off and tucks it in his belt. He's got the gun under the flap of his jacket.

My throat closes up. There's a crew member on the back of the boat. But of course there would be. He's not even looking at us but at the side of the tender, his hands extended, waiting to grab the rope. I push it with my dark trainer. And Easton gets the hint. He picks it up and tosses it to the guy. The guard ties us up without glancing into the tender.

Easton climbs out of the boat as I turn the tender off. I need to play the part—leaving the engine on would be a dead giveaway.

Easton's after him. He cocks the gun and has it up when he stands from tying the tender. "Quiet."

"No, no kill me." His English is different than the others, less of a French accent and more a British one. "I'm . . ." He's clearly searching for a word. This is the lazy guard. "They take me . . ."

"Are you a prisoner?"

"Yes, *mga lalaki*." He shakes his head. "*Les hommes.*"

"Like the men?"

"Men, yes. Come." He reaches out and pushes the barrel of Easton's gun down. He steps to the port side.

Easton and I lock eyes.

"It seems reasonable. He's not really trying to guard anything," I say.

We follow him. Easton has his gun tucked under his jacket. And the man turns and stares at the gun. Then he points to the island. "*Fantôme.*"

"Ghosts?" Easton says.

"*Oui*, no good."

I shiver. They know about the massacre on the other side of the island. "Are you taking us to our friends?" I ask.

"*Oui*," he says. But then I get the feeling he might agree to anything with a gun pointed at him. I don't blame the guy. He's not that old, maybe twenty.

He stops at a hatch in the deck. There's no one around. But then a ship like this . . . needs what—maybe seven to ten to run it? Three are dead, another three are on the island. There's whomever radioed earlier.

The guy flips the latch and pulls the hatch open. It's pitch-black down there.

"If you're going to piss on us again, you could try and have a little better aim. You missed me last time, mate," Zane says.

"Zane," Easton calls out.

It's killing me to not speak, but we both decided the longer we can hide that I'm a woman, the better.

"Easton?"

"Get up here," Easton says.

Zane's up first, followed by Calvin. He takes a glance at me but then lunges for our captive helper.

"No, Green. He's helping us." Easton blocks Calvin from hitting the guard.

Sam and Dante are up the ladder now too.

"What's the plan?" Sam asks me, and I want to laugh.

I want to say *this* is *the plan*, but I counter with, "Take over the boat?"

"Love it, Sugar."

Our captive friend gawks between Sam and me, then he cocks his head at me, squinting. It's dark, but I'm pulling off my best teenage boy voice.

"Let's go, Hal," Calvin says, but he's glaring at Easton like he wants to smash him for bringing me.

Dante asks the captive something in rapid French. "He's been on board for two years. They took him from his village. He learned French from a visiting nun. And he made the mistake of speaking it to one of the other pirates. They threatened to kill his family if he didn't go with them. He says we should kill the rest of them. Oh, and the captain isn't on the bridge. He's drunk in his cabin. They're expecting a big payday tomorrow when they deliver us."

"Deliver us where?" Sam asks.

Dante relays the question. "He doesn't know, only they said they would let him go after they get paid, but they've said that before."

"Big, lots time," the captive says.

"Let's get this captain while he's drunk." Calvin moves from the hatch to the cockpit.

"Belay that, Green." Sam's pointing to the horizon. "I think we've found who's giving the payday."

"Holy shit," Zane says. "That's got to be 120 meters."

"And a good 100 million more expensive than the Rock Candy," Sam adds. "A Lürssen by the looks of the upper decks." It's one of the most expensive luxury yachts, and it's coming right at us.

"In pirate-infested waters?" I ask in my best alto voice. But I know the answer. It's who paid the pirates to capture us. "It could be your dad." I turn to Easton.

"My dad has a code word. He would have given it to anyone who was trying to help us. And he wouldn't have hired this lot. No. If he knew we were here, he would have hired English-speaking mercenaries with high-tech equipment," Easton says, crossing his arms over his chest. "We could make a run for it."

Dante shakes his head. "That, my friends, looks like an organized crime yacht if I've ever fucking seen one. And I've seen plenty—when I was working for the Russian mob."

Chapter 43

Rocket

Sam

Fucking hell. I'm staring at a Lürssen, maybe a 120-meter Project Thunder. It was one of the ones that Rocky wanted, but I talked him out of it. They're too big, like a jacked-up pickup truck with undermount lights. You buy a Lürssen because your dick's too small and you've got a point to prove. Rocky never brought more than ten people to the Mermaid's Tale. The Rock Candy is a better yacht—so long as you don't have someone intentionally trying to break it.

There hasn't been anyone in these waters for the last year, and there's a good reason. They're too dangerous. So it's too much to think the Project Thunder racing toward us is here for anything but nefarious reasons. Even though a small part of me hopes that maybe Rocky put a reward out for his son and the Lürssen is here to help us. But Easton's right: a private SEAL Team Six operation is more Rocky's style.

Right now, I just want Haley safe . . . and I can't help

thinking that this is definitely an out of the fire and into the frying pan situation. Unlike the pirate ship, it's got every damn light in the vessel burning. They're more than announcing their presence—the only thing more blatant would be them playing musical horns like an over-powered cruise ship.

The presumed pirate captain bursts out of the galley. He takes two steps and stumbles. He's yelling, and it's not English or French.

It's our new friend who takes a gun out of his waistband and shoots the captain in the chest. The man drops to the deck, dead.

"Shit, you had a gun the whole time?" Easton says.

He shrugs and tries to hand it to Easton.

"Keep it, my friend," says Easton.

"Rodel." The guy taps his chest and wiggles his eyebrows.

"Don't be a bloody fool, Easton." Zane takes the gun. "No offense," he says to the man.

"No." He shrugs back.

Dante points at the approaching ship. "We need to worry about that, not his feelings." He launches into French, and the guy replies. "Rodel says there are another three crew members on board, but they're all sleeping. They left another six at their port, thinking this was going to be an easy job. Then there's the three back on the island, looking for Easton and Hal . . . They left with twelve. Normally, they are eighteen to twenty."

"Three on the island?" I turn to Easton and Haley.

"We stole their tender. They could take ours, though," Haley says.

"Except I disconnected the battery wires and turned off

the battery switch. Given enough time, they should be able to figure it out," Calvin says.

"That would have been nice to know," Easton grunts.

"You stole the tender?" I say under my breath to Haley, and she smirks back at me. "You're . . ." I pull her in for a quick hug. "Sorry, I smell like rotten fish."

"I don't care." Our new friend, Rodel, pulls the feet of his deceased captain across the ship to the starboard rail. Dante grabs a leg and helps him roll the body overboard. Then Rodel opens the galley door, grabs a board like he didn't just throw a body to the fish, and locks the door, trapping anyone below deck. He nonchalantly chats to Dante while he rounds the galley, takes another board inside the galley, and locks it from the other side while Dante follows along. I get the feeling he's never done this before, but he's definitely had it done to him. It's the smirk of almost glee when he pushes the second board into position. The megayacht slows. "It's going to be on our port in five minutes," I say.

"Yeah, they wanted us alive. I think that's the only thing going for us," Calvin says.

"Unless they wanted to make sure they're giving the reward money for the right people. Before they kill us," Dante says, crossing his hands over his chest.

The eyes of our new friend go wide.

"Did he understand?" Zane asks.

For the first time since he let us out of the fish hold, Rodel looks nervous. "Rodel." He points to himself, smiling at Haley.

"Oh, I'm Hal," Haley says.

"Hi, Hal." He smiles, and I now want to drop Rodel into the fish hold.

The closer the Lürssen gets, the more I can make out.

It's not traveling with its fenders flapping in the breeze. And it's not one guy sitting on the aft deck smoking. There's a half-dozen armed guards positioned all over the ship: the communications platform at the top, either side of the bridge, and the front bow.

"There will be more," Dante says, seemingly reading my mind.

"It's not a rescue." Haley's dropped her deep voice.

"You came in smart, Sassy, dressing like a teenager. Don't worry, your voice will change soon enough. We'll figure a way through this." He puts his arm around her like we aren't waiting for our doom to arrive. But fuck, maybe he's got the right idea, touching her.

He drops his arm when the yacht pulls right up next to the fishing boat. Their bow's a good ten feet higher. The crew of the yacht hook onto the fishing boat and toss a boarding ladder over. Guard after guard jumps down onto the deck next to us. They scatter around the ship, one of them staying with us.

He's not pointing his gun at us, but he's not out for a stroll either. "Weapons," he says in an accent I can't place. His furrowed brow stays focused on us.

Easton and Zane place their guns on the deck. Zane has placed Rodel's a foot away from the stain the captain left. If the guard notices, he doesn't react.

Another guard drops from the ladder and pats each of us down. He's thorough but not invasive. He takes a radio from Easton.

When he's finished, another beefy guard rounds the deck. "Clear."

Five minutes later, which feels more like an hour, a tall, dark-haired man drops to the deck. He's got that casual appearance that says *I'm wealthy, but I don't care.* Other than the Audemars Piguet watch on his wrist.

"Ah, good to see all of you." His eyes scan the group. "Where are your hosts?" He looks briefly at Rodel before he dismisses him as not the captain.

His guard motions to the spot on the deck and the smear of blood that crosses to the other side.

"Well, I suppose you don't survive on an island for nearly a year without having some resources. Easton Rockwell, Zane Morris, and Calvin Green. And then there's Dante Jones. I have an associate who says you make the best hamburgers. He said that when I find you, I should be sure to tell him." The billionaire cocks his head like he's considering whether he should do it or not.

Dante glares back at him.

"And Samuel Miller? Interesting . . . You weren't known to be on raft number two. Yet here you are." He raises his eyebrows at me. If he doesn't know about the Rock Candy, I'm not going to be the one to tell him. "Then you must b-—"

"Hal," Rodel says, and points to himself. "Rodel."

"Hal?" The man laughs and ignoring Rodel he turns to Haley. "As in Haley Brewster." He takes the skull cap off her head. Zane slips his hand onto Calvin's forearm. But it's Dante who takes a step forward.

"Take your hands off of him," Dante says.

"Oh, I see," the ass says. "Have you been playing Balthazar for a whole year with these men? Or just for today?"

Her blue eyes are steel as she looks up at him.

"Indeed." He hands her back her hat.

"And you are?" I ask.

"Mr. Z. But you can call me Thayer." Thayer, unlike his

men, has an American accent—or rather the lack of one, like most yacht owners from the States. He's not looking at Haley's face but her bound breasts, and Zane's going to have a hard time holding the three of us back. "Interesting shirt." His hardened exterior cracks for a brief second. "Where are the rest of the crew for this boat? Have you disposed of all of them?"

"There are three crew below deck. There are three alive on the island. And four bodies," I add because I'm not sure what Thayer is yet. I know the crew of this boat is an enemy.

"And Rodel here. I should put a bullet in him. He'll become just like his former keepers. He'll be the mussels on someone else's hull if I let him go."

"Or he'll go back to his family and try to forget his past," Haley says.

"Oh, Hal. You're an optimist. How nice. I don't meet many in my line of work. Fine." Thayer turns to Rodel. They have a short conversation before he turns back to Haley. "Well, Hal, it appears you're right. I offered him this ship and some cash or a ticket back to his home with no cash. He took the ticket." Thayer motions to one of his guards.

"Where are you taking him?" Haley asks.

"You might be an optimist, but I am not. Rodel here will be below deck in our special accommodations until we get to port."

Haley purses her lips, and I see a bit of her optimism slide into the ocean. Dante hasn't stopped glaring since Thayer stepped on board. I want to kick him before he ends up in the special accommodations with Rodel.

It's clear that we're playing by Thayer's rules, at least for now.

"I see." Thayer nods to me. "Thank you." He turns to

the guard behind him. "Clean up the island and this ship. Drive it out to deeper water and sink it. Let's get off this dirty thing, shall we? You first, Hal." He motions to the ladder.

Haley snaps into charming first stew mode. "Thayer, there are a few things we would like to get off the island."

"Yes, I imagine there are." His eyes flick to Easton. "Let my men clean it up. Tomorrow they'll take you over."

"Um, so . . . our dog and cat are over there."

Thayer inclines his head to the one whom I'm assuming is the head guard. "They'll bring them back after they finish."

She nods.

"Ladies first," Thayer says.

But Dante grabs the ladder and climbs up it with speed to the mega.

"Or chefs first—I suppose it's the same thing." Thayer laughs. It's a good thing he has guards, because I guarantee that Dante would be paying him a visit while he slept if he didn't. "Hal," he says again.

Haley steps up onto the ladder, and the rest of us move in unison to go behind her. But I'm a step faster. I stay as close as I can while not impeding her progress to the top of the ladder.

Stepping onto the deck, the first thing I notice is how protectively close Dante's standing next to Haley. I fall right in line on the other side of her. Then it hits me—the smell. It's like fucking coming home. Then I see the crew lined up like we're guests, standing next to giant guards with semi-automatic guns dressed all in black. It's overwhelming. But there's a whisper of hope that Thayer's not going to feed us to the sharks.

Zane, Easton, and then Calvin pour over the side. I

understand the shocked expressions on their faces. I take Haley's hand and squeeze it like she does to me all the time. Her blue eyes glance up at me, asking, *are we okay?* And fuck, I only have hope.

"Wonderful. I'll have my chief of security, Holloway, and my head stew, Kennedy, show you to your rooms."

"Mr. Z," Haley says.

"I won't forget about your pets, Hal." He nods to us and the crew. And then we're being whisked down two flights to a row of cabins.

"Hal, this is your cabin," Kennedy says.

"It's Haley." She nods at him but doesn't leave my side.

"Of course," Kennedy replies. Haley sucks in her lips but doesn't step into the cabin. "Is it not okay?"

"Oh, I'm sure it's lovely. But I haven't been by myself for a . . ."

"Did you want to share a cabin?"

"Yes, please," Haley says.

Kennedy studies the five of us guys. I can see him trying to figure out which of us are connected. "With whom?"

"We could all share one cabin."

Kennedy pauses. "I'm not sure Mr. Z would . . . I'll ask him." His eyes flick to the chief of security.

"Makes things simpler for me," the chief grunts.

"Come this way." Kennedy moves down three doors. "You can all wait in here while I clear things with Mr. Z." He opens the door of a suite with two large beds. There's a walk-in closet and an attached bathroom.

We file in quietly. The door closes behind Calvin, the last to enter. And a lock turns from the outside.

"You don't lock your guests in their cabin," Calvin says.

"No, no, you don't." I stare at the doorknob.

Want bonus stories from the island? I've got some free micro episodes https://BookHip.com/WSSFKJG

Read the finale Wayward available now.

XOXO

Ellie

Also by Ellie Pond

Dark Wing

Resisting the Bear

Claiming the Wolf

Courting the Bear

Redeeming the Dragon

Tempting the Bear

Defying the Dragon

Chasing the Wolf

Dark Wing Series, Hidden Valley Wolves

Hidden Heart

Brilliant Heart

Bewildered Heart

Mated (completed series of Hidden Valley Wolves)

Mermaid Why Choose—Enchanted Elements

Wicked Water

Rugged Rock

Western Winds

Fire Falls

Veiled City

Captured by the Dark Commander

Tempted by the Forbidden Mate

Caged by the Ruthless Thief

Bound by the Golden King

Seduced by the Mermen: Men of Stele

Claimed by the Mermen

Dark Wing Series, River Divided

Crafting Love

Fighting Love

Dark Moon Rising

Guard

Protect

Honor

Wrecked

Adrift

Uncharted

Unmoored

Wayward

Revenge and Surrender (Emily's series)

Savage Vow

Stolen Promises

Scandalous Devotion

About the Author

Ellie's had many professions, including costume designer, contract archeologist, organic farmer, fabric store owner, and airline gate agent. She's happy to be a full-time writer now. She lives in New England with her three teenage sons, husband, and father. It's a lot of testosterone. When time allows Ellie likes to travel. You can follow her on social media for her travel adventures, and more.